IMPRISONED

Matt Rogers

ISBN: 9781520103037
ISBN-13:

"It is these very dangers, this alternation of hope and fear, the continual agitation kept alive by these sensations in his heart, which excite the huntsman…"

— *Horace-Bénédict de Saussure*

PROLOGUE

The shipyard had been abandoned by port control officials years ago.

Now it held dozens of vessels that had been decommissioned by the Bolivarian Navy of Venezuela over the years. They were nothing more than rusting carcasses, dumped in this vast expanse of concrete and forgotten. No-one came here anymore.

Which meant it perfectly suited the man striding along the dusty land inside its walled perimeter.

He was tall. Around six foot two and dreadlocked, with olive skin. There wasn't an ounce of fat on him. He had the lean, wiry build of someone raised on the streets. Someone who'd lived a life full of hardship.

But that past was a distant memory. Now he relished the success and prosperity that his operation had provided him with.

It didn't mean he slowed down. In fact, he found that the richer he became, the harder he worked. It was necessary in his line of work. Brutality and ruthlessness were keys to survival.

He passed in between derelict ships, walking fast, knowing exactly where he needed to go. Despite the lack of sun, he wore a tattered singlet and khaki shorts. The clothing exposed sinewed muscles carved from years of living on the streets. It was the same outfit he'd worn for years. He wasn't cold. Venezuela's temperature barely fluctuated year-round. It was always warm. Always humid. Nothing changed.

At least, temperature-wise.

Today, his whole world had changed. The operation he'd spent years constructing had been thrown into jeopardy by an unfortunate chain of events. He would do everything in his power to ensure that it continued to prosper. It was his life's work.

He would not lose it, under any circumstances.

He made for the port facing the Caribbean Sea. The water stretched as far as the eye could see. The shipyard was situated in the state of Vargas, which was partly why he was there. In 1999, devastating floods and mudslides killed tens of thousands and decimated the state's infrastructure.

They'd called it a tragedy.

He'd called it a tantalising business opportunity.

When his men seized the shipyard a year later, no-one cared. No-one batted an eyelid. The state officials were as corrupt as they came. Those who showed even a shred of interest had been quickly paid off.

The man made for the most prominent feature in the shipyard — an enormous cruise ship, resting in the shallows of a massive inlet that had been carved into the concrete port. It had docked there years ago and never left. It contained the majority of his assets, spread across hundreds of dilapidated rooms.

He passed two men loitering by the port, resting on a rusting car wreck and smoking cheap cigarettes. Assault rifles — Kalashnikov AK103s, purchased in bulk — lay by their side. They didn't make eye contact as he strode by. Normally they would, but they knew he was in a rage. The man was not known for having a level-headed temperament.

He crossed a narrow makeshift bridge that had been erected after their arrival, connecting the ground floor of the cruise ship to the dock. The floating behemoth had long ago lost its sense of awe. Years of neglect had taken their toll. He walked through corridors with paint flaking off the walls and passed rooms that smelled of fetid dampness. The ship was gargantuan. It wouldn't take much for a stranger to become lost in its bowels. But the man had walked its halls too many times to count. He knew the structure inside and out.

He headed up three floors, ascending a staircase that felt as if it would collapse at any moment. He walked down another corridor, indistinguishable from the rest, and turned into a large room. Along the far wall, sliding glass doors led to a balcony facing out over the shipyard. He'd converted it from a deluxe bedroom into a makeshift office.

Two men sat in front of a sweeping oak desk resting in the centre of the room. Both nervously shifted in the tattered chairs. They were anxious to share the recent developments with their boss.

The man crossed the room and came to a halt behind the desk. Facing them.

'News?' he said in Spanish. 'Good?'

They paused for a second too long. By the time the bald guy on the left shook his head, indicating that the situation had gone south, the man had turned and thundered a fist into the wall. It was made of plaster, and weak. It caved under his rage-induced blow. He let the sound reverberate through the sparsely furnished room, then turned back.

'Negotiations broke down,' the bald guy said. 'They're furious. They're threatening to cut off our supply.'

'You realise what this means?' he said.

'There's more,' the bald guy said. 'It seems it was an American who ruined us.'

'You're joking?'

'I wouldn't dare.'

'Has he been seen before?'

The bald guy shook his head again. 'Never. He's new. Big guy. Taller than you. Short brown hair. Seems well-built. That's about all we know.'

'So someone's hiring tourists to fuck with us.'

'I don't think he's a tourist. Not after what he did.'

'A mercenary?'

'I can't be sure.'

'Where's he staying?'

'We're still trying to figure that out. Once we do, we'll kill him.'

The man behind the desk held up a finger. 'No. Too messy, especially if he's as dangerous as you say he is. We don't want to cause a scene. Especially not in that district. And I want answers.'

'So we take him alive?'

'You think we can?'

The bald guy shrugged. 'I can't be certain. We rounded up a few witnesses and they say he's the real deal. I wouldn't risk it.'

The man in charge grinned. 'I have a better idea.'

He lifted a satellite phone off the desk and switched it on. He punched in a number that he knew by memory. Requests like these were often necessary, and incredibly useful. His call was answered before the second ring.

'Tomás,' the voice on the other end said, answering the call with his name. 'CICPC.'

Which stood for "Cuerpo de Investigaciones Científicas, Penales y Criminalísticas". A name that was far too long and as such had been abbreviated. They were one of many police agencies in Venezuela. It helped that the country's law enforcement consisted of a multitude of separate entities. It meant certain divisions could be targeted.

Paid off.

It was not necessary for the man in the singlet to respond with his own name. 'It's me.'

'What do you need?' Tomás said.

'There's an American who has caused us a great deal of trouble. I will send my men to provide you with a description. Find him and arrest him.'

'Murder?' The standard false charge.

'Murder.'

'Where do you want him?'

'Which prison is your worst?'

'All of them.'

'Any in particular?'

'I imagine El Infierno is the harshest on newcomers.'

Hell. Aptly named.

'Then throw him in there.'

'Why?'

'I want to see what he's capable of — before I kill him. Test him against the inmates. Maybe get some answers.'

'Consider it done.'

They ended the call without saying goodbye. There was no need for formalities following such a discussion. The officer on the other end of the line knew what was necessary. He would deliver, as he always did. And he would receive another duffel bag of laundered bolivars at the end of the year for his assistance.

'Who else knows the American's description?' the man said to the two men before him.

They looked at each other. Shrugged.

'Almost everyone,' the bald guy said. 'Rumours spread quickly.'

'So this information is not exclusive to the two of you?'

'No.'

'Perfect.'

The man in charge wrenched one of the desk drawers open and pulled out a loaded Taurus 24/7. A reliable handgun, smuggled across the border from Brazil a couple of years ago. He'd lost count of the number of times he'd used it. He always kept the safety off. For situations just like these.

Barely suppressing blinding rage, he shot the bald guy three times in the head. Each impact created a fresh geyser of blood. The 9mm rounds killed him instantly. He turned to the guy on the right, who now sat rigid in his chair, bolt upright. Pale with shock. He squeezed the trigger another couple of times and wiped the expression off the man's face.

The bodies keeled backwards off their chairs, thudding into the carpeted floor.

Another pair of bloodstains to add to the ever-growing collection.

There'd been no particular reason for what he'd done. These men were not at fault for the destabilisation of his operation. But killing calmed him. He did it because he could. Nothing more.

Breathing out the fury inside his chest, he left their corpses on the floor and went to find more men. He would send them to assist the police with their enquiries, then watch as El Infierno Prison tore the American scum apart.

CHAPTER 1

Six hours earlier…

Jason King surfaced from an undisturbed sleep, which was something of a rarity these days. He took note of his surroundings. A lavish hotel room, booked the night before on a whim. A sixty-inch television hung on the far wall. Floor-to-ceiling windows faced out over the Caribbean Sea. The curtains were drawn halfway, shrouding the room in a lowlight that added to the coziness. He lay prone in the middle of a four-poster bed, one of the largest he'd ever slept in.

Beside him, someone stirred. He glanced across and saw a bare shoulder and long brown locks spilling across one of the oversized satin pillows.

Ah, yes. That's right.

A bartender from the night before. He imagined she hadn't come across many foreigners of his stature. She'd been overly forward with her flirting. He'd noted the miniskirt and the long legs toned from years in the gym and couldn't help but respond accordingly.

He threw the covers away and crossed the length of the room, still naked. It took some time. The penthouse suite covered much of Diamanté Resort's top floor. He couldn't quite remember how much he'd paid. Whatever the case, it would leave no sizeable dent in his bank account.

Not much could.

He gazed out across the city of Maiquetía — a popular tourist destination in Vargas state — and let the calm of the morning wash over him. The silence was absolute. He guessed the walls were strongly insulated. He admired the view for a moment longer, then dressed quickly in a pair of workout shorts and a loose-fitting tank top. He shoved a change of clothes into a sports bag and left the room. The woman did not stir.

The corridors in this section of the hotel were just as luxurious as his room. Booking a suite like that was an all-inclusive experience. It came with high ceilings and quality bedding and plush carpets and dozens of unnecessary expensive amenities. All things he'd spent countless years without.

His life had not been one of luxury.

He took a private elevator down to the marble lobby. Now mid-morning, the enormous reception area was alive with activity. Peak hour. He didn't often wake up so late. Tourists bustled to and fro, some relaxed, some stressed. Most pasty and soft and innocent. He watched them as he passed by, holding a strange fascination.

He overheard a middle-aged British woman lecturing her husband for making them late to some kind of tourist attraction. King pondered her distress. It all seemed so fickle. Then again — when juxtaposed with the things he'd seen in the past — not much of ordinary civilian life warranted any kind of negative reaction whatsoever.

He found himself taking pleasure in every moment he wasn't being shot at.

The man behind the broad reception desk greeted him with an overly fake smile. "Diamanté Resort" was plastered in huge bold lettering across the wall behind him. 'Morning, sir. How did you enjoy your stay in the Deluxe Ocean-View Suite?'

He rattled off the name like it meant something.

'It was great,' King said.

'Did you want to reserve it for another day or two? You only booked the one night.'

'No, that won't be necessary.'

'Ah. Heading home?'

King shook his head. 'Got nowhere to be.'

That changed things. It meant he was hanging around in Maiquetía. Which meant he would likely go to the competition for tonight's stay.

It added a slight air of hostility to the receptionist's demeanour. 'Very well, sir,' he said curtly.

King smiled, recognising the shift in tone. 'Don't be too offended. I rarely spend two nights in the same place. Nothing personal.'

The man nodded, settling a little. 'May I assist you with anything else? Check out is at two in the afternoon, so—' he glanced at his watch, '—four hours from now.'

'Is there a gymnasium in this hotel?'

'Of course, sir. Eighth floor. Your room key will give you access.'

'Thank you.'

King headed back to the same plush elevator and slapped the number "8". Just before the metal doors slid closed a skinny man in a bucket hat darted through. He wore brown sandals and corduroy shorts and a cheap short-sleeved shirt.

'Morning,' he said, nodding in greeting.

King nodded back.

'On holiday?' the guy said.

Small talk, King thought. Nothing he enjoyed better.

He shook his head. 'Recently retired.'

'Nice!' the guy said. 'May I ask you a question?'

'You can ask me whatever you want.'

Doesn't mean I have to answer.

'Well, I was behind you in line,' the guy said, 'and I couldn't help but overhear that you're staying in the penthouse suite.'

'I am.'

'What's it like? I was looking into staying there with my family but it was just too expensive.'

'It's very nice. I'd recommend it.'

'How can you afford it?'

'That's very intrusive.'

'Sorry! Was just wondering. You're young, that's all. Thought you might have some secrets to success.' He scoffed, as if indicating that he was joking. King didn't respond. He stared straight ahead, unsmiling. The atmosphere quickly turned awkward.

The elevator ground to a halt on the eighth floor and its doors opened. At the other end of the hallway, a glass door led through to a vast exercise room. King stepped out and looked back.

'Sorry, buddy,' he said. 'But you really don't want to know.'

'I don't?'

'Stick to whatever it is you do,' King said. 'I'm sure you'll be happier.'

He left the man to ponder such a statement as the doors clicked close once again. Now alone in the hallway, he walked across its carpeted floors and went into the gym, revealing a large space packed with heavy iron plates and a few powerlifting platforms running along the far wall. Exactly what he was looking for. None of the psuedo-bullshit of commercial gyms. He didn't need rows upon rows of treadmills.

He crossed to the deadlift platform and settled into his regular routine. Three warm-up sets with escalating weights, all ten repetitions each. He kept his back straight, his head aligned with his torso. He made sure to activate his glutes as he ripped the barbell off the floor.

The actions always calmed him. He'd been powerlifting his entire career. Even when the world had seemingly fallen apart around him, the weights were still there. When every ounce of effort in your body is primed and focused on heaving hundreds of pounds off the floor, there's not much room to mull over past memories.

It helped keep his mind in the present.

A task he'd been trying to accomplish more and more with each passing day.

He loaded another plate on each side and stared at the weight before him.

Six hundred pounds.

It had taken him years of training to reach this point. He dusted his hands with chalk, settled into position, took a deep breath and tapped into something primal. Something animalistic. He grit his teeth and wrenched at the bar, activating each muscle simultaneously. It rose. He locked out his legs, then lowered it, then raised it one more time.

Two reps. Face crimson, veins pumping.

He let the weight crash back down and took some time to recover.

The rest of the workout passed quickly. He followed the deadlifts with a range of accessory movements, then thirty minutes of steady-state cardio. All the power in the world was useless if he couldn't keep aerobically fit at the same time.

Sweating from seemingly every pore at once, he crossed the room and spent a short gruelling stint in the sauna, flushing out his body. It was therapeutic. He let droplets of sweat cover the floor below. Hunched low. Head bowed. Exercise was just that.

Temporary discomfort for long-term benefit.

A cold shower cooled him down and closed up his pores. He dried himself and dressed in the spare clothes he'd brought. A casual T-shirt with a cut in the neckline and jeans. The sports bag went into one of the empty lockers and he took the elevator back to the ground floor.

An hour of gruelling exercise. Yet now he was refreshed and invigorated for the day ahead.

He had no particular destination. No pressing matters of concern. It had taken some time to become accustomed to such a lifestyle. Years upon years of following orders had taken their toll. In the back of his mind, a tiny voice told him there were responsibilities he was avoiding.

You should be at war.

He shrugged it off, and stepped out into the humid glow of a late morning in Venezuela.

Diamanté Resort stood out against its surroundings, shiny and vast against the dusty, dilapidated buildings around it. It was situated right near the beach, making it a prime tourist destination. King figured he would get away from its lure. See Maiquetía for what it really was. That meant no tourists. No fake luxury. He needed a break from the unrelenting niceties of such an expensive hotel.

He crossed the busy street, weaving between traffic. He passed tourists weighed down by bags and seaside convenience stores complete with roller security shutters. It seemed in this area there were CCTV cameras on every corner. Food trucks lined the promenade facing the Caribbean Sea, all painted in an array of bright colours to attract the eye of potential customers.

A local man at the bar the night before had told King of a bazaar just a ten-minute walk from the hotel. He'd spoken of steaming native food and ice-cold drinks. The recommendation had come with a demand that King try something called *tequeños*. He wasn't one to turn down a good meal.

Besides, he had nowhere else to be.

Overhead, clouds formed on the horizon, threatening to roll in later in the day. For now it was sunny. The humidity hung thick in the air, drawing sweat from his pores again. It was seemingly impossible to avoid such a dilemma in this country. He didn't care. The conditions were pleasant when he contrasted them with a previous life.

A few local pedestrians shot him quizzical glances as he headed further away from the main tourist district, wondering what a foreigner was doing moving away from relative safety. Many ignored him. They probably figured that — given his stature — he could handle his own.

They were right.

He found the bazaar easily enough. A chaotic babbling rose from one of the streets branching off the main road. He turned down it and found himself in between two long rows of rickety wooden stalls, all covered in various forms of fabric. Most had been faded by the sun long ago. Enthusiastic vendors spruiked their deals to the crowd, comprised mostly of locals. The customers haggled back. It resulted in a cacophony of shouting and gesticulating that would have scared away many tourists unfamiliar to the sights and sounds.

King had seen enough of the world. He was unperturbed. He started wandering along the street, glancing at stalls on either side.

Then he saw three men heading for him.

No, not *for* him. *Past* him. They strode purposefully, coming from the other direction. There was something important on their minds, that was for sure. They moved with the confidence and the wide gait of a trio that exerted control. Customers in the bazaar hurried out of their way. A few nearby civilians made sure not to come into contact with them.

The men weren't used to taking shit from anyone.

One was short and fat. He wore an open singlet and a faded tracksuit. His rosy cheeks had reddened under the morning sun. He walked in front, striding with an exaggerated swagger, chin up, beady eyes flicking over the crowd, searching for anyone who might have the gall to initiate a confrontation. The other two were a few inches taller. Similar dress. Similar demeanour.

From where he stood, King realised he was in their path.

Without giving it a second thought, he decided not to move.Something about them already irritated him.

He pretended to browse one of the stalls, keeping himself firmly rooted in place. The stocky guy in front came within range. He went to brush past, expecting King to scurry out of the way.

King did not.

The stocky guy sensed this a second before they touched and took the effort to drop his shoulder down and drive it into King's torso, adding power to the shove. Sending a message. *Don't get in my way, asshole.*

It didn't work.

The thug simply bounced off King's frame, unable to shift him even an inch out of place. The guy had to take an awkward step to the side in order to correct his footing and save himself from toppling off-balance. He hadn't expected to run into a brick wall.

Which made him look like an idiot.

Something he certainly didn't appreciate.

CHAPTER 2

He squared up to King, eyes wide, temper flaring. 'Got a fuckin' problem, *extranjero?*'

King peered down at the little man. 'Don't think so.'

'American!' the guy said, cackling. 'Ey, boys, we got ourselves an American! Do you know where you are, gringo?'

'I do.'

'You clearly don't. Otherwise you would have got the fuck out of my way.'

'I'm in a market,' King said.

The guy paused for a second. Confused. The smile disappeared. 'What?'

'See? I know where I am.'

'You think you're clever?'

'Reasonably.'

'Not clever enough. You didn't recognise me. You're *loco.*'

'Am I supposed to be scared of a circus midget?'

'You cut that shit, gringo. You don't know who I work for.'

'I really don't care.'

The guy glared at him. King could tell he would shortly resort to blows. A ball of anger had been building over the course of the conversation — and now it would finally culminate in a swing, or a shove, or something along those lines. He kept himself primed, ready to react to any sort of explosive movement. The thug was an angry little ball of rage.

Napoleon complex in full effect, he thought.

'You want us to hurt you?' the fat guy said.

'Not really. I don't like getting hurt.'

'Then apologise.'

'Apologise for what?'

'For bumping me. And calling me a midget.'

'Why would I do that?'

'Because we'll fuck you up otherwise.'

King raised two eyebrows and smiled like he'd been told the funniest joke in the world. 'And how are you going to do that?'

The guy let out a loud, sardonic laugh. 'You just wait and see.'

King was done with conversation. The trio could attempt to intimidate him as much as they desired, but it wasn't going to work. So they would either try something — or they would move on. He was prepared for either option.

The fat guy decided on the former.

He swung a balled fist in a wide uppercut, charged with the fury of a man who had been provoked. A big looping haymaker. King saw it coming from a mile away. He simply leant back on his heel and moved his chin back a few inches. Even if he'd stayed put, the impact would have been nothing more than a glancing blow. It went swinging past, almost in slow-motion. Barely any effort was involved in the evasive manoeuvre. King knew he had the speed and dexterity to avoid pinpoint-accurate shots from trained martial artists. The man in front of him was nothing of the sort.

The fat guy in question went stumbling past, dropping his head low. He'd overcompensated. Thrown himself off balance for the second time in a minute. King wrapped two hands around the guy's singlet and used brute strength to heave him along, adding an abundance of forward momentum to the stumble. The guy's feet scuffled against the dusty ground and he tripped and slammed head-first into the brick wall between two of the stalls. Vendors on either side watched in quiet bemusement as he slumped to the ground and sat there, staring up at King.

Dazed and disoriented and confused all at once.

King turned around, expecting adrenalin-fuelled confrontation from the other two. He found none. They stared at him, hesitant to make a move. Their feet remained firmly planted on the baked asphalt. He registered the look in their eyes and knew he would face no further issues. They were angry, sure. Furious, even. But behind that mask of fake aggression there was shock and awe.

Not many people reacted to violence the way King did.

'We're done here?' he said simply.

They did not respond.

'We're done,' King said.

He turned his back on them and set off down the bazaar — the way he'd been heading in the first place. Little had changed. The incessant drone of chatter had not dimmed during the confrontation. Clearly the locals couldn't care less about a minor scuffle. They'd seen worse.

As he strolled he took a final glance behind him and saw the fat guy still on the ground, arms on his knees, staring at King. His face sported an expression somewhere between disbelief and embarrassment.

Not a good combination, King thought.

He figured they would come for him. For a few reasons. When confronted, the fat guy had instantly highlighted his own importance. Meaning the trio were probably part of some kind of gang. And several passersby had witnessed the altercation. These men could not be made laughing stocks. They prided themselves on their reputation. Which meant they would need to make an example out of the man who had just made them look like fools.

King figured if further action was necessary, it would do good to get it out of the way quickly.

So he turned left at the end of the bazaar and made for the quieter streets of Maiquetía.

He spotted an alleyway running between two high-rise apartment buildings, both shoddily constructed, seemingly on the verge of collapse. He paused at the entrance and assessed its contents. The narrow lane reeked of urine and garbage. He saw dried puddles of vomit on the ground and overflowing dumpsters lining the walls. It was uninhabited.

Perfect.

He strode into the alley, and there he waited.

It didn't take long.

The three of them rounded the corner less than a minute later. This time, they were armed. King spotted the shiny glint of knife blades and he felt his body react accordingly.

Instantly his adrenal glands released the hormone cortisol. He experienced this sensation through the usual symptoms — a churning gut, a dry mouth and cold hands. He knew that the sole purpose of cortisol was to tap into the body's energy reserves. Recognising a life-or-death situation was imminent, he felt an unnatural vigour. He knew things were drastically more serious given the emergence of weapons. The instinctual fight-or-flight mechanism kicked in.

Usually he gave leeway to thugs and common criminals who wanted nothing more than a fight. He showed mercy, because most of them were too dumb to know any better.

But not when weapons capable of fatal wounds were thrown into the mix.

Now he would respond with everything he had.

The two taller men brandished traditional box cutters, probably extracted from their pockets. The fat guy had something a little heftier. His porky fingers were clasped around the handle of a sizeable machete, more than likely picked up from one of the stalls on the way to the alley. It looked devastating. Sharpened to perfection. Probably on sale for an exorbitant price.

The three of them advanced simultaneously. *Smart,* King thought. They could certainly overwhelm him if they attacked all at once. He had to break their formation.

For the first time in months, he felt true fear. It didn't happen often. Usually the odd confrontation he found himself in — like the altercation in the bazaar — quickly resolved itself without any sort of real threat to his wellbeing. A long and violent career had conditioned him to embrace physical incidents as nothing more than an ordinary part of life. He thought nothing of them. He'd moved on from the scuffle in the market seconds after he walked away.

But now the atmosphere had shifted. His pulse increased. His hands were clammy. The natural physiological response to fear reared its ugly head. He welcomed the sensation. It provided a sort of tunnel vision as he responded cognitively to the threat. He zoned in, ignoring the behavioural instinct to escape. It was human nature to run away from a threat when faced with one as dire as this.

King's life experiences had allowed him to almost completely eliminate that sort of natural reaction.

He grit his teeth and forced himself to fight.

The response came as if it were second nature.

Back-pedalling down the alley, he snatched one of the fat garbage bags off the top of a dumpster and hurled it like a fastball at the fat guy. It hit him in the torso, which caused absolutely no damage. But that wasn't the point. Upon impact the bag squelched and its material slit open. The contents erupted from the gash. Garbage juices splashed across the man's singlet, covering his bare arms. Droplets sprayed over his mouth.

One of two things would now happen.

Either the fat guy would fall back, recoiling away from the disgusting occurrence. Or he would be blinded by rage and charge forward. He didn't possess the discipline or experience to ignore the provocation and concentrate solely on the task at hand. King knew enough about human nature to be aware of that.

The guy sprinted at him.

Perfect.

He ducked under the first machete swing, a maximum-energy horizontal slash aimed at his throat. As he dropped and felt the blade whisk through the air above the back of his neck, he couldn't help but feel relief. The first shot was always the most dangerous. Once again the man had put all his effort into a single action. Perhaps he would never learn. Perhaps he would continue to suffer the consequences of such behaviour for the rest of his life.

Whatever the case, he wouldn't forget what happened next anytime soon.

Now well in range, King thundered an uppercut into the guy's mid-section, targeting the soft tissue on the side of his torso. Searching for the liver. If he placed it perfectly, he knew the guy would be incapacitated for hours.

At least.

The liver was a solid organ coated in a tough fibrous membrane. This membrane did not like to be stretched in any way. King's balled-up fist landed with all the upper body strength he had. And he had plenty. His knuckles crunched into soft pudgy skin, shooting a vicious amount of power into the guy's liver, resulting in one of the most painful sensations the human body could experience.

The guy dropped his hands and his legs buckled and he collapsed to the dirty alley floor, moaning and crying. His body reacted without his brain's approval. An instinctive response. He curled into a fetal position and let out a sob, paralysed by the pain.

By then King had already stepped over him. His eyes darted left and right, scouring the expressions of the two remaining men. Both were shocked by the sudden turn of events, yet the man on the left seemed to have his focus still locked on King. The man on the right stared past him, observing the fat guy's agony in disbelief. Distracted.

King had a split second to deal with the more focused man.

The guy swung the box cutter, fast. King shot out a hand and wrapped it around his slight wrist, halting the momentum of the swing. Now the strength advantage came into play. He pushed off one leg and drove the guy back-first into the alley wall. The action was accompanied by a brutal *thud*, knocking the wind out of the man's lungs. King kept a vice-like grip on the guy's wrist, preventing any more opportunities to stab out with the knife. With the right he swung an elbow. He twisted his body into it. It crashed against his adversary's chin, breaking bone. Elbows were short and sharp. It didn't take long to throw one. He wound back and hit the guy with another pair, each knocking teeth loose. Three total, rapid fire. *Bam-bam-bam.*

When he let go, the guy dropped like a rag doll.

King spun. Eyes wide, veins pumping. Searching for the last guy.

Just in time.

The man had come to his senses and charged head-long, his knife hand outstretched, looking to drive the blade into him. King used the length of his legs to his advantage. He lashed out in a front kick. Two fluid motions. Bring the knee up, leg bent. Then extend it, pushing off the other leg, driving power through the hips. The heel of his foot met the guy's chest with enough force to stop a bull. The man had been sprinting full-pelt, so the change in momentum sent him skittering away. He let out a surprised wheeze, suddenly clawing for breath.

King rushed in and wrapped two beefy arms around the guy's mid-section. He pinned his arms to his side, preventing any further attempts with the knife. Then he threw him like a child discarding an unwanted plaything.

The man smashed head-first into one of the dumpsters.

The skull-against-metal contact made a *clang* which King associated with a concussion. Just to make sure, he soccer-kicked the man in the face, whipping his head back before he even had time to fall to the ground.

Three men down. The whole thing had taken a little under ten seconds.

King adjusted his shirt and assessed the damage. The fat guy had taken one of the more powerful liver shots he'd ever landed, sunk with the power created from a threat on one's life. He wouldn't be getting up anytime soon. One of the tall skinny guys had a broken jaw. The other probably had a sternal fracture from the front kick. Both were severely concussed.

Job done.

King left the alley a minute after entering it, receiving several bewildered stares from passing pedestrians. Three armed members of what seemed to be a terrifying local gang had followed him in, and he'd emerged unscathed with no sign of the assailants.

He assumed they were not used to witnessing such a sight.

He avoided their gazes and headed back the way he'd come.

CHAPTER 3

By the time he made it back to the hotel and took the elevator up sixty stories, it was approaching midday in Maiquetía. He pulled the keycard from his jeans and unlocked the door to the penthouse suite. He entered to find it empty.

No sign of the girl from the night before.

He shrugged. Neither of them had assumed that the encounter was anything more than a fling. Besides, at this stage in his life he was far from ready for anything more. He'd spent his career alone; he would heal from it alone.

He crossed the room and picked up the landline phone beside his bed. The number he dialled had been ingrained in his memory for years. He hadn't forgotten it since he'd retired, and he knew he would not forget it anytime soon. Not after what the man on the other end had done for him.

The phone was answered quickly. 'Dirk Wiggins.'

He smiled. 'Hey, old friend. It's King.'

'Jason! Thought you were dead for a while.'

'Because I didn't call?'

'Nah, I knew you were out there somewhere. Didn't blame you for falling off the grid after Australia. It's what I told you to do. How are you doing?'

King thought back to that turbulent period. The never-ending woods of the Victorian countryside. Mysterious enemies. Attempts on his life. Savage violence. His body had taken several weeks to heal from the trauma it had been put through.

'Much better than when you saw me last,' he said. 'How did the investigation go?'

'As they all do. Slow as shit. You caused quite the stir. It took an insane amount of manpower to keep the journalists from sniffing around.'

'I hope you were compensated for helping out.'

'Ah … you know me. Never get rewarded for my troubles.'

'You're back in Delta now?'

'Wouldn't dream of anything else.'

'Enjoying yourself?'

'You could put it that way. It's just what I do. Always have, always will. Where'd you end up?'

'I'm currently in Venezuela.'

A sigh. 'Didn't I tell you to stay out of trouble?'

'How do you know I'm in trouble?'

'You're in Venezuela,' Dirk said matter-of-factly. 'Of course you're in trouble.'

'Don't get ahead of yourself.'

'Let me guess; you're staying in the slums, picking fights with cartels?'

King looked around the lavish penthouse. 'Far from it. Haven't had to deal with anything more than a few local thugs.'

'You dealt with local thugs in Australia,' Dirk said. 'Look what that caused.'

'I'll be careful.'

'No you won't.'

They both laughed.

'I can handle myself,' King said. 'You know that. Good to hear you're doing well, Dirk.'

'You too, brother. Take care.'

King dropped the phone onto its cradle and sat back against the bed frame. He felt the expensive linen sheets and listened to the total silence of the suite. He stared out the windows at a gorgeous view of the Vargas coastline.

All foreign sensations.

He was used to the coarse brittleness of sand and the sound of enemy gunfire and the feeling of warm blood gushing from bullet wounds. These feelings still came to him, late at night. He feared he would never shake them. A man couldn't live the life he had and emerge unscathed.

No-one could.

He drifted into an afternoon nap. Outside, clouds rolled in, obscuring the sun, plunging the room into lowlight. But King didn't witness it. He slept soundly for the first time in weeks. He dreamt nothing. When he came to a couple of hours later, he baulked at the fact that he had napped undisturbed. It meant that something had changed in his life. Some kind of order had been restored.

And it seemed clear what that something was.

Violence.

He hoped that was not the case. He dreaded that he might have become so accustomed to combat over his career that it was now impossible to feel at ease without confrontation. He mulled over the predicament. Clearly, ten years as a combat operative had a profound effect on his life. He wondered just how far its reach would stretch into his retirement.

Then the silence broke.

He heard sudden rapid footsteps in the corridor outside. His senses heightened. At least four men, probably more.

You fucking idiot, King.

He'd simply assumed that Diamanté Resort would be immune to the thugs from the alley. Surely preventative measures were in place to limit the infiltration of a luxury hotel by local gangsters…

But it seemed they had rallied some friends and come back for thirds. This time, they probably had guns. King wondered if the next few moments would be his last.

He sprung off the bed and crossed the room. Searching for some kind of weapon. Anything he could use to defend himself. For the last two months he had travelled unarmed, following certain principles to try and acclimatise to a peaceful existence.

Leave everything behind. Don't invite trouble.

That had come back to bite him in the ass.

He eyed a heavy paperweight resting on the desk by the door, holding down a stack of brochures and informational pamphlets about the resort's features. It would have to do. He snatched the weight off the wooden surface and crept quietly to the door.

Definitely more than four men. It sounded like there was an army headed his way. Perhaps it was useless even attempting a fight. But it wasn't in his nature to accept death, not even in the face of massive odds. He would go down swinging.

The footsteps outside reached the end of the hallway and someone rapped on the door. They waited a beat. Then they pounded against the wooden frame, knocking hard enough to draw the attention of anyone in the nearby vicinity. King hesitated, crouched on the other side, listening to the knocking.

Would the thugs knock?

He doubted it. So who was this?

The door crashed off its hinges, struck by some kind of battering ram, either makeshift or the real thing. Whatever the case, it did the job. The entire door struck King and he felt men on the other side, pushing against it, threatening to throw him off-balance. He shouldered the door aside and it crashed to the penthouse floor. He gripped the paperweight in his right hand and primed himself to throw a devastating right hook.

Then he stopped.

Half a dozen men in police uniform bustled into the room, guns drawn. They surrounded him on all sides. King saw emblems labelled 'CICPC', embroidered into the breast pockets of their khakis. They weren't ordinary police. These men wore Kevlar vests and brandished formidable-looking weaponry. They'd been expecting a firefight.

No-one spoke. King let the paperweight fall to the ground. He glanced around at the wide-eyed expressions. They thought he was some kind of monster.

'What the hell is this?' he said to the room.

CHAPTER 4

Again, no-one responded.

King's gut twisted into a knot. Perhaps the thugs' reach extended further than he thought. He'd heard tales of the corruption rife within Venezuela's law enforcement. He'd never expected to find himself on the other end of it.

Or maybe…

'What is this?' he said again, looking at each man in turn.

One stepped forward. He possessed an air of seniority, as if he were the one in charge. Age lines creased his cheeks. He looked at King with unbridled contempt.

'You're under arrest,' he said. He spoke good English. Barely any trace of an accent.

'I figured,' King said. 'What for?'

'Murder.'

So it had nothing to do with the thugs' injuries. He would not be charged with assault, or anything of the sort. This was a clearly false allegation.

'Murder of who?'

'That is not my business to discuss.'

The penthouse descended into silence once more. King stared at the five barrels pointed his way. He didn't dare move a muscle. It only took one trigger-happy bastard to overreact and put him away forever.

'Will you co-operate with us?' the leader said. His name badge read *Tomás*.

'Will you explain what this is about?'

'I told you.'

'I didn't murder anyone.'

'That is not for me to determine,' Tomás said.

It seemed the argument had become circular. Tomás and his men refused to budge on their position. King looked around and came to the inevitable conclusion that he had little choice in the matter. In his peripheral vision he saw the cabinet against the far wall containing his passport and wallet. *Would they find it?* If the police seized it, he could forget about fleeing the country in the event that he managed to slip away at some point in the near future.

Backup plans are always beneficial.

He raised his hands above his head, pulse beating fast.

'Will I get a trial?'

Tomás said nothing. He tugged a pair of battered old handcuffs from his belt and pulled King's arms behind his back. He locked the cuffs tight. Too tight.

'Easy there,' King said.

'What are you going to do about it?' the man spat.

They marched him out of the penthouse and down the decadent corridor. Tomás kept one hand in the small of his back the entire time, pushing him forwards no matter how fast he walked. A policeman rested a hand on each of his shoulders, creating a triangle that would be impossible to escape from. His hands were pinned behind his back anyway. He would not run. That would cause far more problems than it solved.

They manhandled him into the elevator and began a tension-filled descent to the ground floor.

'I didn't kill anybody,' King said again.

'Shut the fuck up.'

The elevator ground to a halt and the doors swung open. The congregation headed through the marble lobby, attracting surprised looks from all the tourists. King kept his head down and focused on walking. He had too much on his mind to worry about what everyone else thought of him. He could be heading straight for a gulag.

Thrown to the wolves.

A police van waited outside the hotel, its engine idling. Were it not for the Spanish logo on the side indicating it was an official government vehicle, King would have thought he was being kidnapped. It seemed to be on the verge of collapse. Black paint flaked off all sides. He guessed the budget for the police force was considerably low. It was certainly reflected in their vehicles.

Probably why there was so much corruption.

They put him in the back. He sat on one of the rusting metal benches and hunched over, resting his elbows on his knees. Three policemen piled in next to him. The doors slammed shut. There was a brief period of silence, then the tyres spun and they peeled away from Diamanté Resort. King guessed it was the last time he would lay eyes on the hotel.

There were no windows to try and deduce the van's destination. A small interior light with a weak bulb was built into the roof overhead. It flickered every time they turned a corner. Which was often, and fast. The driver took the van recklessly around various bends, trying to disturb the suspect in the back. King planted both feet on the floor and stabilised himself as the cabin lurched from side to side.

He kept his mouth shut. All the necessary talking had already taken place. He knew that he had not killed anyone, and that the police refused to believe otherwise. There was nothing to do but wait to arrive at their destination. Wherever that was.

Ten minutes later, the van stopped and the driver's door slammed and harsh light flooded into the cabin as the rear doors were pulled open. Tomás looked up at him with a gleeful smile.

'We're here,' he said.

'Where?' King said.

'Your home for the next few days. While we get you processed.'

The policeman on either side gripped his arms and forced him out of the car. He stepped down into a deserted street filled with cheap, indiscriminate residential buildings. No houses around here. Just tiny offices and dilapidated apartment blocks and the sounds of babies crying and men shouting.

A relatively nice part of town, King figured.

They'd pulled up in front of what could only be a police precinct. The entire cluster of buildings was painted a stark, unforgiving blue. A collection of military and police vehicles were parked at the entrance, resting idly in their lots. The sun had come out again in the late afternoon. It beat down mercilessly, cooking the asphalt. The humidity drew sweat for the millionth time that day. He ducked his head and wiped his brow against his shirt as they led him inside the station.

There was no air conditioning in the building whatsoever. He was marched through disgusting hallways with dim lighting and through to a small processing room. On the other side of the room sat a large steel door. Even while shut, King could hear feral screams behind it. The shouting and cackling seemed to echo, meaning whatever lay beyond was a large place.

'The hell is this?' he said, turning to Tomás, angered by the lack of answers.

Tomás slapped him hard. A stinging blow that cracked against his cheek and sent him veering to the side. The officer laughed, a short sharp burst of cackling.

'Don't you dare talk to me like that,' he said. 'You're scum.'

'Please explain what's going on.'

'You're going through there,' Tomás said, pointing to the steel door.

'And what's through there?'

'Holding cells. We keep everyone there while we process them.'

'Process them? You don't even know my name. Aren't you going to question me?'

'Why would we do that?'

'To get answers.'

'We don't want answers.'

'What do you want?'

'We want you behind bars.'

'Where's my trial, you corrupt fuck?' King said, his blood boiling.

Tomás crossed the distance between them and squared up to him. King considered head-butting the man, but figured the temporary satisfaction would be outweighed by the severe consequences.

'You get a trial if I say you get a trial,' he said, saliva bubbling in the corners of his lips. 'I'm God in this place. You understand?'

King didn't respond.

'I said — do you understand?'

King still said nothing. He simply stared at the man in disgust. Tomás scoffed.

'The silent treatment, eh?' he said. 'Very well. Let's see how you like it in here when I tell them you're a wealthy American.'

'I think I can handle myself.'

The officer bowed his head and grinned wryly. 'We'll certainly find out.'

Two policemen patted him down, removing the sparse possessions he had in his pockets. The hotel key card and a thick roll of bolivares, equivalent to a few thousand U.S. Dollars.

'No phone?' Tomás said.

'Don't own one.'

'Shame. No chance for you to call home and beg for help.'

'You can't honestly expect to get away with this?'

Tomás laughed cruelly in his face. 'We can get away with whatever we want. You think you're the first tourist to disappear? If anyone comes poking around, we'll bury you. Pretend you never existed.'

King stared straight ahead. Silently fuming, yet at the same time uncomfortable. Because Tomás was right. No-one would ever know if they decided to kill him.

To his surprise, the officer tucked all of the Venezuelan currency back into his jeans.

'Thought you'd take that,' King said.

'I don't want you to die too quickly. You'll need it to stay alive. Plus, we have plenty.'

A harsh digital buzz erupted from the loudspeaker in the corner of the room. The steel door clicked a second later, unlocking. Tomás wrapped his fingers around its sturdy handle and wrenched it open.

A hand shoved King forward and he stepped into the madhouse.

CHAPTER 5

The holding cells were situated on either side of a long, high-ceilinged hallway, roughly the size of a church. It paralleled such a building in dimensions only. The whole place was filthy. The unmistakable smell of old faeces and urine emanated throughout the corridor, triggering King's gag reflex. He fought the urge to cough. It would look weak. Tomás would revel in his discomfort. He swallowed hard and pressed on.

The cells were separated from one another by dirty brick walls. Their fronts were made of steel bars, thick and narrowly interspersed, preventing escape. They ranged from rooms the size of small houses to tiny individual cells. The men in the single cells had mattresses and pillows. Their living conditions were a little cleaner. It was the large cells clustered with local thugs that worried him. The men were rabid and drug-crazed. Their eyes locked onto him like he was fresh meat ready to be torn apart.

'This isn't the prison?' he said to Tomás.

The man laughed cruelly. 'Far from it. If you think this place is bad, you don't know what you're in for if we throw you in El Infierno.'

King knew enough rudimentary Spanish to translate the name of said prison.

Hell.

He certainly hoped he didn't make it there.

The officers frog-marched him to the largest cell and stopped outside its door. Tomás roared a command at the screaming men within. They withdrew from the doorway, shrinking away. Completely insane, yet obedient to authority.

As Tomás unlocked the door, King sized up the situation. At least twenty men inside the cell. All twitching and shivering. Most hopped up on some kind of narcotic. They would all want a piece of him. They'd want to prove themselves to their fellow miscreants.

He knew what needed to be done. It would mean lashing out in an unprovoked attack, but it was necessary to preserve his own wellbeing. At the end of the day, he had to put his own safety first.

They pushed him in and slammed the door shut behind him. None of the men inside moved. They stared at the congregation of officers outside with vacant glassy eyes and twitching lips. When the policemen turned their backs and made for the processing room they'd come from, King knew that it would be seconds before one of his cellmates attacked.

They were itching for a fight.

He watched Tomás lead the three other policemen back down the hallway. Then he spun and shot out both hands, seizing the nearest man by the collar. This guy had the look of a meth addict. He was skinny and gaunt and aggressive as all hell. King activated his muscles and lifted the guy off his feet before he could mount any kind of offence. He kept him elevated with a single arm, and with the other wound up and crashed a fist into his nose. Blood spurted from both nostrils. The guy let out a cry of pain.

King let go and he fell to the ground in a heap.

The animalistic grunts and screams ceased. Everyone stared at the aftermath in awe.

'*You see that?!*' King roared, loud enough for every cell to hear. He pointed a finger at the curled-up addict. 'The next person to fuck with me gets exactly that! *Do not fuck with me!*'

The speech had its intended effect. Instantly the atmosphere inside the cell shifted. The undercurrent of aggression faded away. He assumed none of the men spoke English, yet they had received the general tone of his message well enough. They dispersed, breaking the formation of the group, turning their attention back to whatever it was they'd been doing before he arrived. Some sat on the rusting steel benches lining the cell walls. Others sat on the ground, lighting cigarettes. They'd seen enough. They knew he meant business.

Not an easy target — which was all they seemed to be interested in.

When the crowd cleared, King saw a man sitting on a bench in the far corner. He had his legs up on its surface. His head rested against the concrete wall. He was European, dressed differently to all the other thugs. They wore tattered clothing, covered in stains and full of holes. He wore an expensive polo shirt and a pair of designer jeans. The clothing had started to turn filthy from his time in the cell. But it was still a considerable step above the other men.

King crossed the room and sat down next to the guy.

'I'm Jason King,' he said. 'You speak English?'

The man turned his head and made eye contact for the first time. He had tanned skin and defined cheekbones. His long black hair was tied back. He stared vacantly at King.

'I guess not,' King said.

'You guess wrong,' the guy said, affected by only a slight trace of a Spanish accent. 'Name's Roman.'

'Pleased to meet you, Roman.'

'Pleasure's all mine.'

'What are you doing here?'

'Taking a vacation.' Silence. Roman's expression remained dead-faced. Then he laughed. 'What the fuck do you think I'm doing in here, buddy?'

'I meant — what are you in for?'

Roman didn't respond. He withdrew a long cigar from the pocket of his polo; a fat Cuban. He placed the head between his pearly white teeth. Pulled out a silver lighter. Lit the foot. Took a long puff. Exhaled a cloud of smoke and rested his head against the wall once again. A nearby cellmate noticed the scent and looked up from his position on the floor, eyes wide. Roman shook his head and the thug bowed back down.

Defeated by a single gesture.

'They do what you tell them?' King said.

'Of course.'

'Who are you?'

Roman took another long draw on the cigar. 'I think the real question is — who are you? They know me around here. I know them. None of us know you.'

'I'm new in town.'

'I know. You're either new, or not important.'

'You know everyone important?'

Roman nodded. 'Almost.'

'What do you do?'

'I'm in the import-export business.'

King nodded his understanding. 'So what are you doing in here?'

'Got into a fight. They weren't happy with me. Threw me in for the night.'

'You can't pay them off?'

Roman shrugged. 'Usually I can. Not today, it seems. Caught them on a bad day.'

'Unlucky.'

'So who are you?'

'Nobody,' King said. 'I'm retired.'

'Terrible way to handle retirement. What'd you get arrested for?'

'Murder.'

'Did you do it?'

'No. I'm hoping that will come out soon enough.'

Roman exploded in laughter, a bellowing cackle from somewhere deep in his stomach. He coughed from the cigar smoke and slapped his knee. 'My friend, nothing comes out in here.'

King stared at him. 'What?'

'There doesn't have to be a reason,' Roman said. 'That's how this place works. "Murder" is bullshit. You're in here because someone wants you in here. Simple as that.'

'And when will they let me go?'

'Impossible to say. From how angry the captain looked —
I'd say never.'

'They can do that?'

Roman smiled. 'Welcome to Venezuela.'

CHAPTER 6

A long row of dirty glass windows were built high into the opposite wall. They showed nothing more than a sliver of sky, but a quick glance out revealed that it was approaching late-afternoon. King had sat in silence for the best part of an hour, observing the cell. Staying wary for any signs of danger. Mulling over his options.

He had few.

He quickly realised that an escape attempt in the lobby of Diamanté Resort would have been the smartest move. A public space, with plenty of variables. A lot of room for error by the police. A vicious elbow to the left, a headbutt to the right, a thunderous kick into Tomás' groin — and he would have bought a few precious seconds to disappear into the crowd. It might have worked. Probably not. But a bullet in the back was preferable to whatever awaited him in El Infierno.

There was nothing to do now but play their sick game.

He turned to Roman, who had drifted into a doze. 'Hey.'

The man opened his eyes. 'What?'

'What happens to you?'

'They'll probably let me go in the morning. My business partners will contact the station. Might pay a bribe. Whatever the case, it shouldn't take long.'

'Can I pay a bribe?'

'You got a lot of money?'

King shrugged. 'I have enough.'

Roman raised an eyebrow. 'What brings a rich man like yourself to a place like this?'

'The travel bug, I guess.'

'Well, to each their own. What business were you in?'

'I was a soldier.'

'A rich man and a soldier are mutually exclusive.'

'Not the case for me.'

'Ah — you were specialised?'

'I won't go into details.'

'It's pretty clear from the way you demolished Hector. The guy's got a bit of a name for himself out in the streets. Would be embarrassing if people found out he got manhandled by a tourist.'

'What are you saying?'

The cigar flared as Roman touched it to his lips. 'Retaliation might be in order.'

King sighed. They looked across the cell at the man he'd attacked on the way in.

Hector, apparently.

He sat with his arms wrapped around his legs on the other side of the cell. Blood had caked dry under his nose, covering his lips. He rocked back and forth, muttering under his breath, staring at them from afar. Scrutinising King.

'If he tries anything, it won't be pretty,' King said.

Roman looked across. 'What are you telling me for? You think I care?'

'I'm worried the police will care.'

The man laughed. 'No-one will give a shit. Anything can be bought in this place.'

'Except my freedom, apparently.'

Roman raised a finger. 'Fair point. Except your freedom. Can I ask you a question?'

'Sure.'

'Were you looking for drugs in Vargas?'

'What?'

'Drugs. It might be why you're in here. If you were too intrusive.'

'No.'

'Did you get any requests? To carry out favours for anyone?'

'No.'

'A man of your skill-set … might be appealing to some of the criminals in this state.'

'That's a wild assumption.'

'Is it correct?'

King cocked his head, taken aback by the barrage of questions. 'No, Roman. Stop asking.'

Roman shrugged and settled back against the wall. 'Fair enough.'

They lapsed into silence once more. The sky outside darkened and the air seemed to grow thicker. It was stifling in the cell. The stench seeped into everything. King's shirt had long ago been soaked through with sweat. He saw some of the thugs peeling off their clothing in an attempt to cool themselves. He did the same, removing the shirt so he just wore jeans. He draped the wet shirt over the bench.

'Do we get dinner?' he said.

'If you have money,' Roman said. 'Do you?'

King nodded. 'In my pocket. I'm not sure about pulling it out in front of these guys.'

'Smart move, my friend. Wait for one of the guards to walk past. Then let him know what you want. He'll get anything for the right price.'

It didn't take long for a man to stroll down the hallway, throwing a brief glance into each cell. Checking that no bodies needed removing, King presumed. He got up off the bench and powered through the crowd of resting thugs. A few grumbled as he brushed past, but no further action was taken.

They'd clearly decided he was too much trouble to bother antagonising.

'Hey,' King said.

The guard stopped. Turned. His dishevelled thinning hair had been matted to his forehead by the heat. 'Huh?'

'Can you get me some food?'

'Food?'

His accent was thick. King guessed he spoke barely any English. He made a gesture with both hands, miming eating from a bowl. He nodded at the same time.

'One hundred bolivares,' the guy said.

Ten dollars. Not a bad price for a meal, all things considered. King shoved a hand into his pocket and withdrew a cluster of twenty-bolivar notes. He handed five over and shoved the rest back into his jeans. The guard turned on his heel and walked back the way he'd come.

A low hum started in the cell. It began with a pair of men chattering to each other in Spanish, gesticulating at King. Then more joined in, until it seemed every man in the cell was discussing him.

They'd seen the money.

Bad news.

He stared at Hector, who had a newfound glint in his eyes. Now — if the man decided to attack — he would not just be motivated by revenge. He could get *rich* in the process. A tantalising thought, no doubt.

King leant against the wall. He glared at anyone who dared to make eye contact. They quickly averted their gaze, yet it seemed the atmosphere had once again changed. Tension and nervous energy crackled in the air.

The guard returned five minutes later, carrying a plate heaped high with potato gnocchi. King had seen the same meal in several bazaars since landing in the country a week ago. It seemed to be a popular dish in these parts. He took the plate through a small opening in the cell bars and the guard left once again. No cutlery. No clean dishes. He didn't care. He was more accustomed to this way of life than Diamanté Resort's lavish buffet breakfasts.

He wolfed the food down, drawing the attention of every man in the cell. No-one spoke. They just watched him. He finished quickly and tossed the plate out into the hallway, his hunger satisfied.

Roman stared at him as he made his way back to the bench.

'They won't like that,' he said.

'I don't care,' King said.

'You should. You can't stay awake forever.'

'I'll kill anyone who tries to rob me.'

'You might need to. I'm not sure if you've entirely proven yourself yet.'

'What are you saying?'

'If I were you, I'd go rough a few of them up.'

King shook his head and sat down on the bench. 'I already proved my point. I'm not going to attack anyone else without provocation.'

'That'll get you killed.'

'What will?'

'Being noble. No room for nobility in a place like this.'

'It's not noble. Just fair.'

'Nothing's fair in here. Get used to that. You might be here a while.'

With nothing further to be said, the two men settled into somewhat comfortable positions. King sat upright, leaning against the warm concrete. He felt sweat run down his bare chest. His hair was soaked. His face was soaked. The skin of his back stuck to the wall. The conditions were unpleasant, to say the least. Nevertheless, the food began to settle in his stomach and he felt his eyes grow heavy. It had been a rough day. When he'd first risen out of bed this morning, he had never anticipated events would unfold this way.

From the luxuries of life to this hellhole.

He closed his eyes and slept fitfully, interspersed with brief periods of waking up bathed in sweat. He would look around the room, note each cellmate's position and drift back into unconsciousness.

Sudden movement pulled him awake in the early hours of the morning.

He heard the slight rustling of a body passing through space, brushing their feet against sleeping thugs, heading rapidly in a certain direction. He opened his eyes and saw it.

Hector running across the cell. Headed straight for him. Eyes hard and determined and cruel.

He clasped a homemade knife in his hands, sharpened from some kind of household object.

He would reach King in a couple of seconds.

CHAPTER 7

King darted to his feet as soon as he saw the weapon, instantly awake. The sensation brought back memories of the alley the previous day. It also stirred feelings from years past. All these situations were the same.

Another human being would try everything in their power to end his life in gruesome fashion, and he would try everything in his power to save it.

Hector came in swinging with the knife. Short, sharp, scything. Much more effective than the wild attacks from the amateurs in the alley. King knew he needed every bit of his reflexes to survive what came next.

The blade sliced through the air inches from his neck. It would have connected had he not thrown his head back just in time, slamming the rear of his skull into the concrete wall. It hurt. But a bruise did less damage than a slit throat.

He used the near-miss to power away, juking to the side like a wide receiver dodging a defender. Hector crashed into the wall and spun around, righting himself after the momentum-filled charge. King sensed a few thugs behind him scrambling to their feet, but they would do no harm. They would simply watch the conflict.

He knew he had to end it quickly. The longer Hector drew the confrontation out, the higher the chance he would sink the blade into King's vital organs.

King burst forward.

He stayed within range of a blade swing for less than a second. Just enough time to land a kick. He placed the blow well, targeting Hector's knee. The joint was locked in place, meaning it would take less effort to bend in the other direction. He put two-hundred-and-twenty pounds of bodyweight behind the impact, pushing hard for a single moment. Then he back-pedalled violently, darting out of range just as fast as he'd entered it.

Hector's screams highlighted the damage done.

His leg buckled and he started to collapse to the putrid floor. King assessed the nature of the injury in the blink of an eye and knew ligaments had been torn. The pain would be significant enough to impair his reaction speed for the next few seconds. King rushed in and seized the knife hand. Yet disarming Hector would not end the conflict. An attempt had been made on King's life, which sent shivers of fury down his spine. He squeezed his massive forearms and used all his strength to send the knife plunging into Hector's abdomen. He targeted the blow with precision. Aiming for the intestines, not the liver.

Enough to wound him, but not to kill him.

Hector collapsed to the floor in a puddle of his own blood.

'Keep pressure on it,' King said to Roman.

The man raised an eyebrow. 'You just broke his leg and stabbed him and you want me to tell him everything's going to be alright?'

'He's in pain. Which he deserves to be in. But he'll live. Which he also deserves.'

'Pretty sure he tried to kill you.'

'There's a slight difference in experience here,' King said.

'What?'

'If a young toddler tried to stab you, would you kill them in return?'

'Probably not.'

'That's how I feel right now.' King crossed the cell and stuck his face in the bars. '*Hey!*'

It didn't take long. A policeman he'd never seen before heard the cry and came running through the steel door, his face a pale sheet. King took one look at him and presumed that stab wounds were on the lighter side of the injuries he saw. He'd come in expecting the worst. He made it to their cell.

'He's hurt,' King said, pointing at Hector, who was in the process of clutching his stomach and moaning.

The man realised no-one was dead and visibly relaxed. In fact, he seemed bemused at King's urgency.

What type of shit goes on in here? King thought.

'So?' the policeman said.

'What do you mean?'

'What you want me to do?' he said in stunted English.

'Help him out…' King said, astonished. 'He'll die if we just leave him there.'

'No my problem. One thousand bolivares.'

'You're joking.'

The policeman sniggered. 'Seems like he's friend of yours. You pay for us to help. Or I make sure you stay here longer.'

King didn't feel like explaining that Hector had just tried to end his life, or that he had no idea how long he was scheduled to stay in the first place. But at the end of the day if they took Hector away, the man would be permanently removed from the equation. A price King was willing to pay.

He peeled a pair of five-hundred-bolivar notes off the roll in his pocket. Handed them across. 'It was an accident.'

'Of course. He trip and fall. Stab himself.'

'Is that a common occurrence around here?'

'Oh, yes,' the man said, nodding vigorously. 'Happen daily.'

The policeman pulled a two-way radio out of his belt and shouted instructions into it. In an instant the steel door slammed open and a pair of officers came through carrying a white cloth stretcher. King briefly considered making a break for it. Then the door clicked shut behind them. He sighed. Even if he made it out of the cell, he'd be trapped in the hallway.

One of the new arrivals brandished a shiny assault rifle. King recognised its make. A Kalashnikov AK-103. Standard issue for the Venezuelan armed forces. The officer tossed it to the original guard, who caught it and slid the safety off.

'Anyone moves — they die,' he said in Spanish.

King believed him. It wouldn't take much to cover up his death. He imagined he would be buried in the middle of nowhere and forgotten.

The officers with the stretcher unlocked the cell door and entered. They moved tentatively, wary of the many pairs of eyes studying their every movement. A couple of men sucked phlegm into their throats, threatening to spit at them at any moment. The policeman with the rifle saw this and screamed commands, gesticulating wildly.

King stayed frozen by the entrance. The situation was volatile due to its unpredictability. Anywhere else he would have a little more confidence. In here, anything could happen. He knew he was one wrong step away from a bullet in the brain.

They lifted Hector onto the stretcher. He moaned throughout the whole process. Blood pooled onto the white material, soaking it through in an instant. With twin grunts of exertion they rose and exited the cell. King noted their hurried steps. He didn't imagine they were comfortable in enemy territory. When the cell door slammed shut — separating them from the horde of prisoners — the trio of officers visibly relaxed.

They carted Hector away without another word.

King watched them go with a semblance of relief. The cell shortly returned to normal. He headed back to Roman, noting the lack of tension in the air. It seemed the more serious threats on his life had left with Hector. Danger had stagnated. For now.

Roman's hands were crimson. He'd done his best to try and stem the bleeding. King sat down next to him and took a deep breath, sucking air into his lungs. The jitters of combat had yet to fade.

'I have more questions,' Roman said.

'You seem full of them.'

'You're better trained than I thought. You must have been the best of the best.'

King shrugged. 'Big assumption.'

'Which makes me ask you again — what are you doing here?'

'In prison?'

'In Venezuela. If you have as much money as you say you do, you could be anywhere in the world.'

He shrugged again. 'No particular reason.'

'Who hired you?'

It was the straw that broke the camel's back. Before then King had put up with the man's interrogation, passing him off as simply inquisitive. But this was something else. Roman wanted to know exactly who he was, and which non-existent employers he was working for.

He turned his head when he saw movement out of the corner of his eye. Roman reached behind his back, slotting a hand into his waistband. He came out with a small compact pistol. His finger rested inside the trigger guard.

Ready to fire.

CHAPTER 8

King exploded into action.

As he saw the weapon he brought his left fist off the bench. A short, sharp jab that covered the distance to Roman's chest in half a second. It slammed against his musculature with enough force to knock the breath from his lungs. With the other hand he seized the pistol out of the man's hand, using the fact that he was winded to his advantage.

He sprang off the bench and aimed the gun at the man sitting before him.

A wry smile crept across Roman's features. 'Thought that might happen.'

'Who are you?'

'Not your concern.'

Roman got off the bench, coughing violently. King took the opportunity to study the make of the gun in his hands. It was a double-action semiautomatic with an exposed hammer. It seemed to hold 9mm rounds, although he wasn't sure. He couldn't ascertain the exact model. Probably a local firearm, manufactured somewhere in Venezuela.

Therefore exclusive only to those with inside connections.

'Where'd you get this?' he said.

'It's a Zamorana. Made in-country. We're supplied by CAVIM factory.'

'A military factory?'

Roman nodded.

'So how do you have access to it?'

'Friends in high places.'

The cell had become eerily quiet. Every man in the room watched with fascination. Roman turned his back and walked away, heading for the door. King let him go. There was nothing else he could do. As if on cue, the same policeman who'd demanded one thousand bolivares reappeared. He unlocked the gate and let Roman through without a second glance.

The pair exchanged a knowing nod and the door clicked shut behind them. Before Roman left, he turned and peered through the bars at King.

'You can put that gun down now,' he said. 'Won't do you any favours after I leave.'

'What's going on?' King said. 'Who are you?'

'You're interfering with things you don't want any part of,' Roman said. 'Should have stayed out of them while you had the chance.'

With that he turned and left with the policeman. They spoke softly as they went, exchanging information. Clearly the entire thing had been a setup. Roman had never been a prisoner. He'd been inserted into the cell in an attempt to extract information from King. The relentless questions and constant probing had soon become suspicious.

And now he was gone.

King tossed the Zamorana pistol under the cell bars with grim resignation. It skittered away and came to rest on the other side of the hallway. There was no use holding onto it. It would only invite trouble. He couldn't imagine Tomás being lenient if he discovered King was armed.

He sat back down on the same bench, now alone. His cellmates studied him like he was an exhibition at the zoo. Peering in fascination, puzzled by the complicated chain of events. Their drug-addled minds would struggle to comprehend what had happened. In their eyes, a man had just walked free without repercussion.

King closed his eyes in an attempt to dull a pounding headache that had sprouted to life. He sighed. It seemed trouble was destined to follow him wherever he went. He didn't know who had him falsely arrested, or why, but he was certainly not who they thought he was.

You'll never escape it.

Violence and death and chaos.

All he'd ever known, and seemingly all he would continue to know. Especially if Tomás kept his word of transferring him to prison without a trial. He'd heard the horror stories of Venezuelan prisons and began to regret ever stepping foot in the country.

Gang wars. Drugs. Stabbings. Shootings.

The system was a nightmare. If he ended up in its bowels, he doubted he would ever escape. Suddenly it dawned on him that no-one on the planet knew his location.

Ten years of work for Black Force had taken their toll. It was a classified secret project by officials at the very top of the food chain in the United States military. All of it kept off the books. All of it accompanied by handsome financial compensation. All of it death-defying insanity.

King had lost count years ago of the number of times he'd narrowly avoided death. They'd sent him into war-torn wastelands, put him up against ruthless cartels, used him as a one-man hostage extraction team. The memories had blurred together into a relentless barrage of warfare that visited him almost every night.

So he'd retired.

After an eventful stint in the countryside of Australia, he'd travelled slowly through Europe, healing up, enjoying life. Two months later he was in the state of Vargas. He'd seen a pamphlet outside a travel agency and decided to fly here on a whim.

He'd never been to Venezuela.

It meant he'd arrived with zero possessions. In an attempt to escape his past life he'd made himself uncontactable. No phone. No-one had been informed of his location prior to the trip. There wasn't a soul on the planet who knew where Jason King was.

He should have known better.

The sound of the steel door grating open brought him back to the present. He opened his eyes and saw Tomás stride into view, pausing on the other side of the bars. He made eye contact with King and his features twisted into a grotesque smile. King stared back. His stomach tightened. He knew the worst had yet to come.

By far.

'We've processed you,' Tomás said.

'What?'

'Time for a change of scenery.'

'I'm getting a trial?'

'You've had your trial. You're guilty.'

King didn't respond. With two sentences the policeman had condemned him to a lifetime inside one of Vargas' hellholes. Just like that. No official processes. Not a shred of diplomacy. Nothing but a quick trip to the nearest prison and a lifetime of suffering.

'This is beyond illegal,' he said.

Tomás just laughed. 'We determine what's legal and illegal.'

'So what happens now?'

'You're being transferred to El Infierno. You've been sentenced to life.'

'Fuck you.'

'Oh, I'd be angry too. Nothing you can do about it though.'

Tomás turned on his heel and disappeared from sight. None of the cellmates spoke English but they seemed to notice King's change in demeanour. A quiet fury. Rage behind his eyes.

Someone would pay for what had happened to him.

CHAPTER 9

They came for him at mid-morning.

The hours between Tomás' departure and their arrival later that day passed in absolute silence. King didn't open his mouth the entire time. At one point, one cellmate got a little too curious. The man scurried over to him, wide-eyed, still high on something. He prodded at him with a single finger. King lashed out, throwing a punch but deliberately missing. It scared the man away into the corner.

As he sat he mulled over what options he had. If he managed to get to a phone he could contact old friends from the military who would tear any prison apart to get him out. But he imagined he would not get the chance to. Tomás seemed good at his job, and his job entailed keeping King locked up, for reasons still undetermined.

Four policemen entered the hallway at once, weapons raised, pointing them into the cell. Tomás led the group. He unlocked the cell and beckoned for King to come with them.

'It's time,' he said.

'What if I don't move?'

'We'll beat you to death.'

King nodded and rose. He knew they wouldn't be able to touch him, but if he fought back one of them would get a shot off. It was useless to bother trying. He stepped out into the corridor, leaving the filthy cell behind. His cellmates watched him leave with a mixture of confusion and anger. Perhaps they thought he was an ally to the four men standing before him.

He certainly wasn't.

They handcuffed him again and marched him back the way he had come the previous day.

'How do you get away with this?' King said.

Tomás shoved a hand in his back. 'Don't talk.'

'I'll talk if I want to.'

The butt of the man's rifle struck him in the abdomen, sending a flare of pain up his torso. It hurt, but he didn't let it show. He stayed upright. Masked the burning sensation in his ribs. Stared at Tomás with bemusement.

'That was cute,' he said.

It angered Tomás. The man had put a considerable amount of force into the swing in an attempt to send a message. Any other victim would have crumbled.

King made it look like the blow hadn't bothered him in the slightest.

Tomás wrapped a hand around the back of his collar and quickened his pace. They exited the police station almost exactly twenty-four hours after entering it. The congregation of officers led him to the same van that had brought him from Diamanté. They threw him in the back. A pair of them followed him in and the other two entered the driver's compartment. Tomás drove.

As they tore away from the station, King considered Roman's involvement. The man had been working for whoever was responsible for his arrest, that much was certain. Perhaps it had something to do with the three thugs he'd beat down in the alley. Perhaps he *had* messed with the wrong people. A gang with inside connections in the law enforcement system, throwing him in prison to send a message — that they were not to be fucked with.

But that made no sense. Such an elaborate procedure would be far more time-consuming than a simple bullet to the back of the head. If these people had such a widespread reach, it would not have been difficult to kill him. No, they wanted *information*. Roman had been loaded to the gills with questions, determined to try and snatch an answer out of him before he wised up to the man's true identity.

An answer he did not have.

There was more to this. He was sure of it. But as the van rattled and shook, bouncing over potholed roads towards prison, King figured he may never find out what that may be.

They screeched to a halt after a twenty-minute journey. The doors opened and King stepped down onto dusty earth, an officer's hand wrapped around each arm to ensure he didn't make a break for it. They had parked in an empty lot without another car in sight. Tomás rounded the van's side and came face-to-face with King. He was smiling.

'Welcome to your new home,' he said, gesturing at the massive structure before them.

From their position it was impossible to tell how large the prison truly was. King stared up at an enormous rectangular building, made of a haphazard amalgamation of brick and metal. Guard towers were positioned along the length of the structure, towering over everything else, complete with glass windows running the entire diameter. Reinforced, he assumed. Bulletproof. The top of the building had been coated seemingly at random with hordes of barbed wire. Bars ran along the windows facing out onto the street they stood on.

'This is it?' King said.

Tomás laughed. 'This is one side. It's a square, my friend. The prison's in the middle.'

The sheer size of the place dawned on King. This long building acted as one wall of the prison, clearly guarded around the clock. From here, it seemed impenetrable.

King guessed he would not be breaking out anytime soon.

One of the battered steel doors on the ground floor opened and a prison guard stepped out onto open ground. He was tall and wiry, dressed in an official-looking uniform. His wide eyes flicked over the group and came to rest on King.

'There he is!' he cried. His English seemed good, despite a thick Spanish accent. 'The American pig!'

King noticed the holster at his waist contained a pistol. He looked like he knew how to use it.

'I'm Rico,' the man said, approaching Tomás with an outstretched hand. 'I'll be looking after this guy for his stay here.'

Tomás clasped his hand and exchanged a look with Rico. 'He's all yours.'

'How long will you be looking after me for?' King said.

Rico turned. 'The rest of your life, gringo. Which I'd say won't be long. They don't like foreigners in here.'

'I'm sure they'll like me.'

Rico cocked his head. 'Tough guy, huh? You haven't seen a prison like this before.'

'I'll manage.'

'No you won't.' The man turned to Tomás. 'I'll take it from here.'

The policeman nodded and signalled for his men to return to the van. As he walked off, he took a final glance at King.

'Hope they make life hell for you, American,' he said.

'You'd better hope I die in here,' King said.

'And why's that?'

'You know why.'

He shut his mouth and refused to elaborate. Inside he seethed with rage, yet he did not let it show. Tomás scowled and climbed back into the van. Ten seconds later its wheels spun and it peeled away from the prison. In a cloud of dust it crawled back down the narrow entrance path and exited onto a cracked asphalt road.

King stood in the dusty parking lot and watched, his hands cuffed firmly behind his back. He felt Rico's eyes on him.

'Don't bother running,' Rico said. 'There's three guns trained on you as we speak.'

King turned and looked at the guard. His yellow teeth had curled into a smile. It was clear he got a sick satisfaction by introducing newcomers to the prison. He probably revelled in watching them break under the conditions.

King would not break.

That much he knew.

'You're in on this?' he said.

'In on what?'

'I had no trial. I was arrested yesterday for something I didn't do.'

Rico laughed, a cruel cackle. 'You think you're special? You wouldn't be the first, and you won't be the last.'

'Didn't think you were all this corrupt.'

'Well — I'm a free man, and you're in prison. So who wins?'

Rico led him into the building. The interior was a maze of dilapidated corridors, outfitted with a state-of-the-art security system. Cameras monitored their progress from every corner. The conditions were horrid. King passed under damp ceilings dripping water onto the floor. Lights flickered and half the paint had peeled off the walls. But the reinforcements that mattered were sound. All the doors were made of steel, and required a keycard to open. They passed several soldiers dressed in Venezuelan military gear, all brandishing high-powered assault rifles.

Then Rico pushed open a final door and bright sunlight flooded King's vision once again.

They stepped out into the prison grounds.

The centre of El Infierno was an enormous space, at least the size of a football field. From here he could see the multi-storey building curving around the perimeter of the prison like a giant outline, boxing them in. The guard towers dotting the walls had undisturbed views over the grounds, complete with turrets ready to fire at a moment's notice. King wondered how often they were used.

The prison had a sickening atmosphere. He felt the tension in the air as soon as he stepped onto the dusty earth. He heard sounds similar to the holding cells at the police station, but tenfold in volume. Rabid screaming far in the distance. Vicious arguments in Spanish. The general air of testosterone, like a thousand men vying for dominance. Without even laying eyes on another prisoner King could tell he had entered a brutal world.

'What are the rules here?' he said.

'What rules?' Rico said. 'You do whatever the fuck you want. So does everyone else. As long as no-one touches the guards, it's not our business what you get up to.'

'What about food?' King said. 'Water?'

'I'm not here to hold your hand,' Rico said. 'Work it out yourself.'

They headed down a narrow dusty path between concrete buildings, all indiscriminate and bare of any kind of decorative touch. Utilitarian structures, nothing more.

'These are the private cells,' Rico explained. 'But don't worry about those. You'll never see them.'

'Where am I going?'

'The pavilion.'

King didn't like the sound of that. Rico refused to elaborate, and he didn't prod any further. The Venezuelan sun beat down on the back of his neck. He found himself sweating for the hundredth time that day. He hadn't changed clothes since he'd been arrested. He probably smelt disgusting, but it was hard to tell when surrounded by so much filth.

Hopelessness began to plague him. Until now he'd held onto the possibility of escape. Now it seemed futile. El Infierno was an enormous complex, protected by millions of dollars worth of security features. He didn't fancy his chances of walking free, either.

They rounded a corner and King saw the pavilion.

It was a cage the size of a large warehouse with a concrete roof and walls that were nothing but reinforced steel mesh. Mud caked the floor inside. It was packed with men in tattered clothing, all lean and wide-eyed and animalistic. There were no uniforms. The pavilion seemed to contain a functioning society, shut away from the civilised world and left to their own devices.

From a brief glance, the building appeared immensely overcrowded. King listened to the yelling and hollering and grunting from inside and gulped back his apprehension.

It seemed they were throwing him into a madhouse.

'This is where you'll spend the rest of your life,' Rico said, leering. 'Like it?'

King said nothing. Just clenched his fists and rode out the unbridled spite coursing through him in waves. Whoever had put him here would pay for it. He would use all his skills to ensure he stayed alive. And then he would find a way out, and he would slaughter whoever had done this.

They'd chosen to throw him in here.

He would make them regret it.

The determination kept him charged, kept the energy rippling through his muscles. As they approached one of the entrances, King saw dozens of men notice him at once. They stopped what they were doing and gripped the mesh, staring out at the newcomer. But this wasn't just any newcomer.

This was a foreigner. Easy prey.

King didn't know what to expect as Rico barked a command in Spanish, ordering the prisoners away from the entrance. Many of them fell back, making it safe to open the door. The guard slotted a keycard into the side of the gate. He entered a code, then withdrew a bundle of keys from his uniform pocket and slotted one into the lock on the gate. An elaborate system that would ensure no man managed to break free.

The door buzzed, and swung inward.

'I have a few questions for you later,' Rico said. 'But I'll let you get acclimatised first.'

The guard didn't keep the door open for long. He shoved a hand into King's back, pushing with surprising strength. King stumbled forward, through the gate, into the pavilion. The door grated shut behind him. He heard another buzz, this one indicating it was locked. Then Rico turned and walked away from the cage. Probably back to one of the guard towers.

King found himself facing off against at least a hundred prisoners. The floor all around them was littered with discarded syringes and homemade pipes; a sanitary nightmare. The inside of the pavilion was permeated by the sickening stench of body odour. He imagined general hygiene wasn't a priority in this place.

At the moment, he was priority number one.

Every man in the compound was interested in the tall, well-built Westerner who had just entered their territory.

They all wondered if he would put up a good fight.

CHAPTER 10

King let the adrenalin rush hit him. He'd need it.

Every ounce of his reaction speed would be required to fend off an attack. If a cluster of them decided to jump him at once, then all the combat prowess in the world would be rendered useless. There was a point where resistance became futile. With this many hostile eyes on him, he knew it would only take the slightest hint of mob mentality for dozens of the thugs to join in and collectively beat him to death.

Then he saw the weapons.

At first his brain didn't process what his eyes were registering. It seemed every man in the pavilion was armed. Some brandished homemade shanks. Some had their grimy fingers tightened around handgun triggers. It began to dawn on him that he had entered a world unlike anything he'd experienced before.

A man stepped out of the cluster of prisoners and approached him.

He was elderly. At least sixty, maybe older. His hair had fallen out long ago. His skin was cracked and weathered, probably from years in this hellhole — yet he carried an air of authority that seemed to permeate through the hordes of prisoners.

'My name is Tevin,' he said. He spoke English, too.

'Okay,' King said.

'Who are you?'

'Jason King.'

'What are you in here for?'

'I don't know.'

Tevin nodded. 'Suit yourself. They all end up talking eventually. How long are you here for?'

'I don't know that either.'

'You don't know a lot of things.'

'I'm still trying to process.'

Tevin shrugged. 'I've seen it before. Reality will hit eventually.'

'They all look like they want to kill me,' King said, gesturing to the pack of prisoners behind Tevin, all filthy and angry and wild.

'Newcomers don't get treated too kindly. Some get killed. That's just the way it is.'

'Is it a dominance thing?'

Tevin shrugged again. 'They prey on the weak. New arrivals tend to be weak.'

'Then how are you still alive?'

'I run the place.'

'Ah.'

'How tall are you?'

King cocked his head. 'Odd question.'

'Answer.'

'Six foot three.'

'Weight?'

'Two-hundred-and-twenty pounds. Roughly.'

'Can you fight?'

'Want a demonstration?'

Tevin paused for consideration. King knew that he wanted something from him, and also knew that he wouldn't be satisfied without witnessing what he could do. He would ensure that he got the message across fast and early — that he was nothing like the usual new inmates. He was not a timid Westerner, out of depth in a brutal foreign prison.

They would quickly learn.

Tevin made up his mind and nodded. He turned and peered into the crowd, searching for someone. When he found who he was looking for he clicked his fingers and beckoned them over. A man stepped forward, roughly the same height as King. A little slimmer, probably from the lack of nutrients in prison food. He still seemed powerful. Like he took good care of his body.

Which wouldn't matter.

'This is Santiago,' Tevin said. 'He's one of my bodyguards. You need to show me why you deserve the position more than he—'

He didn't get to finish his sentence, because by then King had already begun to stride forward. Tevin stopped talking and watched the altercation unfold.

King took three big steps, covering the distance in seconds. Santiago stared at him with pure rage in his eyes. They seemed to boggle in their sockets, in disbelief that a newcomer would be so brash. King saw the man's wrists twitch and his fingers tighten into balls and knew the guy would come at him like a freight train.

He wanted that.

Brute force had its advantages, but only if one knew how to use them. King had the experience. It gave him confidence. It allowed him to control his emotions as the giant swung a massive fist directly at his head.

The punch came at him the same way he'd seen a million identical attacks head his way before. The benefits of such an unbelievable and dangerous military career meant that he had been thrust into fist-fights and gruelling training tasks so relentlessly that his brain had entered a state of 'overlearning'.

The reflexes that were relevant in a time like this — reaction speed, timing and the ability to harness the flood of cortisol — had progressed to the point where his responses were automatic. He knew exactly what to do, and how to do it.

When confronted with a furious adversary, he treated it like nothing more than a casual training exercise.

He slipped to the side, jerking his head off-centre, re-positioning himself in the mud. The punch flew by, exposing the guy's chin like a shining beacon. King twisted at the waist and cracked a fist across Santiago's jaw. He didn't wind up. He didn't grow reckless. He knew it would take nothing more than a stiff jab in exactly the right spot to put the guy out on his feet.

Santiago's head whipped sideways, carried by the force of the jab. His neck muscles twisted. In the half-second after the connection King noted his eyes had already begun to roll back in his head. At that point he knew it was all over.

King turned to face Tevin even before the bodyguard's legs gave out and he collapsed to the mud, on the receiving end of a flash knockout. He would come to in seconds, disoriented.

Out of the fight for good.

Of course, the thugs around him had no knowledge of the thousands of hours King had spent training for combat. They didn't see the blood and sweat and mistakes of his past. They weren't aware of how many times he'd failed, how many instructors had beat him into the ground. They just saw a man step into El Infierno and drop the most imposing bodyguard in their pavilion with a single, precise blow.

To them, he was a freak of nature.

'Anything else?' King said.

Tevin peered down at his bodyguard, lying limp on his side on the dirty floor. He shook his head. 'I think I've seen enough.'

He barked a command and two prisoners gripped Santiago under each armpit and hauled him away. They disappeared into the crowd.

'You're now my bodyguard,' Tevin said matter-of-factly.

'Do I have a choice?'

Tevin stared at him. 'Do you want me to keep you alive?'

'That'd be good.'

'Then no, you don't have a choice. Feel free to wander off on your own. You'll find yourself stabbed in the back by a hallucinating addict before tomorrow morning.'

King nodded his understanding.

'Come with me,' Tevin said.

They set off through the pavilion. As the inmates noticed King had earned Tevin's trust they began to disperse, returning to what they'd been doing prior to his arrival. The air of violence and murder dissipated — at least for now. They probably knew that to mess with one of Tevin's friends was a death sentence.

'You own the pavilion?' King said as they walked.

Tevin laughed. 'I wish. I'm not here of my own accord, Jason. I'm a prisoner, just like you. Been here twenty years. Worked my way up. Now everyone answers to me. I can get them drugs, weapons, certain luxuries. No-one will touch me.'

'How many of them work for you?'

'Enough. If anyone laid a finger on me, my men would feed it to them. Then kill them. Slowly.'

'So I'm safe with you?'

Tevin looked at King, then searched in the crowd for Santiago's still unconscious body. 'Oh, I was exaggerating before. I'm sure you're safe either way. They're not used to someone who fights back.'

'You get many Westerners in here?'

'A few. Most die within the first few days.'

'Jesus.'

'We're a different breed,' Tevin said. 'The foreigners are hapless drug-runners. Think they can make a quick buck smuggling shit into Venezuela. Never pays off for them. They turn into cowards as soon as they get in here. Never turn into a coward. These *paisanos* thrive on weakness.'

'You think I would?'

'Oh, I know you won't. Doesn't seem like it's in your blood. What did you do before you came here?'

'I was a soldier.'

'Ah…' Tevin nodded. 'Of course. You've got that air about you.'

'What air?'

'I don't think any of us could break you if we tried.'

'I hope nobody does try.'

They came to a halt by the far side of the pavilion. Tevin paused and took a glance back at Santiago. Two tough-looking men were coaxing him back to consciousness. He groaned as he came to. He would have no memory of the fight.

'Mind explaining how you did that?' Tevin said.

King shrugged. 'Practice.'

'My men practice. They hit heavy bags, they spar with each other. You made him look like a child.'

King shrugged again. 'How often do they *fight*, though?'

Tevin cocked his head. 'What do you mean?'

'There's a difference between hitting a bag and hitting an enemy.'

'Explain.'

'Look, I'm not some kind of superhuman. If they snuck up on me from behind and cracked me, I'm sure it would hurt all the same. But what about the rapid decisions you have to make when someone's looking to take your head off? Are they used to that? Will they react properly?'

'Probably not,' Tevin said. 'We don't get much competition. I've had control for years.'

97

'Everyone gets wrapped up in the heat of the moment,' King said. 'Fighting has certain stressors. It makes people panic. I don't panic. I respond calmly and rationally. That's really all there is to it.'

The bodyguard in the corner made it to his feet for a couple of seconds. He righted himself, shoving his friends away. He took a single step and then collapsed back to the mud, punch-drunk.

'You make it sound so easy,' Tevin scoffed, shaking his head.

Then he turned and led King away.

They left the main area and strode into a corridor branching off from the pavilion. The hallway was home to two long rows of open doorways, each leading into small private rooms. Aggressive music blared from portable speakers, drifting through the doorways. Prisoners in scraps of filthy clothes were strewn across the floor, too high to function. King gazed down at their pathetic forms and wondered just what he'd got himself into.

'These are living quarters?' King said.

'Yes,' Tevin said. 'For those who have earned my respect. There's a hierarchy in here. I'm on top. If I don't like you, or I don't know you, you sleep out in the pavilion. In the mud. Men who treat me with respect might be lucky enough to get a mattress.'

King felt relief that he'd got on Tevin's good side so quickly. It seemed crucial to his own survival in this madhouse. All the ruthlessness and combat prowess in the world would be useless if he had to sleep on exposed ground, open to a blade or a bullet in the skull while he slept. At least a room offered some form of temporary safety.

'This is mine,' Tevin said as they approached the very end of the corridor. He pointed to a locked metal door.

'I'm allowed in?'

'You work for me now,' Tevin said. 'Of course you are.'

He withdrew a small rusting key from his oversized trousers and unlocked the door.

King followed him through.

CHAPTER 11

They entered a spacious living quarters, populated by a trio of tough-looking men in singlets and tattered shorts. The three of them lounged on old sofas and recliner chairs, huddled around a battered old television playing a Spanish drama show. It took King by surprise. This somewhat civilised place seemed a world away from the vicious doghouse of the main pavilion. There was a clear shift in attitude, too. These men appeared relaxed, calm, quiet. It directly contrasted with the sensory overload out there, filled with screaming inmates and prisoners passed out from drug overdoses — many too fried by narcotics to muster anything more than mindless salivation.

Up the back of the room there was a toilet built into the wall, complete with a small partition for privacy. King assumed the object was a rare sight in the pavilion. Above the toilet, a dirty glass window faced out onto an open field of dead grass, running all the way to the prison's perimeter. An unimpressive view, yet a view all the same. Cooking appliances were scattered across the floor, most homemade. They were nothing more than electric rings mounted on paint tins, but they would heat food well enough.

The height of luxury.

'King, meet my other three bodyguards,' Tevin said.

The three men approached him warily, as he expected. The sudden arrival of a new prisoner would warrant suspicion. He had been let into Tevin's personal quarters almost immediately. And he was foreign. King imagined signs of favouritism were treated with hostility by men who had worked hard to earn their positions. Nevertheless, they listened to their boss. They shook his hand, a couple grunting and nodding in greeting. King nodded back.

A row of beds rested against the far wall. Tevin crossed the room and lay down on one of them, sinking into the mattress. He rested his head against a filthy pillow.

King sat on one of the empty chairs.

'Someone put me in here for a reason, Tevin,' he said. 'They framed me.'

Tevin said nothing. Just stared at the ceiling, smiling to himself.

'I need to get out,' King said.

The man continued smiling.

'Tevin…'

He turned and made eye contact with King. 'You're living in a fantasy.'

'What?'

'You don't get out of here. Don't you think — with the influence I have — I would have escaped years ago if there was a way?'

'I was under the impression anything could be bought.'

'Anything except freedom, my friend. Especially if you've been locked up for a reason. Are you a rich man?'

King patted his jeans pocket, checking that the roll of bolivares was still there. 'I've got enough. On the outside I've got much more.'

'Then you can afford a decent life in here,' he said. 'You work for me, and you buy your way to basic amenities, and you'll manage. But don't consider anything else. Don't get your hopes up. They'll only be torn down by reality.'

'I can get out of here.'

Tevin chuckled. 'Just because you were a soldier doesn't mean you're above the guards. There's no way out.'

'How do I find out why I'm here?'

Tevin turned to him. 'Do you think you're special?'

'What?'

'Half the men in here used to be good citizens of society. But they pissed off a politician, or angered a gang. Now they're in here for the rest of their life. If you keep denying it you'll end up just like them. Useless drug addicts on the verge of death.

They realised too late that they're never getting out, and it tore them apart. Don't let that happen to you, my friend.'

King lapsed into silence, mulling over what had occurred. A small window built into the end of the room faced out onto the prison yard, exposing the setting sun melting into the horizon.

He stayed quiet as it grew dark. A bulb in the ceiling flickered to life, casting a dim glow over the contents of the room. The knot in his gut had yet to loosen. In fact, it grew tighter with each passing moment. He knew his motivation would fade the longer he spent in El Infierno.

Which could well be the rest of his life, just as Rico had said.

One of the bodyguards left the room and returned five minutes later carrying a large bowl of curry. Probably purchased from one of the guards for a hefty fee. They ate in silence. Tevin noticed King's change in demeanour and didn't probe him any further.

The rest of the evening passed in similar fashion. Several times Tevin attempted to strike up conversation, yet King had withdrawn into himself. He was not in the mood to talk.

Finally, late at night, when the five of them were ready to fall asleep, he opened his mouth.

'What are you in here for, Tevin?' he said.

The man turned from his position on the lower bunk. 'Murder. Three counts of it.'

'Justified?'

'Not at all. They were my competition. Three brothers, setting up a hardware shop across the road from mine. They had family money. It wouldn't have taken long for them to put me out of business. So I beheaded them while they slept.'

With that he rolled over and grew quiet, drifting into sleep.

King relaxed back into the chair and stared up at the damp ceiling, wondering just how he'd ended up in this mess. It seemed that wherever he turned, trouble followed. It had his whole career, but that came with the job. Now he could not shake the past. Peace and relaxation were concepts that hovered on the horizon, seemingly in reach. Whenever he tried to grab them, chaos would occur. Perhaps he was destined for this.

He used the toilet, unperturbed by some of the room's occupants watching him as he did so. The partition gave him partial privacy — a lot better than what he was used to out in the field. It put his career into perspective somewhat. Even in the bowels of corrupt Venezuela, he felt as if he were living in relative comfort.

He returned to the chair and closed his eyes as a wave of tiredness washed over him. The stress of recent events had taken their toll. The grounds outside grew dark and the constant screaming within the pavilion began to subside.

Apparently even the junkies had to sleep at some point. King drifted into short restless bouts of unconsciousness.

He came to at some point in the night. It was pitch dark outside. The sound of rustling had woken him. It came from somewhere nearby, and — while it could have been one of the bodyguards — he opened his eyes. The noise was frantic. Panicked. He took one look across and saw a stranger inside Tevin's quarters, one hand dipped into the man's possessions. The guy's beady eyes darted from body to body, searching for any sign of movement in the lowlight.

He didn't know King was awake.

The man continued to rustle through piles of clothes, searching hurriedly. His skin clung to his bones like a walking skeleton. The guy was emaciated. King waited until he withdrew a roll of bolivares from Tevin's belongings, then vaulted off the chair and wrapped a hand around the guy's shirt.

The man almost jumped out of his skin. He shrieked, a rabid cry, flecks of spit dotting King's shirt. He slapped a feeble hand against King's chest, trying to fend him off. King ripped the bolivares out of his hand and threw him out into the hallway. The door had been pushed open while they slept. Someone had accidentally left it ajar.

The guy clattered to the floor outside in a loud tumble of limbs, waking everyone in the room. Tevin was up in an instant, feet planted on the floor before King had time to blink. He'd produced a crude semi-automatic pistol from somewhere in his bunk. An instinctive reaction ingrained by years of living on edge.

'All clear,' King said.

'The fuck was that?' Tevin said.

'One of the inmates. He was looking for money.'

'Did he take any?'

King held up the roll of banknotes. 'He tried.'

'Fucking *prick!*'

He gestured to one of his bodyguards, the biggest of the three. A short sharp signal that could have meant anything. But the man got the message. He grunted his understanding and reached under one of the sofas. He came out with a heavy machete. Its edge was serrated, and clearly sharpened regularly. A formidable weapon.

'What's that for?' King said.

Tevin looked at him like he was stupid. 'These wild fucks need to be kept in line. How do you think I've stayed on top all these years?'

'Clearly by being a reasonable and kind leader.'

'You need to set an example,' Tevin said, ignoring the retort. 'Show the whole pavilion what happens to those who try and disrupt the order of things.'

The man with the machete made for the doorway, scything it through the air in short practice swings. He got halfway across the room when Tevin stopped him.

'Wait!' he cried.

The bodyguard paused and turned to face his boss. Tevin spoke rapidly in Spanish, gesticulating to get his point across. Just from his actions alone, King understood the gist of his demands.

'No,' King said even before the bodyguard could pass him the machete.

Tevin locked eyes with him. 'You will do it.'

'No, I won't.'

'If you work for me, Jason King, then you will do as I say.'

'I guess we're going to have to disagree on that.'

'You do not disagree with me.'

'I just did.'

A palpable tension crept into the room. Tevin snarled. 'Kill him. Or we will kill you. Just like I have killed many *sapos* before.'

'Any other options?' King said.

The other two bodyguards rose off the sofa in the corner. They shifted from foot-to-foot, staring at their boss. Obedient as always. Ready to fight at a moment's notice.

'No other options.'

'*Loco,*' one of the bodyguards whispered, which King knew meant "crazy". He didn't imagine prisoners talked back to Tevin very often.

'There's always a third option,' he said.

He jerked forward and broke Tevin's nose with a single head-butt.

CHAPTER 12

The fierce high of life-or-death combat ripped through King's system. In an instant his entire demeanour changed. A second ago he'd held a casual stance with his arms relaxed, his shoulders slumped, his head bowed. Not a hint of aggression or hostility. That was the key. If people saw an attack coming they could prepare themselves. Tense up. Dodge the first blow.

Tevin couldn't.

The sharp crack of broken nasal bones echoed off the walls. Blood fountained from his nostrils and he fell back onto his bunk, reeling from the shock of such a painful injury. By then King had already moved past him, throwing him aside, charging at the man wielding the machete. He was most dangerous. So King would deal with him first.

He hoped that the opening blow had its intended effect. In groups, many rely on the leader for commands. However he acts often carries over to his men. Tevin howled from the pain of his injury. The sharp outcry ripped through the room. His men heard it. They hesitated.

If one man shows fear, King thought, *then it will spread.*

He came within range and delivered a second vicious head-butt, thrusting the thick skull of his forehead into the guy's nose. It was the most effective method of taking the fight out of a dangerous opponent at such close quarters. Get so close that a machete swing is impossible. Then lash out with a blow they'd be least expecting.

The guy peeled away, groaning in agony, clutching his shattered septum. The machete dropped out of his hands.

King scooped it up by the handle and threw it across the room at the two remaining bodyguards charging at him. It turned end-over-end in the air, whistling past them, and buried itself in the far wall. Both men remained unharmed. But that was never the intention. A large knife hurtling through the air towards you creates an involuntary reaction. They both flinched, bringing both hands up in a rudimentary shield, closing their eyes for a moment, praying the blade didn't slice open their organs.

Perfect.

King surged across the room and threw a four-punch combo at the man on the left. He alternated between the body and the head. The first winded him. The second cracked across his chin. The third struck the liver. The fourth hit him just above the ear and rattled his brain around inside his skull, putting him out on his feet.

His legs gave out at the same time that the last bodyguard pulled out a gun.

King's heart spiked. A pang of shock ripped through him. The guy was too far away. He brought the pistol out of his waistband and levelled the barrel at King's head. For a fleeting moment King looked death in the eye. He ducked as fast as he could, contracting the available surface area that the man had to aim at.

The guy squeezed a single shot off. The report tore through the room, deafening inside the confined space, accompanied by a blinding muzzle flare.

King didn't care where it went. All that mattered was it missed. He didn't feel the explosion of nerve endings that signified a bullet wound. He dropped low and powered off the floor, tensing his glutes. He charged across the room. He wrapped both arms around the guy's legs and drove him back off his feet.

Before the man could fire a second round, the back of his head crashed against the concrete. It made enough noise for King to recognise that the fight was over. A concussion would be the least of his problems. Spurred on by blind rage, he snatched up the pistol and fired a round through the base of the man's skull.

You try to kill me. I try to kill you.
That's fair.

The aftermath of sudden massive violence settled over the room. It became eerily quiet after such an intense brawl. Ears ringing, King clambered off the dead bodyguard and crawled onto the nearest chair. He clutched the gun between his fingers. The weapon was another Zamorana. Purchased from either the local or national police forces. He panted for breath, sucking air into his lungs, recovering from the high of combat. He checked the repercussions.

One bodyguard was dead. Blood pooled from his head onto the concrete floor, coagulating with the dust to form a viscous brown substance. Another was unconscious, lit up by King's barrage of punches. The guy who'd held the machete rested in the doorway, clutching his bleeding nose and moaning. Tevin was in a similar position. Both nostrils poured blood onto his white bedsheets, ruining them. He looked across the room at King with disbelief plastered across his face.

'You don't know what you've done,' he said, spitting a mouthful of blood onto the floor.

'I have an idea,' King said. 'Looks like I just fucked you all up.'

'You'll regret this. You haven't been here long enough. You don't know who I am.'

King rose off the chair. He towered over the now-feeble old man. 'I think you've got things the wrong way around, Tevin.'

'What?'

'You don't know who I am.'

'A soldier. Who cares? I've seen plenty of tough guys in my time. I'll get my men to kill you as soon as you turn your back.'

'I've seen some shit that makes this place look like Disneyland,' King said. 'So if you think you're going to scare me, or intimidate me, then give it your best shot. I'll be outside. Send anyone. I'll fucking tear them apart.'

He let the threat hang in the air, then left the three men in their sorry states. He stepped out into the hallway and saw the skinny thief still resting on the dirty floor, staring into Tevin's room in a state of shock.

'Lay low for a while, kid,' King said. 'They'll be angry.'

The guy stared vacantly, completely unaware. No English, evidently.

King walked past him and set off down the corridor, heading back for the pavilion. He kept the Zamorana in his grip, eyes flicking left and right, searching for confrontation. He found none. Whether due to the look in his eyes or his imposing stature, the prisoners left him alone. It must have dawned on them that he was a different breed. Not a clueless drug smuggler, crawling into their territory weak and feeble and cowering. Something else.

They were in his territory now.

He shoved past a group of Spanish thugs and headed for one corner of the pavilion. There was no furniture of any kind in the cage. It was nothing but a bare room packed with inmates. No room for cover. King felt his stomach sinking as he sat down with his back resting against the wall. Tevin was right. He had a gun, but he would have to fall asleep eventually. It wouldn't take much to outnumber him. Unless he decided to kill half the men in the pavilion, he would end up catching a knife in the back or a bullet between the eyes soon enough.

Most of the prisoners were asleep. Outside it was still dark, with a faint glimmer of light creeping over one of El Infierno's walls. He could make it through the coming day, and probably the entire night after. He'd kept watch longer than that during his time in the special forces. But then what? Eventually he had to break. He couldn't sleep deprive himself forever.

One by one, the inmates stirred as the sun rose. All of them were caked in mud, gazing around the putrid room with glassy expressions. They didn't care about the conditions, as long as they could get their hands on the next fix. King watched them all. Some seemed to have their wits together. They communicated with each other in hushed whispers, minding their own business. Others drooled onto the floor, scratching at scabs and staring into space.

King gripped the Zamorana tighter. There seemed to be no threats in this area of the pavilion. His line of sight was obscured by the crowds, so he couldn't see if Tevin or his men had emerged from their room yet. He imagined they would, looking for revenge. He would be ready.

It was an uncomfortable position to hold. He had to stay constantly wary, never letting his guard drop, scanning the crowd for any kind of threats.

He heard a noise from outside the pavilion. A foot scraping against concrete. He glanced out through the steel mesh and saw Rico approaching the cage. The man kept his hands behind his back, strolling leisurely, as if he had all the time in the world. He noted the gun in King's hands and grinned.

'Bet you're not used to a prison like this,' he said.

'I'm not used to any prison,' King said.

'I'm sure you aren't, scum.'

'What's to stop me shooting you right now?'

'You won't do that. It's the rules.'

'What if I say fuck the rules?'

'Then the guards will slowly torture you to death. You don't want that.'

'Any luck on my trial?'

Rico looked away. 'Didn't they tell you at the station? You've already had it.'

'So I'm in here forever?'

'You're a murderer. Of course you're in here forever.'

'I deserve better than this.'

'You deserve what we say you deserve. Now, I see you're in a bit of a tricky situation at the moment. I'd guess that you've pissed off Tevin and his friends. Am I correct?'

'I did a little more than piss them off.'

'Ah. So you're fucked.'

'I'll kill them if they try anything.'

Rico paused. Surveyed the yard. 'Come to the gate.'

'Why?'

'Those questions I mentioned before,' he said. 'It's about time I asked you them.'

CHAPTER 13

Rico took the Zamorana away from King and shoved it into his own waistband. Then he cuffed him and led him out of the pavilion, much to the dismay of the other inmates. They barked insults in Spanish, hurling abuse at the gringo prisoner who seemed to be allowed special privileges. King didn't look back at them. He stared straight ahead and let Rico lead him towards the fortress surrounding the prison.

He was unnerved by what questions Rico could have in mind.

The guard took him through dilapidated hallways until they came to a heavy steel door. He unlocked it and gestured for King to follow him in. It was set up like a conference room, with a large wooden table in the centre surrounded by rickety chairs. There were no windows. The air was stifling. An uncomfortable atmosphere permeated the place. As they entered, Rico signalled to a pair of prison guards at the other end of the corridor. They drew their weapons and approached the door, keeping watch on the other side. Rico slammed the door closed.

'What is this?' King said.

'We need to talk,' Rico said, sitting in one of the chairs. He beckoned to the opposite side of the table. King sat.

'About what?'

'Do you want to get out of here?'

'Obviously.'

'Then I need answers.'

King hesitated. 'Are you saying you're a factor in me being locked up in here?'

'I'm not saying anything. But you need to say a lot if you ever want to see outside these walls again. If not, I'll just leave you to rot.'

'You're a prison guard.'

'Am I?'

Silence.

'The three men you beat half to death yesterday,' Rico said. 'I need to know exactly who put you up to that task.'

King froze.

The only way he could know about that was if…

Rico leant forward, resting both elbows on the table, studying King like he was a science experiment. The two stared at each other across the room. Tension ran thick in the air. King saw the man in a new light.

'Do you really work for the prison?' he said.

Rico smiled. 'Maybe. Maybe not. None of your concern. Now, those men…'

'I've never seen them before in my life.'

'I'm not saying you had. Who put you up to it?'

'No-one.'

A flicker of rage flashed in Rico's eyes, as if he thought he was being played with. 'Bullshit.'

'I was minding my own business and they provoked me,' King said. 'So I fought back. I do that.'

'I don't believe a word of it. *Especially* given the timing.'

'The timing?'

'You know what you did.'

'I'm not sure how many times I have to tell you I have no idea who they are, no idea who you are, and no idea what party I crashed. But if you're really the one responsible for me being in here, then I suggest you let me the fuck out.'

Rico cocked his head. Like King had just asked to be made President of the United States. Like he was offended by such stupidity. 'And why would I do that?'

'Because this whole thing is a giant misunderstanding.'

Rico leant even further in. 'I have you right where I want you. I'll keep you in here until you give me answers or the other prisoners drive you insane. Or kill you. I know someone put you up to this, but I'm trying to piece together which faction it was.'

'Who are you?'

Rico shook a finger in his face. 'You don't get to ask questions.'

'I don't care.'

'You have two options,' Rico said. 'You tell me what you know, or I throw you back in there and Tevin's boys tear you apart.'

'I don't know anything,' King said. 'So I guess that leaves you with only one option.'

'Suit yourself.'

The man let out a rapid burst of Spanish, loud enough to be heard out in the hallway. On cue the door swung open and the pair of prison guards entered. Both were well-built, each around two-hundred pounds of solid muscle. They lifted King off his seat and marched him back the way he had come, giving him time to think about what had transpired.

Rico had thrown him in here. Which meant the three goons he'd beat down in the alley had worked for him. So he wasn't a guard. He'd paid his way into El Infierno to monitor King in an attempt to get answers that he didn't have. He thought King was some kind of hitman, put up to the task of disabling the three men. But why?

What had he accidentally disrupted that warranted such an extreme reaction?

He didn't get to spend any more time with his thoughts. The guards hurried him towards the pavilion under the warmth of the morning sun. Once again, the nearby prisoners stared at him with rabid curiosity. The activity of the newcomer intrigued them. Word had likely spread regarding what had happened to Tevin and his men. He would either be a target, or a hero.

He quickly found out which.

The hostility was tangible as they thrust him back into the cage. Many of the same weapons King had seen when he'd first arrived were back in the hands of the inmates. He was an outsider again. An intruder. Tevin had turned most of the pavilion's population against him while he was gone.

He turned to speak to the guards, but they were in the process of leaving. The gate had been bolted shut behind him. He was trapped.

He sighed and faced the rapidly forming crowd, outfitted with knives and guns and all kinds of weaponry supplied by either the guards or Tevin's goons.

He prepared for the last conflict he would likely ever have.

CHAPTER 14

It was a sickening feeling. The realisation that nothing he could do would have an effect on the resulting conflict. If they wanted to, they could light him up with bullets or stab him over and over again until he was dead. He would never be able to fight them all at once. His heart rate quickened and his pores opened up once again. Sweat trickled down his forehead. He gulped back the thick humid air.

He saw no sign of Tevin. The old bastard would be cowering in his room, relying on younger and stronger men to do his dirty work.

There might have been a hefty reward promised for the man who brought King's head to Tevin. He sensed it in the expressions of the thugs. An air of opportunity hung over them all. They stared at King like he were a prized possession, some grinning from ear to ear.

Then everything changed.

It began with a blaring klaxon, sounding far in the distance behind King. Instantly the attention shifted away from him.

The prisoners who had lived in El Infierno long enough to know what that meant looked away, staring wide-eyed through the steel mesh. Suddenly fearful.

King had no idea what was about to occur.

But it couldn't be good.

'*Raqueta!*' one of the men screamed, breaking the tense quiet.

Pandemonium erupted in the pavilion. Men scrambled for their measly possessions, gathering up small packs of food and water, shoving their weapons away in an attempt to hide them. King waited by the entrance. He made sure to control his breathing. Panic raged all around him, but he would not let it consume him.

Not until he had reason to worry.

That came next. He heard hurried footsteps outside the pavilion. He turned and saw dozens of men in military-style uniforms hurrying towards the building. They spread out, a cluster entering through each separate gate amidst a cacophony of shouting and screaming.

'Get the fuck away from there!' a voice hissed, speaking English well enough.

King spun back and saw a pair of inmates standing nearby. Both unarmed. No threat. They had to be brothers. Both were reasonably tall, above six foot but still shorter than King. They took care of themselves, evident in their round shoulders and barrel chests. Their facial features bore the most resemblance, sporting striking blue eyes and curly hair. In fact, it was difficult to tell them apart.

'What's happening?' he said, struggling to make sense of the commotion.

'Raqueta,' the man on the left said. 'It's the Guardia Nacional! Run!'

Guardia Nacional.

The Venezuelan National Guard. Whatever a raqueta was, King didn't expect it to be pleasant.

The twins did not elaborate. Just as confused as when he'd first heard the shrieking wail of the siren, King noticed two guards heading straight for him. These men didn't seem like ordinary prison staff. They wore khaki uniforms and brandished batons and shotguns. King's heart leapt in his chest as one of them raised a heavy-duty shotgun and fired a round into his legs.

If the gun had been loaded with actual slugs, both of his lower limbs would have been severed in a grotesque spray of gore. He'd seen it happen before. Not a pretty sight. He would have spent the rest of his life in a wheelchair.

But that didn't happen, because the gun was packed with anti-riot pellets. They tore into the skin of his calves, causing massive neurological pain, making him wince and buckle at the knees. Yet no significant damage was done.

In fact, it just made King furious.

Unable to help himself, reacting the only way he knew how, he burst up off the muddy floor and ripped the shotgun out of the man's hands. It came loose effortlessly. The guy hadn't been expecting any form of retaliation. King imagined that rarely occurred against the Guardia Nacional. He didn't care. He spun the weapon around and swung it like a baseball bat at the man who had shot him. The butt cracked against his temple, halting his momentum, sending him sprawling off his feet.

A cry of outrage sounded from all officials in the vicinity.

'*Shit,*' King whispered under his breath.

They swarmed on him like a pack of rabid dogs. He briefly considered taking down as many as he could, but decided against it. It would do nothing but cause more trouble, which was the last thing he wanted. He'd been foolish to fight back against the first guard.

He took a deep breath and braced for what was coming.

Baton blows rained down from all sides, accompanied by vicious swathes of agony. A crazed mob surrounded him, all National Guard, all furious. A well-placed shot slammed home against his ribcage. The pain buckled his knees and he dropped. He hit the mud and curled into the foetal position in a desperate attempt to protect his face and groin from any direct strikes.

The barrage took a full minute to cease, and when it did King spat out a mouthful of blood and gasped in shock. The rate at which the situation escalated had taken him by surprise. He felt the throbbing and searing and aching all over. It was impossible to pinpoint to a single area. He'd been badly beaten. It would take a moment to assess the damage.

His limbs responded normally. As they dragged him into a sitting position and cuffed his hands behind his back, he found himself somewhat certain that nothing was broken. The injuries appeared to be superficial. They hurt like all hell, but he'd suffered similar harm too many times to count. An ordinary civilian would feel like they were dying, but he knew how to isolate the screaming nerve endings and control the agony, shutting down the emotional response. As long as no significant internal damage had been done, he could manage. Bruises and cuts and jarred limbs would heal.

He stayed on the ground as one of the guards rested a knee on his shoulder in an attempt to keep him in place. If King wanted to, he could explode up and break the guy's nose with a single kick. But he stopped himself from doing so. Now was not the time for anarchy.

He rode out the pain of the beating, watching the chaos unfold within the pavilion. Inmates ran from the guards like their life depended on it. Batons sliced through the air and the racket of anti-riot rounds tore through the enclosed space.

Tough-looking thugs dropped without resistance, cowering from the random beatings. There seemed to be no purpose to the altercations. Just high-ranking soldiers happy to let out all their anger and frustrations on the scum of the Vargas state prison population.

'American fuck!' the guard closest to King said.

He spat a thick gob of saliva onto King's tattered jeans, staring down at him with disgust. King peered back up at the man with the same venom in his eyes. He felt his left cheek starting to swell. It had been caught by a baton at some point during the beatdown. A vicious headache flared to life behind his eyeballs, pounding into his skull.

The twins he'd seen before the violence broke out slammed their butts into the mud near King. They also had their hands cuffed. Another guard pushed a grimy hand into the closest twin's face, making sure he stayed down.

'What the hell was all that?' King said.

'The Guardia Nacional search the pavilion every now and then,' the same one that had spoke earlier said. 'We call them raquetas. Some of the guards like to be violent beforehand. Let out a little steam.'

'I can see that. They confiscate all weapons in the pavilion?'

'The ones they can find. Then the prison guards just sell them right back to us. Along with drugs, knives … whatever we can afford.'

'Seems unnecessary.'

'I think it's all just an excuse to beat the shit out of us.'

'I can believe that.'

'I'm Raul,' the man said. 'This is my brother, Luis. He does not speak English.'

Luis nodded a greeting, a gesture that transcended all language barriers. King nodded back. His head flared even from the slight movement.

'I'm Jason,' he said. 'I'm new here.'

'We know. You're all anyone's talking about right now.'

King scanned the room as the Guardia Nacional arranged the prisoners into a long line in the mud. The men sat side-by-side, heads bowed, all reluctant to make eye contact with the officials. Some glanced across at King with rage in their eyes. It seemed they'd missed their chance for a payday. There was still no sign of Tevin.

'I can't imagine that's a good thing,' King said, sighing as he felt fresh waves of pain course through his system.

CHAPTER 15

The Guardia Nacional turned the pavilion inside out. They seized all visible belongings and upended their contents into the mud. Every gun, knife and satchel of powder was quickly seized. The owners of such possessions were given quick beatings, struck with either the end of a baton or the butt of a shotgun. King had no possessions, and as a result had no reason to be beaten.

They gave him one anyway.

The guard who he'd knocked down with his own weapon strode up and down the row of filthy prisoners. When he found King, he kicked him sharply in the ribs. King rolled with the impact but it still winded him. He doubled over involuntarily. The guard smiled.

King wondered if they would kill him. He didn't imagine it would take much more provocation. Striking a guard was surely more than enough reason to warrant a quick execution, especially since the entire process of his arrest had been off-the-record. He figured men in this pavilion were murdered for a lot less.

But they did nothing. Which surprised him. It either meant he'd chanced upon a lucky day where they felt generous. Or they were under explicit orders to keep him alive.

Rico.

'Hey,' a voice said, snapping him out of his thoughts. He glanced across and saw Raul watching him.

'Yeah?'

'What are you in here for?'

King stared at the ground. His lower legs were caked in dried blood, drawn from dozens of tiny pellet impacts. 'Murder.'

'Damn, gringo. Who'd you kill?'

'No-one.'

'Huh?'

'Just because I'm in here for murder, doesn't mean I did it.'

'They found you guilty.'

'I wasn't given a trial.'

Raul spoke softly to Luis in Spanish, and they exchanged a look. Like they had seen such cases before. 'Then you pissed someone off, homie.'

'I'm aware of that.'

'Who'd you piss off?'

'That I don't know.'

'You must have done something.'

'I've done a lot of things.'

'That's a real big help, my friend. Really narrows it down.'

King smiled. 'I'm in here. Let's just leave it at that. Nothing I can do about that now.'

'There sure ain't,' Raul said. 'If they threw you in here then you're never getting out.'

'Here specifically?'

Raul nodded. 'This is *maxima*, my friend. Highest security in all of Venezuela. And the most corrupt. By far. I'm surprised you didn't catch a planilla.'

'A what?'

'Their bayonets. They usually stab anyone who pisses them off.'

King gulped back anxiety. He knew he would be defenceless to stop them from doing just that. 'And why are you in here?'

Raul looked at him. So did Luis. 'I don't know if I trust you enough to answer that just yet.'

He let the cryptic nature of the statement hang in the air as the raqueta came to an end. The Guardia Nacional finished ridding the pavilion of its most dangerous weapons. They brought each inmate to their feet and began the process of patting them down. King was searched by the same guard he'd struck with the shotgun. A purple welt had sprouted to life over the man's right eye.

'That doesn't look good,' King said.

'*Planilla,*' Raul whispered. 'Watch yourself.'

After he finished the pat-down, the guard gave King an ice-cold look with his good eye and punched him in the stomach. King saw the shot coming and jerked back as it landed, turning it into nothing more than a glancing blow. Dissatisfied with such an outcome, the guard swung for his head. He ducked under it, dodging the wild haymaker. It whistled past, close by. No connection though. This made the man furious. He'd been schooled by a battered inmate in handcuffs. He lashed out feebly with a kick, which ricocheted off King's thigh, doing little damage. Then he turned and stormed out of the pavilion.

If only he was allowed to kill me, King thought.

The handcuffs were removed. The guards kept their shotguns raised high in case a suicidal prisoner got any ideas. The pellets were anti-riot but a spray to the face would risk serious injury — even death. King didn't risk testing them.

He sucked the pavilion's humid air into his lungs and his heart rate began to calm. He realised he wasn't as hurt as he initially expected. He'd done well to cover up during the beating, and as such he was only bruised. He knew he would still be more than capable of holding his own.

The Guardia Nacional began barking commands in Spanish, and the prisoners responded. They formed a somewhat orderly line near the gate, waiting patiently. The hostility in the air had vanished.

'What's going on?' King whispered to Raul.

'We're eating,' the man answered.

At least a dozen guards and prison officials escorted the cluster of prisoners out of the pavilion. King was struck with a couple of rifle butts, forcing him into the midst of the procession. They were led into a spacious yard of dead grass. On the other side of the yard rested a long low concrete building with no windows.

'That's the kitchen,' Raul explained.

King nodded, enjoying the weather for the brief moment he had outside. He quickly deduced that an escape attempt on the walk to breakfast would be a death sentence. He'd seen the officials swap their riot guns over to the real thing as the prisoners left their usual enclosure. One step out of line would be met with a hail of bullets.

The kitchen turned out to be much like a school canteen, only more sterilised. Metal floors, metal walls, metal benches, metal tabletops. Everything was smooth and shiny. It must have been the most sanitary area of El Infierno. King assumed it had been constructed this way to make cleaning easier. A simple wipe-down of all surfaces would make it ready for use again instantaneously.

Under the watchful eye of a small army of prison officials, King lined up to receive a plastic bowl half-full of lukewarm meat and rice, accompanied by a cheap disposable cup filled to the brim with water. Raul and Luis collected identical bowls behind him and the twins sat opposite him at the nearest table. Other prisoners sat down all around them and wolfed their food down without cutlery, most drooling onto the steel tabletops. A junkie with wide eyes and a limping gait slapped his bowl down next to King.

Too close.

The man stared at King questioningly, as if trying to provoke him. King knocked the bowl off the table and pushed the man away. He scurried wordlessly into a corner and collapsed in a heap, succumbing to the truckload of narcotics coursing through his veins.

King turned back to Raul and Luis, ignoring the junkie. The twins had been watching his every move. Almost studying him.

'What?' he said, questioning their looks.

Raul shook his head and took a mouthful of the gruel. 'You're nothing like the usual newcomers.'

'How so?'

'You're not scared. At all. It takes people at least a few weeks to acclimatise to this kind of environment. They spend that time shitting their pants, usually. Taking beatings from other prisoners. Doing everything they're told. You came in here like a force of nature.'

'You don't think I'm scared?' King said. 'Don't be ridiculous.'

'You don't look it. You're the bravest fresh face I've ever seen. And we've been here a year now.'

'That's the point. Fearlessness and bravery are two separate things.'

'What?'

'Of course I feel fear,' King said. 'Who doesn't? I just ignore the instinct to run away. That's all there is to it.'

'I don't think it's that simple, gringo.'

'Of course it's not. You don't want to know what I've done to reach this point. Can I ask a question?'

Raul cocked his head. 'Sure.'

'How come you speak perfect English and your brother doesn't speak a word?'

'He can speak a handful of phrases,' Raul said. Luis's striking blue eyes pierced into King as he watched the proceedings silently. 'But it was a childhood friend who taught me. Every day. For years. Luis preferred the outdoors. He likes soccer.'

They finished eating in silence. It seemed Raul had plenty of curiosity about King's past. He decided to keep the details of his career shrouded in mystery. For now. He didn't know these men well enough to divulge sensitive information just yet. He gulped down the fluid and finished the bowl in front of him.

Breakfast concluded uneventfully and they were returned to the pavilion and shepherded into the enclosure. By the time the gates slammed shut behind them, the atmosphere had changed considerably from when King had arrived back in the pavilion earlier that morning. The raqueta — which Raul informed King was prison slang for *search* — had sucked most of the verve from the more dangerous prisoners. Most of the men had been demoralised by the Guardia Nacional stripping their weapons away. Almost all now found themselves unarmed.

King didn't imagine they would risk a physical confrontation with him after what he'd done to Tevin's bodyguard upon arrival.

'Where is Tevin?' King said, noting the man's absence during the morning meal. He loitered alongside the twins by the pavilion's entrance while other inmates began combing through the room, retrieving their belongings scattered across the ground.

'Probably holed up in his room,' Raul said. 'He gets certain privileges. They don't bother him as much as they used to.'

'Do the guards know what I did to him and his men?'

'Probably not, and they don't care. It's kill or be killed in here. As far as the guards are concerned, we could tear each other to shreds. It just makes their job a lot easier. The prisons here are overcrowded enough.'

'Then why take away the weapons?'

'It's an economy, gringo. Like a reset button. Now we need to pay for new guns. Which goes into the pockets of the prison guards. Which probably goes into the pockets of the Guardia Nacional down the line.'

'Where do you get money from?'

'Outside connections, mostly. The guards sometimes let us make calls. Organise for money to be sent here. That sort of thing.'

'What do I do about Tevin?'

Raul looked up. 'What do you mean?'

'He's angry. He wants me dead. I was close to being killed when the raqueta broke out. I imagine there'll be attempts as soon as these guys get their hands on guns again.'

'You want to take him out?'

'I won't kill him. But I don't think he got the message before.'

'What message?'

'I told him not to fuck with me.'

Raul laughed. It was cruel and full of contempt. 'You're in his world. Why would he listen to you?'

'He's an old man.'

'He's an old man who runs this pavilion. Everyone listens to him. Everyone does what he says.'

'Why? Because he has a room? Because he has better access to guns and drugs?'

'Partially. He's respected.'

King got to his feet. 'I'm sure he's only respected because of what he can get done. No-one gives a shit about a feeble old murderer.'

Raul and Luis studied him with curious looks on their faces. Like he was an anomaly.

'What?' King said.

Luis whispered something in Spanish. Raul smiled and nodded. 'He's still surprised that you don't show fear. Everyone gets scared in this place. It's hell.'

'No it's not,' King said. 'I've seen worse.'

He brushed past them and headed for the hallway. It was time to pay a visit to the man causing all this trouble.

CHAPTER 16

The hallway smelt like piss and shit and vomit. But so did everything else in the pavilion, so King sucked it up and pressed on. He passed inmates coming down from vicious highs, lying prone on the dirty floor. Doors opened and shut and mean-looking thugs passed him by, eyeing him off in the process. The place was alive with chatter and madness. The pavilion in El Infierno was a community in itself. King was just a single cog in a larger machine.

But so was Tevin.

He approached the door at the end of the hallway. It was bolted shut. But its material was flimsy wood. It would give. King strode into range and smashed it open with a single kick, planting his trainer firmly into the lock.

They weren't ready for it.

He burst into the room, scanning his surroundings for any kind of weapon pointed his way. If there was, it would spell disaster, but he had confidence that the brash manoeuvre would take them by surprise — especially so quickly after a raqueta.

The dead man was nowhere to be seen. He'd probably been carted out of the pavilion when King was away with Rico. The two remaining bodyguards were in bad shape, and as a result they were slow to react. They were both sprawled across the couch, one with duct tape covering his badly broken nose and the other spaced out, not all there, still reeling from the effects of the concussion he'd received earlier that morning. Tevin himself lay on the same bunk, identical duct tape plastered across his own face.

The guy with the concussion made it to his feet first. He took a step forward. King twisted at the hip and drove all the momentum in his body through his right leg, whipping it round like a bat. His shin sunk into the side of the man's leg, buckling it at the knee with the loud *crack* of skin-against-skin contact. Leg kicks caused massive damage to those unprepared to absorb them. The guy lost all momentum and toppled backwards, sinking back into the couch cushions. He'd have a sizeable bruise the next morning.

The bodyguard with the broken nose made a move, as if he were about to get to his feet.

King held up a hand, palm open. The universal *stop* signal. 'You want me to break it again?'

The guy paused for a split second, but it was enough to sway control in King's favour. He had all of them exactly where he wanted them. Once again he watched the effect of demoralisation take place. One guy backed away, and the rest instantly gave up on any kind of assault they'd been planning.

'I didn't think so,' King said. 'Stay where you are. Both of you.'

He crossed the room and sat down on the chair closest to Tevin's bed, positioning himself so that he had every member of the room in his peripheral vision. Then he looked long and hard at the old man.

Tevin sneered at him. 'What do you want?'

'A resolution to this.'

'You ruined your chances of that when you attacked me and my men.'

'My chances?'

'What?'

'My chances have nothing to do with it. I'm telling you now, you'd better leave me alone. Or I'll start recruiting inmates and we'll get into a full-scale gang war.'

Tevin laughed. 'With what money? I control this prison.'

'No, you don't.'

'Want to test it? Go ahead. Do it.'

'I might. There's a lot you have to learn, Tevin.'

Tevin sat up with genuine anger in his eyes. 'You do not understand. You walk around here like you know everything about this place, when really you don't have a clue. You think you're tough because you're tall and you can beat people up, but that means nothing in here. I could click my fingers and have you killed. That's the kind of control I have. I was considering doing so, but I'm waiting it out. Seeing how you'll react. It's not often we get a man like you in this pavilion. I'd like to play with you.'

'I think you planned to kill me,' King said. 'But the raqueta interrupted all that. Now you're scrambling for a plan. You can't get your boys to jump me with their fists because I'll send them straight to the infirmary. So you're exuding this aura of control — like you're far above me — when really you're hurrying around behind closed doors like a coward, trying to figure out exactly how to deal with me. That's why I'm here.'

'You don't know what you're talking about.'

'Neither do you, old man. You're a toxic leader.'

'What?'

'You use coercion and manipulation to get what you want. People follow what you say because they're scared they'll catch a bullet if they don't. That's not control. You've got a unique environment here where that type of leadership happens to work. But watch what happens when people start floating across to my side. I'd guess that your little set-up will come to a crashing halt pretty soon.'

'If this resorts to a war, you'll lose,' Tevin said. 'Feel free to test out whether that statement is true.'

'Maybe. Maybe I'll kill you first.'

'How would you do that?'

'I could kill all three of you in this room within a minute.'

Tevin made to retort, but something stopped him. King kept his expression deadpan. He was confident in his statements because he knew for a fact that they were the truth. Tevin must have seen the look in his eyes. He *knew* King had killed many men before.

'You're a pawn in the grand scheme of things,' Tevin said. 'That's why you're in here.'

'You're right,' King said. 'For the life of me, I have no idea why I've been locked up in here. But my worries have nothing to do with you.'

'You sure?'

'Oh, I'm sure, Tevin. I see it. You're trying to capitalise on the unease I'm feeling about why I'm in here. But you're not involved — I know that much. At the end of the day, you're an old criminal. And I'll kill you just like I killed your bodyguard if I even get a hint that you're planning something.'

He didn't wait for the man to respond. He got to his feet and threw a feint. A stiff jab, pinpointed at Tevin's nose but deliberately falling far short. Tevin recoiled like a deranged man, bringing both hands to his face, desperately trying to protect his already broken nose. In that moment he looked feeble.

Which is exactly what he is, King thought.

It left an impression on everyone in the room. They lost a little more confidence. Sagged a little further down in their seats. To exude complete control of the situation, King crossed to the toilet and relieved himself, outwardly uncaring of the tense confrontation. He hoped it gave off the air that he thought nothing of the men in the room. That way, they would subtly consider him their superior.

He turned and strolled out of the living quarters, whistling softly to himself as if he had not a worry in the world.

But he knew he was in trouble.

He'd seen the stubborn look on Tevin's face. Sure, he was an old man, but he was set in his ways. He would not stop until either he or King were dead. King had left the Force to escape a life of killing. He would do everything he could to only kill when it was absolutely necessary.

He would wait until the moment someone showed violence, aggression or hostility towards him. Then he would demolish them, find out who put them up to it, and retaliate.

But before that, it was time to recruit help.

CHAPTER 17

He re-entered the pavilion in a state of heightened awareness.

He didn't doubt that Tevin had considerable control of the general population in the enclosure. Money trumped all in El Infierno, and Tevin seemed to have the most influence in that department. He was certainly a problem. But King had far greater troubles on his mind.

Unless he put together a concrete explanation as to why he had been falsely accused of murder and thrown into a gulag, he would remain in here forever. The prison was too well-fortified to attempt any sort of escape. For the time being, at least. He knew he might be able to do it, given his track record in the military and his widespread expertise in the art of physical violence.

But it would involve killing many guards, and causing general anarchy. It would mean devolving into the man he used to be, the ruthless mercenary hired by the upper levels of the U.S. Government to destabilise entire terrorist organisations and eliminate swathes of hostile threats. He'd left the States to escape that past. He'd sworn it would not return. He didn't want to resort to such measures just yet. There was every chance he would die in the process. Perhaps there was a more pacifistic solution to his troubles.

He passed through crowds of restless prisoners, none of whom bothered him.

Then he saw the entrance.

The pavilion had a new arrival.

A man with pale white skin and thinning hair had been thrust up against the steel mesh by a couple of Venezuelan thugs in tattered singlets. They screamed expletives at him in Spanish, shaking him viciously in the process. Even from across the room, King saw the man trembling. There were tears in his eyes. He'd shown weakness almost instantly.

Bad idea.

King crossed the pavilion, heading straight for the trio. No-one noticed him coming. The two thugs were too preoccupied with terrifying their new slave to bother scanning for any approaching threats. The new guy was too busy shitting his pants to concentrate on anything outside his immediate vicinity.

He grabbed the thug on the left by the back of his collar and wrenched him away. The guy lost his balance and sprawled into the mud, taking a faceful of the stuff. The other man wheeled around.

He saw King looming over him, at least five inches taller and fifty pounds heavier.

He saw the force with which his friend had been hurled across the pavilion by a single tug.

He turned and walked quickly in the other direction.

'Good call,' King muttered under his breath.

The new guy collapsed to the floor, panting, resting his back against the mesh.

'You okay?' King said.

'Yeah, I think so,' the guy said between deep inhalations. 'Just scared. Fuck.'

British, King noted.

'What's your name?'

'Percy Reynolds. I'm from Birmingham.'

'Jason King. I'm from … all over.'

'You sound American.'

'I am. Don't live there anymore though. Haven't spent much time in one place for years. Well, until now, I guess.'

'Clearly. Goddamn, how the fuck did I end up in here…?'

Percy had the distinct look of someone struggling to believe their own reality. King tried to imagine being thrown into this Venezuelan hellhole if he'd lived nothing but an ordinary life. It would be madness.

But his life had been far from ordinary, and due to that he'd grown accustomed to the chaos far quicker than expected.

'You tell me, buddy,' King said.

Percy wiped a sweaty hand over the strands of hair matted to his forehead. He thumbed a finger into each eye, raising a pair of spectacles that had been cracked in the altercation with the two thugs. He let out a single, feeble sob. Then he composed himself and dropped the glasses back down onto his nose.

'I've been a bloody straight shooter my entire life,' he said, speaking quietly. 'Just a normal guy. I work in human relations at an IT firm. Done that for the last ten years. Now I'm here.'

'And how exactly did you end up here?'

'I bought drugs.'

'Ah.'

'First thing I'd ever tried that wasn't what I was *supposed* to do. That's what this whole trip was. Shake things up a bit, try and get out of the nine-to-five — escape the soul-sucking rat race. I'd heard that Venezuela could be dangerous which was exactly why I came here.'

'Mid-life crisis?'

'I guess so. Face my fears, be more outgoing. That sort of thing.'

'I get you.'

'Didn't really work out, did it?' Percy said, staring at his surroundings, still sporting a perplexed expression. Still trying to process his new circumstances.

148

'So what exactly happened?' King said.

'I met this guy at one of the markets. He asked if I was looking for drugs, and I said yes, because I've never done anything like that before. Thought now might be the perfect time to try new things. Branch out a bit, you know.'

'You don't have to justify everything to me, Percy,' King said. 'Buying drugs is very low on my list of morally questionable activities.'

'You sound like you've seen a lot of shit.'

'I have. Continue.'

'Yeah, so, this guy told me to come back the next day and he'd have a whole bunch of good stuff for me.'

'A drug dealer didn't have any product on him?'

'No, I guess not. I don't know. Beats me how any of that stuff works.'

'That's a red flag already, Percy.'

'Like I said, I just did what he said. Came back the next day. He showed up. I gave him the money he asked for. He gave me a quarter of what he promised me.'

'You sure there wasn't a mishap on your end?'

'I'm sure. I'm … tight with money. So I made sure to outline exactly how much I wanted before handing over the money. And he gave me three grams of cocaine when I paid for twelve.'

'What'd he say?'

'Not much. I started carrying on and he shoved me up against a wall. Called a pair of cops over. He talked to them in Spanish for a bit — I'm still pressed against the wall, mind you — and then they carted me away. Threw me straight in here.'

'No trial?'

'No trial.'

'This can't be normal,' King said. 'I didn't get one either. If this happened regularly it would cause all sorts of diplomatic uproar.'

'That's what I was thinking.'

King explained the events that had transpired over the last few days. He gave no hint of his past, and didn't care to mention that one of the prison guards had something to do with it. He needed more time to think about Rico. It would do no good for Percy to have to speculate on that lead too. The man had enough to worry about as is.

By the time King finished talking, Percy had become slack-jawed.

'Wait, so this Tevin guy wants to kill you?' he said.

'Yeah.'

'Does that put me in danger?'

'You're in a pretty terrible situation, Percy.'

'How so?'

'If I leave you alone, the animals in here will beat you, rob you, maybe kill you. They might rape you beforehand. I don't know how rabid they are. I haven't been here long enough. I can protect you from all that. Most of them fear me. But if you stick around me, you'll probably make enemies. Just as many people want me dead. It's up to you.'

'Seems like there's risks either way.'

'You're in a prison in Venezuela. Get used to it.'

'Well, you helped me out. And fuck being in here alone. So I guess we're friends, Mr. King.'

King paused. 'Was that a serious title?'

'Of course not.'

'Good. Don't ever call me Mr. King again.'

Percy smiled, the first flash of teeth King had seen since he'd met the man. 'Got it.'

King held out an open palm and Percy took it. He tugged the man to his feet. 'Follow me.'

'Where are we going?'

'We're too exposed out here. There's nothing to stop someone killing us in our sleep.'

'Doesn't look like there's many alternatives.'

'There's a few.'

'I wouldn't imagine they are pleasant.'

'They're certainly not.'

Percy sighed. 'What are we doing?'

'We're evicting the occupants of one of the rooms.'

'Forcibly?'

King nodded and cracked his knuckles. 'Forcibly.'

CHAPTER 18

The inmates kept their distance as King led Percy through the pavilion, heading for the hallway. A few seemed eager to intimidate the new arrival but King kept him on a short leash so he didn't venture out into the crowds. He wouldn't put it past any of the savages in El Infierno to attempt a murder. They made sure not to antagonise King — fearing he may retaliate — but anyone else seemed to be fair game.

As they crossed the open space a fight broke out nearby between a group of inmates. The sudden commotion caused King to react reflexively. He shielded Percy with a large hand and searched for the source of the screaming.

Two men brawled in the centre of a pack, vying desperately for the upper hand. A third joined, throwing wild punches with venom behind them. One of the original pair caught a glancing blow across the side of his face, knocking teeth loose. He spat blood and reached into his belt.

'Oh, that's not good,' King whispered.

He came out with a makeshift shank, sharpened from a wooden stake. The guy who'd struck him couldn't get away in time. He wrapped an arm around his enemy's neck and viciously punched the tip of the shank into his chest; once, twice, three times. King lost count. The motions had the intent to kill behind them. The victim spluttered crimson and his eyes glazed over. Blood pooled from multiple stab wounds dotted across his torso, covering the attacker. He threw the stake away and let out a primal scream, his arms stained red.

'Jesus Christ,' Percy whispered.

'Let's get out of here,' King said.

They pressed on through the madness. The spontaneity of the killing had taken him by surprise, but he imagined such a sight was a fairly common occurrence within these seemingly lawless walls. Just another reminder to secure a room before he found a shank sliding between his shoulder blades while he slept.

The hallway was dank and decrepit at this time of the day. It was approaching midday, and the sun had reached its apex in the sky. Only a sliver of natural light made it into the corridor. Percy walked timidly behind King. He heard the pitter-patter of the man's feet. Like he didn't want to disturb the residents.

Unfortunately, residents have to be disturbed, King thought.

He chose a room at random. One of the doors close enough to the pavilion to provide a means of escape into open ground should the opportunity be necessary. Far enough away from Tevin's room to be able to prepare for an all-out assault. The door was shut. King looked back at Percy.

'Maybe stay out in the hallway while I deal with this,' he said.

'W-what?'

'They might not be too happy that I'm crashing their party.'

Percy looked at him, still perplexed. 'Who are you?'

'Just a guy.'

King thundered a foot into the door. It was weak, like Tevin's. It sprang open, revealing another pair of bunk beds in a semi-spacious room that smelt like shit, just like everything else in El Infierno. Apart from the thin frames, the room was completely bare. Three tattooed muscle-bound thugs dozed in separate bunks.

One reacted faster than the other two. As King stormed into the room he swung his legs off the flimsy mattress and got to his feet.

'*Qué coño haces, gringo?!*' he roared.

King punched him in the teeth, mid-sentence. Blood sprayed and he fell back in a tangle of limbs. The other two launched out of their bunks, spurred on by adrenalin. They charged across the room at him. One had both hands up, balled into fists. King ignored him. The other was in the process of reaching for something in his belt, running with an awkward gait to compensate for the movement.

He's a problem.

King bolted directly at the man scrambling at his waistband. It wasn't a large room. By the time he produced the pistol, King was on top of him. He tackled the guy into the concrete wall, knocking him senseless. The gun clattered away. King pinpointed where the sound came from. In one motion he turned and dove. Fingers scrambling for the weapon. He saw it a second before he snatched it up.

Another Zamorana.

Seemed like the only thing going on the black market around here.

They must have missed it during the raqueta.

He sensed movement directly behind him. He turned and put a bullet into the third man's foot. A geyser of blood fountained from the wound and the guy dropped like a sack of shit, reeling from the nerve damage. King had suffered a similar injury back in Australia. It had taken months to fully heal. The scar tissue remained.

He tucked the gun into his own waistband and took his time hurling the three men out into the hallway, one by one. The first man he'd punched in the teeth put up somewhat of a fight.

He swung wildly, managing to clip King in the ear. He shrugged it off and returned with a blow of his own.

The patented liver shot.

Every ounce of fight in the man dissipated instantly. He groaned from somewhere deep within. King tossed him out after his friends. The three goons collapsed in the mud outside, dirtying their clothes — which were already putrid in the first place.

King loomed in the doorway and tapped the barrel of the Zamorana against the frame.

'Anyone tries to come back and I kill you,' he said, slowly and succinctly in an attempt to cross the language barrier.

To make sure they got the message, he mimed firing a shot at each man successively. They watched him from the ground like he was a lunatic.

He beckoned Percy inside, slammed the door shut and left the previous occupants to pick themselves up.

The dilapidated interior of the room was unpleasant to say the least, but at least it provided protection from a sneak attack. There was one way in, and one way out. There were no windows whatsoever, making it a little more cramped than Tevin's room. But it meant they could barricade the door and take cover in the vulnerable hours of the night ahead, when they needed rest. Then they could head back out into the pavilion during the daytime. Fully alert. Ready to go.

'Are you tired?' King said.

Percy looked at him as if he were crazy. 'I don't think I'll be able to sleep for a week,' he answered.

'You'll manage eventually.'

King selected one of the beds and stretched out on it, keeping a finger tucked inside the Zamorana's trigger guard — just in case. In the sudden quiet, Percy's panicked breathing filled the confined space. King listened to it for a few minutes. He kept his mouth shut, deciding not to overload the man with information just yet. He needed time to process what had happened to him. Even though he could handle the drastic change of surroundings that came with being thrown inside a third-world prison, he didn't imagine an ordinary civilian could.

He drifted into a state of tranquility. It came naturally to him. After spending years scouting enemy strongholds in the far corners of the globe, he found it effortless to tune out and simply *be*. He lay on the bed. He watched the door. He controlled his breathing. He didn't let his mind wander. Percy sat sideways on the bed opposite, intermittently rubbing his eyeballs.

After what could have been close to a couple of hours, the man spoke. The words came quickly, in an outburst, like he'd been mustering the courage to talk for a long while. 'How-are-you-doing-this?'

King rolled on his side and raised an eyebrow. 'What?'

Percy repeated the question, slower, more controlled.

'What do you mean exactly?' King said.

'I've never been more scared in my life,' Percy said. 'I think I'm going to vomit. How are you coping? This seems like just another day to you.'

'Because it's just that,' King said. 'Just another day.'

'It's madness! A few days ago I was holed up in a cubicle, filing tax returns. This is total fucking madness…'

'To you it is. I've had certain life experiences that — to be honest — are far worse than this. These people are civilians. Sure, they're violent drug addicts, most of them, but they're just low-level gangsters and thugs. It's all about perspective.'

'You're not scared of them?'

The conversation oddly mirrored Raul's sentiments at breakfast.

'I'm just as scared as you are,' King said. 'I feel the fear. I experience the same things you're experiencing right now. You feel nauseous. Your throat's dry. Your hands are shaking. But I control it. I compare the situation I'm in to ones I've been in before. Then it doesn't sound so bad.'

'You used to be a soldier, didn't you?'

'You could say that.'

'Prefer not to talk about it?'

'You got it.'

Percy nodded. 'Isn't it ironic?'

'What?'

'The one time I decided to stray from the typical straight-shooter existence that I've been living my entire life, I end up here. In this place. The worst hellhole imaginable.'

'There's worse places than this.'

'But you're some kind of superhuman,' Percy said. 'Us normal folk lose our minds when this kind of stuff happens to us. Not sure if you understand that.'

'Oh, I understand alright. I was exactly like you.'

'I find that hard to believe.'

'That's why I joined the military in the first place. Had high levels of anxiety growing up. Everything freaked me out. I'm naturally introverted. Then I signed up to serve my country and things ramped up from there. First time I got shot at, I thought I was going to die from a heart attack. I know exactly what you're feeling right now. You want normality.'

'And you don't?'

'I don't know. I'm trying to live a peaceful life now. Seems like I keep getting sucked back into shit like this.'

'What happened to you to change you into who you are now?'

'My career happened.'

'The one you'd prefer not to discuss?'

'That's the one.'

'You're scarred from it?'

'I don't know,' King said again. 'I honestly have no idea. I think death became such a recurring aspect of my life that these situations feel like nothing out of the ordinary.'

Percy smiled. 'We're the exact opposite.'

'Are we?'

'I've never been in trouble. Seems like you've never been out of it.'

King nodded, running a hand over the Zamorana. 'Seems that way.'

'I—' Percy began.

King cut him off. 'Look, Percy, I've had a hell of a lot going on the last couple of days. We got ourselves a room. We have all the time in the world to talk later. Right now, I need some rest.'

Percy nodded. 'Got it.'

'If I doze off, just yell as loud as you can if you hear anything suspicious. Or if the door opens. Got that?'

He nodded again. 'Yep.'

The afternoon passed fast. They remained undisturbed. Every now and then King would wake to movement on the other side of the door, but it would quickly dissipate. Just prisoners passing by.

Nothing threatening.

Not yet.

His sense of time all but vanished in the space. The bulb on the ceiling didn't rise or set. It stayed soft and flickering for hours. Without venturing out into the main area, King wouldn't know when it was dark. And he didn't dare leave the room. He'd made a lot of enemies during his brief time in El Infierno. Right now, he was priority number one on many hit lists. He wanted to let the nervous energy dissipate before he considered showing his face again.

At some point, Percy piped up. 'I'm getting really tired.'

King smiled. 'What did I tell you? You dumped all your energy when you came in here. Now you've crashed.'

'Do you mind if—?'

'Not at all. Get some sleep, Percy. I think we're in for a long night ahead.'

King trained the barrel of the Zamorana on the closed door, well-rested and alert. If Tevin or his men or any of the thugs in the pavilion decided to bull rush their room, King would make sure he killed as many of them as possible with the fourteen rounds left in the magazine.

Because that's what you do best, a voice in the back of his head whispered. *That's all you're good at.*

That's all you'll ever be.

CHAPTER 19

Almost exactly four hours later — according to the rough estimate of a clock in his head — King heard Percy jolt awake in a cold sweat. Perspiration dotted the man's brow. He wiped his forehead with a filthy buttoned shirt and gazed around the empty room.

'Fuck,' he whispered. 'Had a nightmare.'

'Think you'll survive?' King said.

The corners of Percy's mouth upturned slightly. He gave King a resigned look. 'Still felt worse waking up to reality.'

'Well, you'll be pleased to hear that nothing happ—'

The door swung open, flooding the room with light from the hallway. Wide-eyed, King whipped the Zamorana into position, barrel fixed on the door. His eyes took a moment to adjust to the brightness. Two figures loomed in the doorway. If he saw they had any kind of hostile intentions, he would empty the contents of the pistol in their direction.

But they weren't armed.

They even had their hands raised in the air, signifying their lack of weapons.

It was the twins from the pavilion.

Raul and Luis.

King recognised them, but he did not yet trust them. 'What do you want?'

'To talk to you,' Raul said.

'So talk.'

'We would both appreciate it if you lowered the weapon.'

'Close the door behind you,' King said.

The pair moved further into the room and shut the door, sending the room back into half-light, illuminated dimly by the weak bulb fixed into the ceiling. Raul and Luis sat on the empty lower bunk and rested their elbows on their knees. They both gave Percy a quick nod. He stared back, unsure of what to do. He'd never seen the twins before. King came to the conclusion that neither man was a threat and decided to lower the Zamorana.

'We hear you're in a bit of a predicament,' Raul said.

'I am,' King said. 'Tevin wants me dead.'

'Why don't you kill him?'

'I'm getting close to doing just that.'

'Then what?'

'Huh?'

'What will you do after you kill him?'

'I don't know. I haven't thought that far ahead yet.'

'A lot of men in here depend on Tevin. He brings them good food, he brings them guns, he gives them whatever drugs they're after. I don't think it's a wise idea to kill him by yourself.'

'So what are you suggesting I do?'

'I'm not suggesting anything,' Raul said. 'But we are both willing to help you with whatever you decide on.'

'You are?'

'We've never been huge fans of what Tevin's doing here. He's started charging a protection fee to most of the pavilion. He gets us to ask the guards to retrieve money from our families or friends, and then we pay him to leave us alone. It's getting too much. Most of us don't like him. We just put up with him because he has the final say on everything around here.'

'But he still has a lot of friends?'

Raul nodded. 'Many will still stick up for him if we attack. But if we find enough who dislike him, we might get enough men on our side to lead to a stand-off.'

'Then what?'

'There'll either be an all out war, or nothing. My guess is it will grow too large to justify conflict. If we get enough people involved, a battle will end up killing most of the men in here. I don't think anyone wants that.'

'Why are you getting involved at all?' King said. 'It's probably safer to just keep to yourself.'

'I respect you,' Raul said. 'I respect what you're doing here. You're not just rolling over for Tevin like everyone else does. I think others may feel the same; they're just not vocalising it. It's been a while since Tevin's made an enemy with competence. And I wouldn't mind seeing this place shaken up. It's a madhouse as it is right now.'

'Is this the only pavilion in El Infierno?'

Raul laughed and shook his head. 'I think there's six. Four for men, two for women. Plus private cells for privileged inmates.'

'Why isn't Tevin in a private cell?'

'He's on top in here, but out there he's nobody. He's been in here long enough to wiggle his way into an authoritative position, but that doesn't mean anything to the outside world. It's the businessmen and those with family money that get special privileges — because they can afford it. Tevin makes a bit through profits off his drug and gun running ... but in the grand scheme of things it's very little.'

'Then I say we finish him off,' King said. 'It's doing no-one any good to wait around like this for someone to jump us. I'll go in there now and shoot him and his two bodyguards dead.'

'You do that now,' Raul said, 'and you'll be dead yourself within minutes. He has too many of them on the payroll.

You're a good fighter but you can't take on the entire pavilion at once.'

King nodded. 'So we get more men. I have cash on me which I haven't shown to anyone yet. I can pay for help.'

'How much do you have?'

'Almost fifty thousand bolivares.'

Raul let out a low whistle. 'Any of them catch wind that you have that kind of money on you and they'll swarm you like vultures. Keep that to yourself.'

He turned to his brother and spoke in a hushed tone. King's Spanish was not good enough to translate efficiently. He let the two converse for a minute, then Luis got to his feet and made for the door. On the way out, he nodded at King, a seemingly friendly gesture. Then he left the room, moving fast.

'He likes you,' Raul noted.

'He said that?' King said.

'Many times. He's still in awe, I think. The way you fought back against the guard, the way you fight back against everyone.'

'Just who I am.'

'I like it too.'

'How did you two end up in here anyway?'

Raul sighed and bowed his head, recalling traumatic memories. 'We both were sent here a year ago. I still can't believe it all happened.'

'What happened?'

'We both worked for the Agente De Mudanzas for a few months. In English, that means Movers.'

'I know,' King said. 'I learnt some rudimentary Spanish. Many years ago.'

'During your career?'

'Yes.'

'A man of many cultures,' Raul said with a slight smile. 'Anyhow, they're drug runners. Started as a low-level street gang and built themselves into what they are now. They're the largest importers of narcotics into the state of Vargas. Everyone knows where they do business but they've paid so many officials off that no-one bothers them.'

'They control the authorities?'

'They do.'

'And you worked for them?'

'I did.'

King hesitated. 'Then what are you doing in here?'

'They threw both of us to the wolves. We were dealing recklessly, thinking we were invincible because of who we worked for, and we got caught. We had close to a kilo between us. I never heard from any of the Movers again. They just let us get arrested and charged. Abandoned us as soon as we found ourselves on the wrong end of the law.'

'Is that what they usually do?'

'Exactly the opposite. From what I've seen, they protect their own. But our boss started getting more and more ruthless as time went on. He doesn't have time for incompetence. I'd say he saw us as two idiots and let El Infierno swallow us up.'

'Who is he?'

'He's the reason they run half the state now. They were nothing before the mudslide tragedy many years ago. It crippled more than half the state. He capitalised by snatching up an entire shipyard for almost nothing. Now he pays off police, he buys politicians. All to be left alone and increase the cocaine coming in through the port from neighbouring Colombia.'

'What's his name?'

'Rico.'

King's stomach dropped.

Of course it fucking is.

Pieces began to fall into place. He slowly put together a number of different theories as to why he ended up in El Infierno, and why a drug gang's leader was watching over him under the guise of a prison official.

He turned to Percy, who until this point in the conversation had remained completely silent, watching from his bunk.

'Percy,' he said. 'You bought cocaine, correct?'

Percy nodded.

'Where from?'

'Somewhere in Maiquetía. I can't remember exactly what the street was called, but it was near the beaches.'

'I was staying near there,' King noted. 'Raul, did you operate in that area?'

'If you bought cocaine in Maiquetía, it would have come from the Movers. They're the only players in that district. Trust me. Me and my brother used to make most of our money from cashed-up tourists.'

'Used to?'

'Well, up until the Movers forgot all about us.'

'Ah,' King said. 'And are they professionals?'

'What do you mean?'

'Do they make mistakes? Do they mix up orders?'

'Never. That's the last thing they would do. The entire philosophy behind Rico's operation is to be as consistent and efficient as possible.'

'Percy, tell him,' King said.

The British tourist explained what had transpired, from the moment he decided to purchase drugs all the way up until he was thrown in El Infierno. Once again, he stressed the once-off nature of his urges and continued to highlight that he would never dabble in such illegal activities again. Much like King, Raul didn't give a shit. He seemed more concerned with the details of the deal itself.

'Perhaps I was wrong,' Raul said after Percy finished.

'What do you mean?' King said.

'That definitely doesn't sound like the Movers.'

'Which part?'

'Showing up with a quarter of what was agreed upon.'

'Maybe they slacked off in the time you've been here.'

'I guess ... if Rico moved on. But I doubt either of those things have happened. Rico was a wild man in the time I knew him. He lived and breathed his operation.'

King recalled the crazed sneer on Rico and the aggravation behind his eyes when he thought he was being lied to. 'I don't think he's moved on either.'

'What makes you so sure?' Raul said.

'Just a couple of things I've seen.' King paused, thinking hard. 'So say the Movers are still operating in Maiquetía. Why would they stuff up a deal like that? Maybe they thought they could extort some dumb foreigner?'

Percy frowned.

Raul shook his head. 'No chance. That was the one thing they prided themselves on. Professionalism. Always being accurate. They would not be so foolish to start ripping off their customers. Rico would never do such a thing. It's how he grew the Movers into what they are today.'

'So something's off in their operation?'

'Must be,' Raul said. 'Why are you so curious about all this?'

'I think I may have inadvertently been the cause of all this behind-the-scenes turmoil.'

'How so?'

'I'm still trying to work that out.'

Suddenly the room lit up as the door swung open rapidly. It caught King by surprise. He'd been deep in thought, distracted by recent revelations. He'd let his focus falter. As such it took him a fraction of a second too long to bring the Zamorana round and aim it at the door. He knew he could very likely die in the time it took to do so, and his heart froze in his chest.

But that didn't happen, because Luis stepped into the room, followed swiftly by two Spanish men. Both were short and stocky. They waddled with the gait of men who had packed on a little too much weight in the belly area. One had long thin hair and the other was bald.

Luis noted the barrel pointed at his temple and smiled wryly. He said something in Spanish.

'He says you're very trigger happy,' Raul said. 'Always ready to go.'

'Gotta be,' King said. 'Too many people want me dead. I was slow that time.'

'What world do you live in where that kind of reaction was slow?'

'The world where I stay alive.'

Luis introduced the pair as Daniel and Mateo, friends who had been locked up in El Infierno for several years. They had suffered abuse from Tevin and his men for years, for reasons they could not work out. He seemed to hold a hatred towards the pair ever since they'd stepped foot inside the pavilion. As such they'd been treated like dirt for the majority of their time in prison. They were more than willing to lend their services to King in the event of conflict.

Raul translated all this, listening fast and speaking fast. King took it all in, resting the Zamorana on his knee as he thought. He stood up and shook each of the men's hands. The language barrier prevented any sort of meaningful conversation, but he noted the look in their eyes and knew they would help. There was pent-up rage and frustration in both of them. King knew exactly what that felt like.

He knew they could be trusted.

'So we have six,' he said, turning to Percy and Raul, the only two English-speakers in the room. 'This could get ugly.'

'It will get ugly,' Raul said.

'Did Luis tell you anything?'

'A lot of people out there know what's happening. They know tension is brewing. He said he hasn't seen the pavilion like this in years. Everyone's quiet, everyone's scheming. I don't know, King … this could go very badly for us.'

'It could go very badly for a lot of people.'

'What time is it? It's tough to keep track in here.'

'Middle of the night still.'

'And everyone's awake?'

'I think they can sense something large is coming. Apparently a few weapons have crept back into the pavilion already. Guards selling them on the down-low.'

King shook the Zamorana in his hand. 'I have one, at least.'

'Won't do you much good if everyone's after you.'

'Let's worry about that when it happens.'

King studied the members of the room. There was enough men on his side to provide a slight level of reassurance, but nothing more than that. All it meant was that they would not be extraordinarily outnumbered in the event of an attack. Nevertheless, his heart rate began to ease.

He wasn't alone.

'We can take shifts now,' he said. 'Two men watch the door, four sleep. Everyone good with that?'

A collection of nods came back. Daniel and Mateo spoke to Raul in Spanish. He listened and nodded. Then faced King.

'They offer to take first shift,' he said. 'As a thank you for standing up to Tevin.'

King smiled. 'I don't have much of a choice.'

'They're grateful anyway.'

He nodded and rolled over in the bunk. Sleep had been sporadic and restless over the last few days, given everything that had transpired. He'd managed a few restless hours before, but it hadn't been enough. Constant tension and unease made one exhausted.

'How the fuck can you sleep right now, mate?' Percy said. 'I'm shitting my pants.'

'We've been over this, Percy,' King said, still facing the wall. 'I've been in worse situations.'

'You're a nutter.'

'At least being a nutter makes me calm.'

He drifted off, slipping away from the throbbing and aching and burning all over his body as it healed from the dozens of baton swings. He ignored the cramped, humid conditions and the unease which had plagued his every thought since he'd first been arrested. It all went away.

But not for long.

CHAPTER 20

Panicked shouting tore him from unconsciousness.

His eyes flicked open and he came to in an instant. He blinked hard twice, until his blurry surroundings came into focus. Bodies, all around him. Frantic movement. Yelling. Surprise and tension and unrest.

He leapt to his feet, still processing what he was seeing. A cluster of men had stormed into the room, slamming the door open, taking the two sentries by surprise just long enough to capitalise. Now the room was over-populated, bodies against bodies. An air of confusion permeated the place.

King looked at the intruders. They weren't Tevin's men.

Three of them were Guardia Nacional.

The other was Rico.

All four brandished Kalashnikov AK-103 assault rifles, big, bulky guns, all reliable, all pointed in their direction.

'Hey, boys,' Rico said, a devilish smile spread across his face.

Raul made a guttural noise full of rage. King saw him lock eyes with his old employer. Rico's smile did not falter. He kept the leer spread across his face, languishing in the twins' anger. 'Didn't think I'd see you two again. Enjoying the stay?'

Luis spat at him. The glob of saliva landed on Rico's combat boot. He looked down at it, then shrugged. 'I'd normally kill the both of you for that. But I probably deserve it. Anyway, enjoy the rest of your short lives. I have other matters to tend to.'

King took his finger off the trigger of the Zamorana. It would do no good to end Rico here, because he would just take three magazines full of ammunition in return. The remaining Guardia Nacional soldiers would tear him to shreds. He couldn't kill four men before they retaliated. Besides, where would that leave him? Stuck in a pavilion, no closer to freedom, with four dead officials on his hand.

Well, three dead officials. And one drug lord.

'What are you doing?' King said.

Percy cowered in his bunk. Raul and Luis stood side-by-side, fists clenched, ready to attack. Daniel and Mateo looked similar.

Rico let his eyes wander over the ragtag group of men and laughed. It seemed he found everything in life hilarious. 'You six better not put up a fight. We'll kill you and bury the evidence.'

'We're not putting up a fight,' King said. 'Now what do you want?'

'There's rumours spreading,' Rico said. 'That you gentlemen are inciting something you shouldn't be. Care to explain?'

Silence.

'I think I need to talk to the two Westerners,' he said. 'They seem to be the ones causing all the trouble lately.'

'Leave Percy out of all this,' King said. 'I'm the one you have a problem with.'

'Are you?'

'You know I am.'

'You're certainly right that I have a problem with you. But I also have a problem with your friend. So I'll talk to you both. Follow me.'

He instructed the three soldiers in Spanish to keep watch over the other four men, which King deduced by hand movements and general tone alone. Then Rico gestured for he and Percy to follow. Reluctantly, he stepped forward.

'King,' Percy said feebly.

He turned. 'Let's go. You won't change his mind. Just do what he says.'

Percy's shoulders sagged. Maybe he thought King had some magic solution to this problem. But right now, he had nothing.

The air was already thick and humid in the room, warmed by the body heat of ten men. Raul and Luis watched them go with venom in their eyes. King knew every fibre of their being wanted nothing more than to pummel Rico into oblivion for tearing them away from their family and throwing them into hell.

But they wouldn't get a chance.

Not yet.

King powered through the small crowd and stepped out into the hallway. Rico kept the barrel firmly trained on him. His hands did not falter. They stayed deathly still, positioning the gun completely on target, standing just far enough away to negate any kind of wild charge King might decide to throw.

He's well-trained, that's for sure.

Percy scurried out of the living quarters and stopped by his side. King looked through the pavilion, and outside. It was still dark, but not pitch black. The faint glimmer of dawn had begun to creep into the surroundings, turning the buildings outside a shade of blue.

'Out there,' Rico said, motioning with the barrel.

They moved through the pavilion, heading for one of the gates. Dozens of inmates gave King the evil eye as he passed them by. He ignored them and pressed on. He was sure that were it not for Rico escorting them through the compound, he would have caught a bullet in the head by the time he reached the far gate. So far, the prisoners hadn't started trouble with him, but that didn't mean they respected him. He presumed that for the right price they would kill anyone.

And Tevin seemed to have his sights set on eliminating King for good.

They stopped by the gate and Rico scanned his keycard on the sensor. He punched in a four-digit code and the lock emitted an electronic beep. He pushed on the steel bars and the door swung open.

King could have killed him in that moment. Rico had taken his eyes off his prisoners while fumbling with the keypad. It would have taken a single motion to disarm him and light him up with Kalashnikov rounds. But that would result in no answers, and would do more harm than good. So King ignored it and stepped through into the prison grounds.

This side of the pavilion faced a number of neighbouring buildings, all plain concrete, all grey, all unassuming. The prison grounds were a maze of interconnected compounds. Breaking out would be all but impossible. He'd have to navigate down paths that twisted and turned — avoiding all guards — then find a way through the perimeter building.

Rico stood across from them in the low light. Beside King, Percy stood hunched over, hands shivering. He was terrified.

'The fuck are you two doing?' Rico said.

'He's not doing anything,' King said, gesturing to Percy. 'He just got here. I'm the one antagonising Tevin, so you deal with me.'

'Tevin?'

'The guy who runs the pavilion.'

'Ah.'

'You'd know that if you actually worked here.'

Rico chuckled. 'So you pieced together that I'm not a guard. Congratulations.'

'I know more than that.'

'Oh, you do?'

'I know you want me alive because you want answers to all your questions.'

'That's pretty obvious.'

'And I know why.'

'Elaborate, if you really are such a detective.'

'I fucked up your entire operation, didn't I?' King said. Then he grinned, as if showing that he had done so intentionally.

Rico grit his teeth in rage and tightened his finger around the Kalashnikov's trigger.

CHAPTER 21

For a moment King thought Rico would blow his brains across the pavement. But he didn't, because he was curious. King would humour him.

He raised a finger and pointed it at the drug lord.

'The three thugs in the alley,' he said. 'The ones I beat the shit out of. Now I know where they were headed. It seems they were responsible for securing more of your supply. They missed a meeting of some kind because of what I did to them. The suppliers must have high-tailed it out of there. Maybe they suspected foul play. Or they're big on punctuality. Anyway, that's irrelevant. Point is, your supply is non-existent now, isn't it? Seems you've had a communication breakdown with the supplier. I set off a chain reaction. You don't have enough to get you through. And your gang prides themselves on running a tight ship. Now competitors can creep in. Snatch up the eager customers. Am I right?'

'You already knew that,' Rico said. 'Who put you up to it? Which group?'

'That's the thing, Rico,' King said. 'I've been telling the truth this whole time. No-one did. I worked all that out myself. Percy here tried to buy cocaine from one of the Movers and the guy wasn't able to deliver what was promised. You're spread out, and you're losing your hold on the market. Must have really pissed off your suppliers by not showing up, huh?'

'You really have nothing to do with this?' Rico said.

'That's what I've been telling you. You assumed I did because it was an almighty coincidence. I beat down the three most important men in your organisation on that day. But all they did was piss me off. That's their fault.'

'You're some kind of ex-soldier?'

'I am.'

'Just passing through?'

'Uh-huh.'

Rico smiled and raised the Kalashnikov.

In that moment, King knew he was bat-shit crazy, and that he would never be let out of El Infierno voluntarily. Unless he left via a body bag. He had angered Rico, a man used to getting whatever he pleased. Infuriated him, even.

'You think that changes things?' Rico said. 'Just because you didn't have a motive? You put your hands on my men. That's a death sentence.'

'I'm trying to be reasonable,' King said.

'Fuck you. I should kill you myself. But that'd be too quick. I'll just throw you back in there. You won't last long.'

'You're an amateur,' King said.

'What?'

'You heard me. This entire thing is nothing but a temper tantrum. You should let me go, and forget I ever existed. I made you look like a fool. Accept that. Learn from it. Move on.'

Rage flickered behind Rico's brown eyes. He surged forward and grabbed Percy by the shirt. Dragged him over.

'*You want to insult me?!*' he roared, loud enough for most of the pavilion's occupants to hear. 'Are you forgetting where we are? I run this whole state!'

'Don't,' King said, in a voice barely above a whisper. His veins were ice-cold.

'Who's going to fucking *stop me?*' Rico snarled.

For a single fleeting moment King met Percy's gaze. He saw the unbridled terror in the man's eyes. Even worse, he could do nothing to stop what came next.

Rico pulled the trigger.

A barrage of rounds exploded from the Kalashnikov's barrel at close range, all tearing into Percy's chest. The man let out a weak cry as bullets shredded his shirt, pulping his torso with lead. Blood sprayed from the wounds. Rico let him go and he collapsed to the pavement.

King saw his eyes. They had already glazed over. The first two or three rounds had most likely done the job. But Rico made sure to put more than ten into him.

Just to send a message.

Something deep inside King snapped. He felt it give, just like that. One second he had his emotions under control. Perfectly subdued, like a lion on a leash.

Then, as he watched the life fade out of a man who had done absolutely nothing wrong, the leash vanished. He couldn't control what came next. Professionalism and discipline had taught him to battle the primal urges that came with anger. Many times he had successfully done so.

This time, he found it physically impossible to show restraint.

He charged at Rico before the man even had time to stop firing, or swing his aim around, or prepare himself in any way. He seized the gun and wrenched it free. Even in such a state of heightened anger, he felt the strength that fury lent him.

It was a completely different level of efficiency.

He broke Rico's finger as he tugged the Kalashnikov away. The man couldn't get it out of the trigger guard in time, and King pulled with a force that shattered the bone into pieces. He howled and recoiled back, surprised by the sudden pain.

King spun the assault rifle in his hands, feeling its familiar weight. He righted his aim and fired, a short *tap-tap-tap*, three rounds that tore open Rico's leg, plunging deep into the kneecap. He dropped where he stood. Legs buckling. Mouth opening in surprise. King reversed his grip on the gun again and swung with the speed of a Major League batter. The butt caught Rico on his open jaw. The *crack* that accompanied the impact sounded gruesome enough. A couple of teeth flew loose, surrounded by droplets of crimson.

Fixated on causing as much pain as humanly possible, King dropped the Kalashnikov and surged on Rico's battered form. He grabbed one arm and twisted wildly, breaking it at the elbow joint with a juicy *pop*. Then he wrenched it back the other way. Breaking more bones. Causing more agony. He moved with a savage ferocity that he hadn't felt in a very long time.

In the space of five or six seconds, he'd brought a world of pain on the supposedly mighty drug lord. Rico lay in the dirt, curled into a pathetic ball. Still conscious. Nothing had come close to knocking him out. King had made sure of that. But he would be feeling every inch of the trauma inflicted on his feeble frame.

'Been waiting to do that for a while,' King said.

Rico let out a guttural noise somewhere between a sob and a dry heave. He lay on his back next to Percy's corpse, staring at his useless left arm and his right leg now pouring blood into the dirt, creating a grimy viscous putty as the two combined. More crimson ran from his mouth.

Somehow, he managed a sentence. 'They'll kill you.'

'They'll try. But things have changed. Now I need to try and escape.'

'Y-you won't get out of here.'

'I might. And if I do, I won't rest until your entire operation is demolished.'

Rico laughed pathetically and spat blood into the dirt next to his head. 'Good luck. What makes you think you have a chance?'

King leant down. 'Because you don't know who I am. You don't know what I can do.'

He raised the Kalashnikov, aiming the barrel between Rico's eyes. Ready to fire the kill shot.

Wild shouting sounded from somewhere above. King looked up and saw a cluster of guards standing on the balcony of the closest watchtower, peering down at them from the vantage point.

They saw the blood pooling into the dirt.

They saw one of the wounded men was a prison official.

They saw an armed prisoner standing on open ground, unguarded.

They raised their weapons.

King abandoned his position and scrambled across the narrow path, sprinting wildly, searching for cover. The dirt kicked up near his feet, accompanied by the distant din of rifle fire. He ducked behind an indiscriminate concrete building opposite the pavilion. Across the path, inmates peered out through the steel mesh, fascinated by the scene unfolding.

The klaxons around the compound roared into life, shrieking and hollering. They signalled an approaching raqueta.

Guardia Nacional would storm the prison at any moment.

Here we go, King thought.

He clenched his fists, hands now shaking from adrenalin. From his position, there was all likelihood that the Guardia Nacional would tear past him, heading straight into the pavilion. In their haste they might not see his crouching form in the lee of a neighbouring building.

Sure enough, ten seconds later a dozen men rounded the corner, coming into view, all dressed in military uniform, all armed with batons and shotguns.

They didn't notice him. The few that reached the pavilion first spread out across the various gates, punching in key codes, getting ready to swarm the prisoners.

King took a deep breath. He had two options. He could slip past the Guardia Nacional and head back the way they had come. Attempt to find a way out through there. But it unnerved him. The likelihood of stumbling into a dead end was too high. Getting caught was no longer an option. After butchering Rico, he didn't imagine they would be lenient on him.

The second option was tantalising.

He could instigate a war in the middle of a raqueta.

It would cause complete anarchy. At least, for a while. But he had to draw the prison guards away from the wall. He had to create a situation so insane that all prior systems of controlling El Infierno would become shaky.

So he broke free from his cover and quietly followed the Guardia Nacional into the pavilion, with a single word on his mind.

Chaos.

CHAPTER 22

Already, tensions were heightened.

The military guard storming into the compound were entering a different world. The first raqueta had been frenetic, yet largely uneventful. The beatings dished out by the Guardia Nacional that time were savage, but were not retaliated against. They seemed to be the norm. This time, the atmosphere amongst the general prison population was tenfold more hostile. Many had been preparing for a confrontation with King and his men. Testosterone was high. Violent reactions would be easier to provoke.

King knew he could capitalise on this.

Amidst the screaming and grunting of bodies clashing together, he slipped into the fray and waited for an opportunity to kick things off. It came when a soldier wielding a shotgun turned his back, heading for a group of thugs in the corner. King came up behind him and slammed a boot into the back of the guy's knee. His leg buckled and he loosened his grip on the shotgun, clearly surprised by the well-placed blow. King seized the shotgun and jerked backwards, slamming the butt into the guy's helmet with enough force to knock him off his feet.

Then King used the momentum generated by the blow to line up his aim and fire a cluster of riot pellets into two Guardia Nacional soldiers nearby.

It was the first discharge of a weapon inside the pavilion.

The guards grimaced and doubled over, taking most of the pellets to their torsos, winding them, stinging them, surprising them. Soldiers who witnessed the attack cried out in rage and surged towards King. He dropped the shotgun and ducked into the pack of prisoners in the centre of the pavilion, becoming just another body in a sea of brutish men.

He headed straight for the hallway on the far side. On the way through, he made sure to cause as much trouble as humanly possible. He bumped into a tough-looking Spanish thug. He seized two handfuls of the guy's shirt, spun him round and heaved him into a pack of men nearby, knocking several of them off-balance. Then he spun on his heel and slammed a fist into the gut of another random prisoner. The guy doubled over, moaning. King pushed him off his feet and he careered into a second cluster of men, all taken by surprise by the violent action.

That was all it took.

Wild brawls broke out all around him, spurred on by the confusion of the raqueta and the overabundance of testosterone

191

rippling through the air. King knew he'd just created a shit-storm. He ducked low and powered through the chaos, using his size and strength to his advantage, bundling everyone in his way aside like rag dolls. This only seemed to further provoke the inmates. In the sea of men vying for physical dominance, getting pushed over like a feather enraged almost everyone he encountered.

King slipped into the hallway just as the fighting reached its peak.

He noted several things at once. First, the grimy corridor was sparsely populated. The majority of conflict had broken out in the main area of the pavilion, leaving only a few drug-crazed stragglers crawling across the muddy floor, too high to even think about fighting. He glanced down the length of the hallway and saw Tevin's door still firmly shut. The man was hiding in there, avoiding the chaos of the raqueta.

Very likely up to something.

The door to his own room lay ajar. One of the Guardia Nacional had stuck his head out, peering into the pavilion, surprised by the sudden outbreak of hysteria and madness. King knew he had an opportunity to capitalise on the confusion once again.

'Rico!' he yelled to the guard, feigning fear. 'He is crazy! He killed my friend! He's shooting at the pavilion!'

Unable to understand English, the guard cocked his head, attempting to make sense of King's panicked sentences. By the time he began to retort, probably telling King to stay back, he had already come too close. He slammed the door back into the guy, buckling him, then charged into the room.

'*Fight!*' he roared as he slammed into a cluster of bodies.

He wasn't able to deduce the twins' exact location, but he was sure they would get the message.

He locked a powerful forearm around the throat of the guard he'd disoriented and squeezed. The guy bucked and writhed like a mad man, but it had little effect on King's hold. He felt the man slipping into unconsciousness as the four men on his side lashed out in frenzied bursts of anger.

By the time King put the Guardia Nacional soldier out and released him to the floor, the other two men had been dealt with sufficiently. The twins had beat down one guard using his own Kalashnikov as a dull object, and Daniel and Mateo were in the process of raining down savage blows on the third.

'Stop,' King said, and they instantly ceased.

The third guard, still conscious, stared up at them. King held out a hand and nodded a truce, gesturing for him to stay put at risk of another beating. The guy nodded, wiped blood from his nostrils and scooted to the far wall. He sat still and simply watched.

'Where's your friend?' Raul said, looking around.

'Dead,' King said, bowing his head for a moment. He let the image of Percy's bloodied corpse lend him energy. 'I just caused a raqueta. A very violent one. I'm going to attempt to get out of here now. It might mean I end up on the wrong end of a bullet. You four can either come with me, or stay put. Completely up to you. Tell them.'

Raul muttered to the other three in Spanish, translating the message. Daniel and Mateo listened silently, their faces contorted into skeptical grimaces. King already knew they would refuse. Their opinion on him had quickly changed. They thought he was some kind of wild madman.

Perhaps I am.

Luis seemed eager. His eyes widened and the corners of his mouth tilted upwards. Fascinated by the opportunity to escape.

'I think we've made our decision,' Raul said after the four had finished going back and forth.

'You two are coming?' King said, pointing to the twins. 'And the other two are staying?'

'Yes ... how'd you—?'

'Pretty obvious. Let's go.'

He hadn't grown close to either Daniel or Mateo. He had known both of them for less than a day. He couldn't communicate with them due to the language barrier. It was their choice to stay, and he had no qualms with their decision either way. They would probably look back on their choices and smile if he and the twins ended up getting caught and executed.

Either way, he wasn't bothered at all. He nodded goodbyes to both of them and then turned to Raul and Luis.

'This could get messy,' he said.

'We know,' Raul said.

'Any reason you two want to take that risk?'

'Our sister, and our mother. They were dependent on us when we worked for the Movers. That's why we started in the first place. We haven't been able to contact them since we got in.'

'You'd risk your life for them?'

'Of course. It's family. I thought escape was impossible before, but if you're saying there's a chance then we'll take it. Wouldn't you do the same for yours?'

'I don't have any family.'

Raul nodded. 'I guess you can't relate then.'

'I can't relate. But I can understand. Let's go.'

They gathered up the Kalashnikovs dropped by the three guards, so that each man brandished an assault rifle. King checked the safety of his weapon. It had been flicked off before the soldiers had entered. They'd been ready to kill.

Now he was ready to kill.

The old Jason King had resurfaced.

The din of the raqueta had been muffled by the concrete walls, but as they exited into the hallway its volume reached a crescendo. King took in the scene, slightly surprised by how quickly the conflict had escalated.

The pavilion had turned to bedlam.

Guardia Nacional were involved in many of the brawls. Batons swung and the constant *crack* of shotgun discharges ripped through the heavy air. In their primal states, the prisoners had switched from fighting amongst themselves to lashing out at the guards. It had quickly become a skirmish.

King couldn't help but hesitate. He'd planned to charge headlong through the chaos — cutting a path to the nearest open gate — but the sheer intensity of the conflict made him stop to reconsider. Maybe there was another way…

Then he heard screaming behind him.

Coming from the end of the hallway.

He turned and saw Tevin's door flying open. Armed men spilled into the corridor, searching for targets. All their eyes were wide and rabid. He guessed most were hopped up on some kind of drug that Tevin had access to. Maybe speed.

Tevin's hired thugs. They numbered at least seven, and came tearing down the corridor like berserkers. Heading straight for them.

The pavilion to King's rear. Crazed killers to his front.

He raised his Kalashnikov and started firing, and then all hell truly broke loose.

CHAPTER 23

The element of surprise saved his life.

The thugs hadn't been anticipating King and the twins lying in wait in the corridor. They must have planned to seize the confusion and charge to his room, bursting the door open and unloading their weapons into the cramped space. It would have worked, had King not been ready for violence at a moment's notice.

He flipped a neurological switch and was transported back to a time where all he did was kill. When his career had revolved around the deaths of mercenaries and gangsters and terrorists. He swung the barrel from man-to-man, squeezing off just enough shots to put them down. He moved with cold, calculated efficiency. Blocking out all emotions.

It only hindered his aim if he thought of his targets as people.

For a brief millisecond, he considered the dangers of returning to this state. He'd worked so hard to break free from it. He'd retired from Black Force. He'd travelled through desolate countries and kept his head low to try and recover from a career of madness. And here he was, right back in the mayhem.

But it was the only choice he had if he wanted to stay alive.

He killed every thug who was in the process of raising a gun. Two at the front. One off to the side. They sprawled into the mud, bleeding heavily. Firearms clattered from their limp hands. The rest seemed to wield only handheld weapons. Bats, crowbars, machetes. King picked the guy with the machete off. His head jerked back as he took two rounds to the temple in a spray of brain matter.

And then they clashed.

The hallway was too narrow, too small. He couldn't hope to put them all down before it turned to a close-quarters brawl. The commotion had played out so fast that Raul and Luis had yet to get a shot off. Their reflexes were slower. Less honed.

They still had their barrels pointed at the ground when the group of Tevin's goons slammed into them.

A filthy cramped corridor was the worst place for a strategic fight. But that didn't matter, because King thrived in these scenarios — when technique and efficiency went out the window and the upper hand was given to the man with the most sheer power.

He knew that was him.

As soon as two thugs crashed into his chest — knocking the gun out of his hands — he exploded. He threw a vicious slicing elbow to his left. A sharp knee to the right. The men fell away. He seized the man in front of him — a tall, bald Spanish guy baring his teeth — and delivered a colossal headbutt into his nose.

It was the third septum his forehead had destroyed since arriving at El Infierno.

Raul and Luis did their best. Both men were well-built. Tall and solid. They could scrap. More importantly, King knew his own actions would encourage them, spurring them to fight. He hadn't hesitated in the slightest before fighting back against Tevin's assault. He knew from experience that the display of bravery would lend a motivational boost to everyone on his side.

So the twins lashed out at anyone nearby, giving it their all. King tried to ascertain if they had the upper hand, but the brawl was too feverish to get a decent look. He could only worry about himself.

As he lashed out with a two-punch combination that smacked a thug's chin in one direction just so he could wind up for a haymaker on the other side, he took a quick glance to see if Tevin had appeared. So far, still no sign of him.

The guy in front of him dropped, his limbs loose. He'd been knocked senseless by the combination. King sensed Tevin's thugs crumbling all around him and realised that he and the twins had more than likely gained the upper hand in the conflict. He hadn't taken any kind of considerable blow yet. Sure, he was injured from the beatdown he'd suffered during the first raqueta, but adrenalin did its best to mask the effects of all the bruises and cuts.

Then a wave of bodies slammed into him from behind, pressing him forward, knocking him off his heels.

Claustrophobia kicked in. The corridor had become so densely populated by the fresh swarm of men that he had trouble breathing. He wheeled around and saw inmates surging into the hallway, fleeing from the Guardia Nacional.

They must have turned lethal, King thought.

It was the only thing that could explain such a mad rush.

Punches and baton swings whistled through the air around his head. He weaved left and right, ducking and bobbing. He dodged the tip of a baton that came at him so fast it would have broken his jaw had it connected. The displaced air washed over him, chilling him.

A shiver ran down his spine.

He didn't even see where it came from. Just that it almost knocked him into a coma. He slammed a trio of inmates aside and spotted Raul and Luis in the crowd.

'To the gate!' he roared above the din.

Raul nodded and battered a man in his way aside. The guy's slight frame didn't stand a chance in the carnage. He crashed into the far wall and dropped underneath the rampaging horde.

The three of them powered through. King got in front of the twins and used his weight advantage to smash aside anyone in his path. He didn't care who they were. Inmates, Guardia Nacional … they all stood between him and the other side of El Infierno's walls.

A soldier saw the three of them fleeing in the opposite direction to the crowd. He raised a shotgun and aimed it directly at King's face. King looked down the barrel and baulked. Riot pellets or not, they would still shred his skin to pieces. Probably kill him at such a close range.

He ducked and leapt simultaneously. The guy had the extra weight of the shotgun in both hands and couldn't bring his arms down in time to protect his mid-section. King rammed a shoulder into his stomach and took him off his feet. The two sprawled into the mud.

King was momentarily blinded by the mud that geysered away from the impact zone. He wiped it frantically off his eyelids and assessed the location of the guard. The man had landed hard, smashing all the breath out of his lungs, sending the shotgun flying away into the crowd. As bodies moved all around them King drove a fist into his solar plexus, taking out every last ounce of breath. The guy coughed and spat and doubled over. It would take him a few minutes to recover from that.

All King needed.

He saw the tiniest sliver of a gap between two separate brawls, both involving a mixture of inmates and guards. A narrow line leading directly towards one of the gates. He scrambled to his feet and turned to find the twins.

He stared straight into the barrel of an automatic pistol.

Tevin leered from the other end.

Somehow, someway, the old man had made his way through the pavilion in the heat of the widespread melee. Inmates had probably let him pass. Even in such rabid states they still more than likely respected his rank within the pavilion.

He'd made a beeline for King.

King didn't move. Any sudden action would cause Tevin to pull the trigger even quicker than he already intended to. He'd only been staring at the weapon for half a second, but in his mind it felt like an eternity. What could he do?

Nothing.

Except feel a crushing blow in his ribs as a Guardia Nacional soldier crash-tackled him, sprinting in from the right-hand-side, using a running start to drive momentum into the attack. The man must have seen King attack his comrade and decide to return the favour.

King's neck whipped to the side, jarring several muscles at once. He felt a ringing pain in his ears. Either from Tevin's gun discharging at such close proximity, or his brain scrambling from the tackle. Whatever the case, he splayed across the dirt with enough force to slam him into a semi-conscious state. He felt a brutal *thump* as his head bounced off the hard ground. He groaned and rolled over.

Incapacitated.

But alive.

He looked up at Tevin, who had fired at where King had stood not a second earlier. The old man struggled to correct his aim. Battle raged around him. It threw his senses off *just* enough. Added a tiny delay to his actions.

All King needed.

He leapt forward, head pounding, arms outstretched. One hand wrapped around Tevin's lower leg and he wrenched with everything he had, completing what was known as an ankle pick takedown. Usually — if implemented perfectly — the opponent ended up on their back.

But this was not a trained martial artist. Tevin was a frail old man. And King was a powerhouse.

Tevin left the ground and rotated almost an entire revolution, his frail bones doing nothing to resist King's ferocity. He landed on his neck, hard enough to cause major neurological damage, not hard enough to kill him.

King was more than happy to complete the equation.

He scooped up the gun the man had dropped — a Taurus 24/7 — and brought his aim around. He destroyed Tevin's head with a trio of Parabellum rounds. Pulped the guy's temple into a bloody pulp.

Good riddance, King thought.

He'd given Tevin more than enough chances to leave him alone. He'd put up with attempts on his life more than once. Enough was enough. A man only had so much patience.

Raul stumbled over to King, bleeding heavily from the mouth. It was clear that he'd taken a few good punches. Luis emerged from the crowd, shoving aside two Spanish inmates. Blood covered his bare arms.

It wasn't his.

His face didn't bear a single scratch.

'Your brother's deadly,' King said as Raul helped him to his feet.

'He can hold his own, that's for sure.'

King led the trio out the open pavilion gate. He guessed it was the first time the twins had left the enclosure in a very long time. Their feet crunched slowly over the gravel, and they gazed around in awe at the surrounding buildings, all tinged orange under the warm glow of the rising sun.

Dawn had broken.

A volley of gunfire from a distant watchtower sent a spray of rounds across the path in front of them. King ducked low and wrapped an arm around each of the twins' midsections. He spurred them forward. They dove in unison across the path and under the shelter of the same building he'd crouched behind a few minutes earlier.

'We're pinned down,' King said, grunting in frustration as another magazine was emptied in their direction.

Then something happened which he didn't anticipate.

A cluster of inmates had noticed them slipping out of the pavilion. For some reason unbeknownst to King, they decided to follow. Four men spilled out onto the pavement, fleeing the enclosure. Shots rattled around them and they all bolted in different directions.

It set off a chain reaction.

Before King knew it, half the pavilion's population had surged out the open gates, directly defying the Guardia Nacional. Soldiers came sprinting out after them, tackling inmates at random, throwing wild shots. A multitude of fights broke out across the pavement.

King sensed rebellion in the air. It appeared his provocation at the start of the raqueta had created a snowball effect. Years upon years of abuse had turned the prisoners into caged animals. They were unleashing all the pent-up fury. King watched it unfold in awe.

'This is getting out of hand,' Raul said.

'It's exactly what we needed,' King said. 'I didn't expect it to pay off so well.'

'Do you know where we need to go?'

'I know which way I was brought in. That's about all I have.'

'We don't have any other choice, do we?'

'I don't. You two can go back to the pavilion whenever you please.'

'I don't want to be around to experience the aftermath of this,' Raul said. He stared in shock at the carnage raging all around them. 'Neither does Luis. And we have a family that needs us.'

King nodded and waited for an opportune moment to make a break for it. On a whim, he glanced down the track. Percy's feeble corpse lay in the same place. His glasses were shattered. A peaceful calamity had crept over his face. The relief of death.

But he couldn't concentrate on Percy for long at all.

Because the space where Rico had previously lay — cowering from his injuries — was bare. The man had disappeared.

'Fuck,' King whispered. 'Let's go, right now.'

'Why right now?' Raul said.

'Because there's someone around here who will do anything to kill me.'

They broke free from the narrow alley and took off down the pavement, heading for the far wall of El Infierno.

CHAPTER 24

King felt his chest heaving as he ran down indiscriminate paths, blood pumping, hands shaking. The twins followed close behind. The centre of El Infierno had been haphazardly thrown together in its construction. There wasn't a shred of symmetry to its geographical layout. The rest of the prison had become a ghost town. Offices previously manned by guards and prison officials lay bare, paperwork strewn across the floor, swept off the desk as they dashed either toward or away from the source of commotion.

He could hear the violence from here, a soft echo of mad screaming that drifted over the buildings and permeated the prison grounds. Every guard in the complex would be drawn to the chaos. They remained at their stations when order was kept and procedures were set in stone. But King knew exactly how people in positions of power reacted when insanity broke out.

Not well.

He'd succeeded for most of his career by capitalising on the reactionary nature of his enemies. Now he would do so again.

He stopped running as they approached a sharp turn in between two enormous concrete structures. He raised a hand, halting Raul and Luis in their tracks. Ahead, the multi-storey outer wall loomed over everything else. A twisting path would take them right up to its door.

'Wait,' he whispered.

Gunshots sounded from the same direction they'd come. Either inmates had got their hands on weapons, or the Guardia Nacional had reached the end of their patience and turned to more dangerous means of subduing the riot. Probably both. It came with a shift in atmosphere. The situation had turned from barely under control to completely irrepressible.

Now people were dying.

King continued to wait. He predicted what would come next.

He was right.

A pair of prison guards stationed on this side of El Infierno came careering around the corner. They saw King standing in their path and baulked, but their momentum carried them a few more steps, unable to slow themselves in time.

The shiny assault rifles in their hands were useless at such close range. King bundled one up against the wall and kneed him in the gut, hard enough to do significant internal damage. The guy crumpled, letting go of the rifle.

An AK-74, King noted as he caught the gun in mid-air, spun and swung it into the neck of the second guard.

One of my favourites.

The butt of the Kalashnikov slammed home into the soft tissue of the guy's throat. Not hard enough to kill, but enough to cause serious problems. He shot off his feet. As he went down, Raul kicked him hard in the ribs, incapacitating him for the foreseeable future.

They hadn't done anything to provoke King. But sometimes certain situations called for injuries to innocents. Sure, it was unfortunate. But these men would heal up. He would die gruesomely if he stayed within these walls.

He turned to see both twins slack-jawed, astonished at the ease with which he'd dispatched the guards.

'Come on,' he said, hurrying them along.

The twins hustled past the two incapacited guards. Before he followed, King bent down and patted his hands along the first man's olive-coloured vest. He was met with no resistance. The blow to the gut had put the guy out of action for at least the next few minutes as he recovered his breath. King found what he was searching for — the jangle of a set of keys — and ripped the bunch from the guy's pocket. Sure enough, a keycard had been slotted into the keychain, its plastic knocking between two keys. He gripped the bundle in one hand, keeping the other wrapped firmly around the AK-74.

'You think that will get us through?' Raul said.

'Let's hope so,' King said. 'Otherwise I'm going to have to turn to more desperate measures.'

'These aren't desperate measures?'

King looked up. 'Not even close.'

'You used to be a bad man, didn't you?'

King glanced down at the prison guards writhing on the ground, fighting through the considerable pain he'd brought upon them. 'Hard to say. There's too many grey areas.'

'Use those grey areas to get us out of here. Please.'

'I'm trying my hardest not to.'

They continued towards the compound's perimeter, passing under the line of sight of a rusting watchtower. If occupied, it would take little effort to unload automatic weapons in their direction, picking them off from a clear vantage point. But there wasn't a guard in sight. King heard the conflict on the other side of El Infierno escalate in volume, and grimaced.

'Raul,' he said. The man stopped and turned. 'You think they'll get the riot under control?'

Raul shrugged. 'No idea. But don't feel bad. Something like that had been brewing for months. It would have broken out with or without you. I was waiting for the day it all kicked off.'

'To escape?'

He shook his head. 'To fight back.'

Up ahead, Luis called out. They saw him tugging at the handle of a thick metal door built into the side of the multi-storey perimeter. It led inside. Probably into a maze of dilapidated corridors. As King jogged to catch up, he found himself questioning whether he'd instigated all this anarchy for nothing. If they were cornered inside the building, he didn't fancy his chances of being alive by sundown.

He approached the panel next to the steel door and tapped the keycard against a small electronic pad. A beep of confirmation — and a small green light kicking into life above the panel — indicated that the card was compatible.

Luis pulled the handle again.

It didn't budge.

King eyed a grid of numbers under the pad, hovering just above a thin LED screen.

'There's a key-code on every door,' he said. 'Thought that might happen.'

His gut constricted as the situation became clear. A beat of fear arced its way down his spine. His hands grew clammy. Sweat dripped off his brow.

Death would not come quickly if they caught him alive.

'I'm going back to those two guards,' he said quietly.

Raul noted the steely determination in his tone and raised his eyebrows. 'What are you going to do?'

'Get the code out of them.'

'What if more of them catch up? What if we're overwhelmed?'

'We don't have many other choices, Raul.'

Then the door burst open in their face.

CHAPTER 25

A frantic shuffle of bodies. Official-looking military uniforms. Tight lines of tension on foreheads. Furrowed brows. Determined expressions. Bulky assault rifles.

Four Guardia Nacional soldiers stormed out of the building.

King saw them power their way through, carried by the energy injected from approaching combat. At the same time, he heard the whining of an alarm behind them, emanating from within the building.

Reinforcements.

Heading for the pavilion.

He met their eyes, and knew both he and the twins would be torn to shreds in seconds if he didn't act. Almost in slow-motion, he saw their pupils widening in shock, their hands beginning to react, their barrels swinging in his direction. They were very clearly three prisoners *far* away from where they were supposed to be. They were close to the wall. They were armed. They would not be shown mercy.

So King would not show them mercy either.

He dropped, his feet scraping away from the ground. He fell a foot and then his knees slammed into the earth. His jaw rattled. His senses faltered for a moment, stunned by the impact. But he'd driven his centre mass out of the guards' line of sight, meaning it took them that extra second to react to his actions and re-focus their aim.

By which point he'd brought the barrel of his own AK-74 up and unloaded its contents into their legs.

Gunfire rang out across the empty path. Thirty rounds of ammunition tore across the tiny space between them. Bullets sunk into calves and shins and feet before any of the four had time to fire a shot. They fell simultaneously, blood arcing from flesh, screams slicing out of their mouths.

Shocked by such a rapid sequence of events.

Much like any man who crossed King.

Sometimes he imagined how events unfolded from the perspective of his enemies. He knew his reaction speed was inhuman, an extreme outlier amongst the outliers themselves. That's what had secured him a position in a top-secret U.S. black-ops program. That's what had kept him alive through years of vicious combat.

That's what would keep him alive today.

He didn't hesitate to surge forward as soon as the pack of soldiers were taken off their feet. It took a millisecond to assess who his attention had to shift to. Two of the men sprawling into the dust had taken wounds of such a painful nature that their instinctive reaction had been to release their weapons and clutch their trousers, which were quickly turning crimson. Instantly, he disregarded them. He focused solely on the two men that had their fingers slotted inside the trigger guards of their assault rifles.

Kalashnikov AK-103s. Standard issue for the Venezuelan Army.

Very dangerous at close quarters.

He wound up and swung his leg at one of the weapons as if taking a free kick. He targeted the space where the magazine met the receiver, as it provided the least room for error. As soon as contact was made and the gun tumbled away across the dirt he spun and pounced on the last armed guard.

The guy lay on his back, covered in dust, bleeding profusely from exit wounds in his calves. Nevertheless, he possessed the mental fortitude to keep a grip on his firearm. King squashed him into the ground, slamming him chest-to-chest. Minimising the potential to find himself on the other end of the barrel. He grabbed the AK-103 and wrenched it free, then used the stock to drop a blow into the guy's stomach. The man let out a wheeze of protest. Coupled with the other injuries, King didn't imagine he would be putting up much more of a fight.

He got to his feet, surrounded by four groaning bodies. All disarmed. All going nowhere.

Raul and Luis had barely begun to react.

'What the f—' Raul whispered, gazing at the scene around him. He looked at King like he was some kind of monster, like he didn't come from the same planet. Like he possessed skills that bordered on otherworldly.

'Let's go,' King said.

There wasn't time to gawk at his talents. They had all the time in the world to ponder such thoughts when they were free.

King caught the edge of the door just before it swung shut. As his fingers locked around the cold metal, he breathed a sigh of relief. If it had clicked closed, they would have been left in the same position they'd started in.

And now every guard in the compound knew of their presence.

Thirty rounds ejecting from the AK-74 had caused a deafening racket. The noise had echoed across El Infierno. Harsh and sharp. Drawing attention to the other side of the prison.

King knew they needed to move, or they would quickly find themselves in a war.

He used short commands to instruct the twins. They needed to be told exactly what to do. He saw shock setting into their features. Their time in the pavilion may have desensitised them to violence, but not at this level of intensity. Not when every move made the difference between seeing freedom and being carted unceremoniously back to the prison in chains.

Where he had no doubt Rico would relish torturing him slowly to death.

Raul and Luis scooped up two of the AK-103s the soldiers had dropped. Briefly, King glanced at each man's legs. The sights passed through his mind and he checked to see whether any limbs would need amputation.

Probably not, he concluded.

Which was the most reassurance he would get, for a fresh set of alarms exploded from loudspeakers across the compound. These sounded at a different frequency, shrieking with the urgency that highlighted a volatile situation.

He imagined that the three of them had been spotted on various cameras. Now every guard in the compound would be alerted to their presence.

There were prisoners breaking out.

King ushered the twins inside the building, his heart racing, wondering just how on earth a peaceful holiday had turned to this in the space of a few days.

CHAPTER 26

The interior of the building brought with it a different smell.

It was still putrid — but a controlled kind of putrid. Not the filth of untouched faeces and urine that permeated every inch of El Infierno's centre. Prison officials and Guardia Nacional soldiers patrolled these corridors. They had offices in these buildings. As such, the conditions were somewhat passable. Hygiene was tended to. So King inhaled deeply as the three of them tore through white-washed hallways, relishing the smell of civilisation. He tasted freedom, so close now he could almost sense the other side of the building *just there.*

And he'd only been locked up for two days.

He couldn't imagine how Raul and Luis felt.

He saw it in their faces. Something that he hadn't seen since he'd met them. An emotion that began to surface only when escape transformed from a shaky improbability to something very plausible.

Hope.

After at least a year inside the walls of El Infierno, he imagined they had become resigned to the brutal, unforgiving system, shattered by the betrayal of the gang that employed them. Now they might finally be able to start a new life.

King kept his AK-103 raised and his right eye firmly aligned between the sights, but they made it down three corridors in succession without any sign of resistance. He spoke as they moved.

'Where to after this?' he said.

'We're not out yet,' Raul whispered.

'We're close. Will you visit your family first?'

He nodded. 'Of course. Luis and my sister were inseparable. They did everything together. He didn't handle the arrest well. He hasn't spoken to her in over a year.'

'And you?'

'I was closer to my mother. But I cherish both of them.'

'I'll get you to them,' King said. 'Then I'm gone.'

'Where will you go?'

He paused. 'Haven't figured that out yet. Seems impossible for me to escape trouble.'

'I think you can,' Raul said. 'I think you try too hard to seek it out.'

'You think?'

'You don't need to do anything after we get out of here. It's not on you to get us back to our family.'

'I'd like to help.'

Raul raised a finger. 'That's why. You can't help everyone. When you try, you get yourself into this shit.'

'I didn't involve myself in this. I stumbled across it.'

'You beat up the three Movers when you didn't need to. If you want peace, King, you need to refuse to react.'

'Sometimes I can't.'

Raul shrugged. 'Then maybe you're supposed to do this forever.'

The corridor ended up ahead, sprawling out into a security station to process new arrivals. Two separate steel doors were built into each end of a narrow path, walled in by bulletproof glass. A bank of controls lay beside the station, currently uninhabited. Usually, a guard would monitor the prison staff exiting or entering. The setup was designed to ensure that no-one could leave without express approval of a staff member sitting behind the impenetrable glass.

Now it lay deserted. Surrounded by every siren in the prison sounding in unison, King paused by the first steel door and struggled to figure out a way past the checkpoint. The controls to unlock the doors were locked away in the bulletproof cube, usually occupied by a guard.

They had come this far.

He wouldn't let them fail when they were so close to the other side.

He heard muffled movement from somewhere in the complex. Somewhere behind them. He froze, listening intently. It came from behind one of the closed doors, within one of the adjoining rooms. Amidst the din of the alarms, he couldn't confidently assess which one. He dropped into a crouch and headed slowly back the way they'd come, pressing his ear against the wall every few feet.

Nothing.

Maybe they were trapped in this corridor after all.

Sudden commotion broke out directly in front of him, a cluster of hurried panicked movements happening all at once. King saw a wooden door burst outward, thrown open from the inside. A man came charging through into the corridor, his eyes bulging in their sockets. Mid-thirties, King guessed. They were roughly the same age. This man wore an official prison uniform with his buttoned-up shirt tucked into brown slacks. He had a pistol clasped between his fingers with no situational awareness to speak of. The gun looked like a foreign object in his hands. King knew inexperience when he saw it.

A man used to long slow stretches of inactivity behind a desk, watching proceedings through security cameras, buzzing his co-workers in and out of El Infierno all day. A man who had fled into an office at the first sign of losing control of a situation. Then he'd second-guessed himself, and come hurtling out into the hallway in an attempt to save face after such a cowardly gesture.

Noble, for sure. But misguided.

King had no intention of ending the man's life, so he darted forward and jabbed the thin barrel of his weapon into the guy's liver. The metal pummelled into his side with enough force to double him over. From there, it was simple. Like clockwork.

There was no-one more effective than King at physical conflict.

He bundled the guy into the wall and slapped the pistol out of his hands. It barely took any effort at all. Like scolding a small child for touching something he shouldn't. The gun made a harsh noise as it skittered away across the linoleum.

Wide-eyed, breathing heavy, the guard let out a moan that signalled a mixture of frustration and fear. He'd made bold plans with such a brash manoeuvre. It certainly hadn't unfolded the way he'd envisioned it.

King backed off and raised the AK-103. Barrel pointed between the guard's eyes. He wasn't sure if the man had ever had a gun aimed at his head. He assumed the gesture would evoke a specific type of reaction in the event that one hadn't.

He was right.

The guard began to bawl. No build-up. No sobbing or snivelling. Just an explosion of emotions that King knew meant his life had never been threatened before. The man was staring death in the face, and he couldn't handle it.

'You speak English?' he said.

The guard stared blankly, tears trickling down both cheeks.

'English?' King repeated.

The guy shook his head.

Luis approached the stand-off and began to talk directly to the guard in Spanish. He spoke low, barely audible above the sirens. King kept his gun trained on the guard, every so often shaking the barrel for effect. Each time he did so, the man flinched.

By the time Luis had finished his spiel, the guard was fully compliant. From the tone of his voice King guessed it had come laced with threats and promises of death in the event that he didn't help them. By the end of it, the guard had wet himself.

Luis raised his own weapon and prodded it into the guard's back, directing him towards the booth. As soon as King realised Luis had the situation under control, he wheeled his aim away and trained the gun on the other end of the corridor. They'd spent too much time in one place. He knew either Guardia Nacional or prison guards would follow the trail of incapacitated officials and happen upon them in no time.

Unless the riot in the pavilion had turned into a full-scale bloodbath.

Which it must have, because the corridor remained deserted. The absence of conflict unnerved King. He was in battle mode, primed for conflict, ready for a firefight. The extended period of nothingness bothered him more than a shootout would have.

Which isn't natural, he thought.

But neither was running through an entire army of prison officials. And he had done so successfully. It sent a ripple of confidence through his system. To any other man, such a feat would have been impossible. Yet he had cut through El Infierno like a hot knife through butter. And now he would soon be on the other side of its walls.

He kept all his focus directed at the end of the corridor. Behind him, he heard movement. Doors unlocking. Raul and Luis were coaxing the guard into letting them out.

So close.

A harsh buzz indicated that the first door had been opened. King registered the noise, but didn't act. Not yet. It would only take him turning his back for a second to compromise them. Guardia Nacional could charge round the corner and light them up in the time it took to make it through the doorway.

The second door buzzed.

They had a clear path to freedom.

As a deterrent, King squeezed off a volley of shots with the AK-103. They dotted the far wall, taking sizeable chunks out of the plaster. The sound of multiple discharges ricocheted off the narrow walls, blisteringly loud inside the corridor. King felt his ears ringing. He stayed unperturbed. The gunfire would cause anyone nearby to hesitate.

Which gave him more than enough time.

He spun on his heel, dropped the AK-103 and took off for the station. At the same time, he assessed the position of the twins. Raul had been the one to enter the booth with the guard. He was in the process of exiting at full pelt. Luis held the first door open for them. They had to time it so that the guard didn't trap them in the space between the two doors.

King flew past Luis and snatched the second door, which had popped open when unlocked. He held onto its metal surface so that it didn't swing back and lock, effectively trapping them in. Now both doors were open. There was a clear path to freedom. He saw sunlight spill into the glass corridor.

Raul burst through the first doorway and rushed past King, leaving the prison. As he did so, Luis let go of the first door and stepped inside the room.

Then King saw it.

A figure rounding the corner at the other end of the hallway, limping badly. One arm dangling uselessly by his side. Blood covering his uniform. His good hand clasping an automatic pistol.

'Luis, *down!*' King roared.

Luis sprinted for the second door, arms and legs pumping like pistons. Behind him, the first door slowly began to swing shut.

Not fast enough.

A single *crack* tore down the corridor, registering in King's eardrums at the same time that he saw Luis jerk forward like a marionette thrown by its strings. He locked eyes with the man for a split second, seeing the fear in his stark green irises. Then the side of his head puffed open in a spray of brain matter and he slapped the hard tiled floor with a wet smack.

All tension dissipated from his limbs.

Luis was unquestionably dead.

King saw Rico leering in the distance. The grotesque smile seemed to hover for a brief moment — teeth stained red, nose dripping blood.

Then he turned and fled El Infierno, stepping out into the bright Venezuelan heat. He shut the memory away. Perhaps he would need it later, for motivation. But for now he had to focus on escape.

They hadn't come this far for nothing.

CHAPTER 27

He knew what came next would be tough. Beyond tough.

He stepped down into a small courtyard — not the one he'd arrived at. This space was a little more claustrophobic, a little more deserted. It was a small inlet carved out of the surrounding trees. A row of rust-pitted dumpsters lined the nearest wall, each leaking disgusting fluids. Broken wood pallets crawling with cockroaches were strewn across the courtyard's floor. It seemed to be the dumping ground for El Infierno's unneeded waste.

The inlet exited onto a main road with occasional passing traffic. On the other side of the road, steep hills ascended far above them. A shanty town had been constructed in the side of one mountain. Its rickety houses overlooked El Infierno.

Beautiful view, King mused.

But he wasn't concentrating on any of that. He gave his surroundings nothing more than a passing glance, because the real problem lay directly ahead in the form of Raul, standing a few feet away from the entrance.

A man who fully expected to see his brother emerge from the doorway after King.

King passed through the doorway and slammed it shut behind him, shutting them both off from any more of Rico's pinpoint-accurate shots.

Raul's face fell. His features crumpled. He cocked his head to the side, staring right at King, hoping for some kind of explanation. There was so much King wished he could say.

Don't worry, Raul, your brother is heading a different way.

He's perfectly fine.

Nothing to worry about.

He'll catch up with us later.

But King had nothing for him. He looked into Raul's eyes, seeing the hurt flaring within them. They were identical to Luis'. He shook his head, a single solemn gesture that said everything all at once.

Raul's legs buckled.

Whether he was fainting or simply overcome with grief, King could not let him collapse in the dirt. Rico would make his way down the hallway, open the steel exit doors and unload the rest of his clip into the man's crumpled form if given the opportunity.

They hadn't come this far for that.

King scooped a hand under Raul's armpit and hauled him to his feet. Raul sobbed, eyes already watering, tears sliding down each cheek, destroyed by the loss of someone so close to him in the seconds before they both found their freedom. King felt the same emotions deep down, threatening to bubble to the surface and faze him out.

But as always, the necessity to succeed at the task at hand overpowered whatever shock or anger or grief he felt.

He shoved Raul hard, spurring him forward, heading for the main road. The morning traffic passed by frequently enough for King to be confident they could seize a car. Raul stumbled once, and faltered. King saw the expression on his face. He didn't want to leave El Infierno behind, because that meant Luis had been confirmed dead. He clutched onto a strand of hope. He hadn't seen the body for himself.

Perhaps his brother had miraculously survived…

'Raul, there's nothing that can be done,' King said. 'I saw it myself.'

'You can't be sure.'

'I'm sure.'

'We need to go back and…'

'We'll die.'

He pushed Raul again, double-handed, his actions full of urgency. Finally, the man reacted. He took one last look at the enormous brick structure looming in the background. Then he spat on the ground and set off at a jog down the gravel path, his eyes bloodshot.

King followed, glancing back every so often to ensure the exit door remained firmly shut. He didn't expect Rico to be able to make it down the corridor very fast, and he assumed the guard monitoring the station wanted nothing to do with them. Nevertheless, he kept his AK-103 at the ready.

They left the scraggy brush behind and burst out onto a two-way asphalt road. It ran along the lee of the mountains opposite, great sweeping valleys of green and brown that ascended into the sky. The shanty town overlooked them, thoroughly dilapidated. To the north, the road trickled down through the city of Maiquetía until it met the coastline. It ran parallel to the ocean, stretching into the distance for as far as the eye could see.

'We need a place to hole up,' King said. 'Where did you used to live?'

Raul said nothing. He stared vacantly at the cars passing them by, detached from reality.

'*Raul!*' King roared, snapping him back to the present. 'Talk to me. We need to focus these next few minutes. Understand?'

The man nodded.

'Where do we go from here?'

'We're going to die, man,' Raul whispered.

'What?'

'The Movers will want us both dead. They'll tear the whole city apart looking for us. My mother, my sister...'

'Where are they?'

'I don't know. I haven't been able to contact them for a year. But I hope they're still in our old home.'

'Did you used to live there?'

Raul nodded. 'Me and Luis both. Before we were arrested...' He trailed off, choking up at the mention of his brother.

'It's down in Maiquetía?'

Raul nodded again.

That was all King needed to know.

Time was sparse. Even now, word of two prisoners' escape was likely flooding through the prison grounds, drawing the full force of the Guardia Nacional to this side of the complex. They had to get clear of the area before they were overwhelmed.

He waited for a break in the traffic and stepped out into the middle of the road. In his lane, a dirty olive hatchback crawled up the hill a hundred feet away, heading straight for them.

He tucked the Kalashnikov rifle behind his back and held up a hand, feigning distress. There were no visible signs to indicate he was an escaped prisoner. He still wore the same clothes from a few days ago, albeit dirtier.

The car slowed. Through the windscreen, King saw the driver gesticulating, yelling inaudibly in Spanish. Cursing the idiot blocking his path. The tyres bit the asphalt until the man had slowed his vehicle to a crawl. It crept slowly towards King's motionless form.

He brought the AK-103 into sight and held it double-handed, one hand wrapped around the trigger guard, the other tight on the fore-grip. An intimidating pose. With the barrel of a very real, very dangerous weapon pointed directly at him, the driver baulked. He stamped on the brakes and threw his quaking hands in the air.

King sometimes forgot how intensely civilians reacted to death threats. He considered situations like these normal. Which was probably how he'd ended up in such a predicament in the first place. He gestured with the barrel, motioning the guy out of the car.

The man complied.

King passed him as he went to slip into the driver's seat. He took one look at the guy's dirty shirt, straggly hair, oversized slacks and beat-up ride. He didn't imagine the guy was in a comfortable place financially. The loss of his automobile would only make that worse. King didn't ignore his conscience.

He couldn't.

He slipped a hand into his jeans pocket and withdrew the wad of bolivares within. Equivalent to roughly five thousand U.S. Dollars. He peeled off half and tucked them into the shaking driver's shirt pocket. The guy looked at the money and raised his eyebrows.

They didn't speak the same language, but King nodded his thanks for letting the incident transpire smoothly. The guy nodded back. Probably awfully confused. Yet a little reassured by the payment. He shuffled to the side of the road without a word of protest and watched King and Raul drive off with his car.

'The fuck was that?' Raul said, sprawled across a passenger's seat full of holes and cigarette burns.

'A bit of decency,' King said. 'Been a while since I showed any.'

'Luis, man…'

He grew quiet. King spun the wheel and floored the vehicle in the other direction, slicing in between two nondescript sedans heading down into Maiquetía. The sun had only just risen and it cast a warm glow over the seaside city. At any other moment in time, King would have enjoyed the scene.

But not when an entire drug gang wanted his head. Not when he had just escaped from a horrid third-world prison. Not when he'd just witnessed the death of an ally.

Right now, he couldn't care less about the view.

They drove in silence. King didn't let his focus fade. He made sure to constantly check the rear view mirror for signs of trouble. Approaching military vehicles, or armed drug dealers, or any of the other countless people that wanted him dead.

How did you manage to end up in a situation like this again?

He knew what would be best for him. Drive straight to the hotel and retrieve his passport and all the other items he'd left in his room, which by this point had probably been cleared out by housekeeping. Head straight for the airport. Catch the next flight out of Vargas state. Leave all this brutality and bloodshed and savagery behind. If he couldn't retrieve his passport, he could get into contact with old friends in high places. They'd sort him out.

That's what he *should* do.

Yet against his better judgment, he found himself glancing across at Raul. The man was an emotional wreck. He had no idea how to contact what family he had left. He'd just lost the brother who'd helped him survive a year in El Infierno. He was in no state to search for his mother and sister alone. Especially not with every Mover in the state hunting for his head.

That brought King to the mental image of Rico firing his rifle into Percy's chest, killing the defenceless man in cold blood without a shred of empathy. King pictured his leering face, and the look in his eyes when he hit Luis from the other end of the corridor. It angered him all the way down his spine.

He gripped the wheel tight, letting out his frustration. Then he continued descending the hills.

He would stay. He would try to help Raul. He would try to find Rico — and finish it.

He wondered exactly what would result from such a decision.

CHAPTER 28

'What will you do now?' Raul said, his voice soft and raw with emotion.

The arid scrubland all around them morphed into rows of dilapidated apartment buildings. They had entered Maiquetía. Passersby saw King driving the vehicle. Their gaze lingered. He guessed that tourists in these parts was something of a rarity.

'I'll get you to your mother and sister,' King said. 'Then I'll try and find Rico.'

Silence.

King looked across. 'What?'

'You don't want to do that.'

'Why not?'

'You just broke out of prison. I don't know how much more luck you think you can have.'

'Luck didn't get us out of there.'

'Then what did?'

'Me.'

'Who are you?' Raul said. 'Like, who are you really?'

'I'm just a guy, Raul,' King said for what felt like the millionth time. 'Same as you. Except I've seen a lot more.'

'You don't know what I've seen.'

'I don't. But no matter what, I know I've seen worse.'

'How can you be so sure?'

'Trust me.'

'Is this your mysterious past we're talking about?'

King nodded.

'You want to get into that yet?' Raul said. 'I'm curious.'

'Not at all. Where's your old place?'

'Stick to this road. I'll tell you when to turn.'

The trip passed uneventfully. They trawled through slums and busy intersections. They passed groups of young children loitering on street corners, smoking cheap cigarettes. They saw men wielding rifles clearly purchased on the black market, who stared at each passing car with open aggression. But amongst all that, King saw families bustling to and fro. Friends laughing. Civilians enjoying life. Hopefully Raul could find his family amongst this crowd.

Raul directed him down a side street branching off from the main road. The hatchback entered a rundown neighbourhood. Some houses had been abandoned long ago, evident by shattered windows and peeling paint and overgrown lawns. Traffic in these parts was non-existent. King drew the attention of every pedestrian in the area as he steered the car down street after street. He saw a muscular thug in a loose-fitting singlet gesture to a pistol tucked into his waistband as they passed.

'You grew up here?' he said.

Raul nodded. 'We managed. But I wanted to get the family out of here. That's why we both joined the Movers. It was only temporary…'

'Don't worry,' King said. 'I'm not judging you in the slightest.'

'We're not bad people, man…'

'I know.'

Raul held out an open palm, indicating for King to stop. He brought the car to a halt in front of an apartment complex that looked as if it would collapse at any moment. The place was an enormous white block of flats. Its once-pristine exterior had long since been stained yellow by the heat and the dust and the filth.

'Here,' Raul said.

King pulled into the small carport out the front of the property. It contained a trio of nondescript vehicles, all at least ten years old and falling to pieces. Yellowed newspapers and shards of glass from smashed car mirrors littered the ground.

'Mamá's car isn't here,' Raul said. His voice turned increasingly quiet as he studied the complex. 'I don't know, King…'

'Do they have a phone?'

He sighed. 'I can't remember the number. It's been a year.'

'There's ways to find out if she still has a residence.'

'Maybe. Let's just check the apartment. I don't have a good feeling right now…'

It was unnervingly quiet as they exited the car. What King imagined was normally a neighbourhood bustling with life had become dead. He couldn't hear a sound save the faint echo of commotion from the main road.

'Is it usually this quiet?' he said as they headed for the building.

'Um … I don't know,' Raul said, only half-interested. 'I can't remember.'

He sounded fazed out again. King looked across and saw his eyes had grown distant. They were damp. King bowed his head. He imagined Luis' death would not stop haunting Raul for years.

'Are you okay?'

Raul sniffed and wiped his eyes with a putrid sleeve. 'Don't know, man. Let's just check it out, please. I just want to see them…'

King's gut twisted into a knot as they pushed the reception doors open and stepped into a humid, claustrophobic lobby area. He shared the same feeling that Raul had described.

A strong premonition that no good would come of this investigation.

An overweight middle-aged woman sat behind a small desk facing the entrance. She didn't smile or utter a greeting as they entered. She simply stared with a deadpan expression. She said something in Spanish to Raul. It came out harsh and obtrusive. Raul responded with a question, and she answered. His face lit up and he turned to King.

'She says they're here,' he said. 'They've been paying rent ever since we left. She's seen them around.'

King felt relief. He didn't want to picture what state Raul would enter if they had stumbled across a pair of bodies. And he wouldn't have put it past Rico and his men to deliver such a statement after both brothers had been thrown in jail.

'How did they manage to afford it?' he said.

'Does it look like I know?'

'Let's go then.'

They entered a dark and cramped stairwell, illuminated faintly by the odd flickering bulb every couple of levels. Raul took the stairs three at a time, motivated by nervous energy. King tried to relate to the man's excitement. But he had no loved ones. He had no connections. That had come with his career. He could have spent the rest of his life in El Infierno without anyone on the planet batting an eyelid.

He followed Raul, scouting each floor for any signs of hostile intentions. Nothing. Each hallway branching off from the main stairwell was deserted. The whole building felt abandoned, even though it was a residential area.

Raul stopped on the sixth floor and led King through several nondescript corridors, all indistinguishable from each other, all filthy. Spiderwebs covered light fixtures and clusters of loose wiring and insulation hung through holes in the ceiling. They paused at a plain black door.

'This is it,' Raul said, his hands shaking.

King debated between leading the way in or hanging back. If Raul's mother and sister were indeed here, he would place himself awkwardly between a family reunion. But if Movers had somehow made it to the complex in time and were lying in wait, he didn't want Raul storming head-first into a slaughterhouse.

In the end, saner heads prevailed. There were no long-term consequences to scaring Raul's family. If they were gunned down upon entering, that would be *slightly* more inconvenient. King pushed Raul aside and placed a hand on the doorknob.

'What are you doing?' Raul said.

'Just in case.'

He pressed his ear against the door, listening intently. He heard nothing. Not a peep. Either Ana and her mother were asleep, or someone had a gun trained on the door, waiting patiently for both of them to step through and be eliminated.

In one motion, King twisted and shouldered the door aside, bursting into the apartment. His blood pumped as he assessed its contents. He was ready to kill.

But that would not be necessary.

For it quickly became clear that the apartment had been abandoned for a while.

CHAPTER 29

King passed through a narrow entranceway into a space containing both a kitchen and a living room — separated by a partition. At first glance, everything seemed normal. The apartment had a homely feel to it. A few quilts lay draped over furniture; maybe a pastime of Raul's mother, maybe store-purchased.

Then, in the corner, he saw it.

A chair lay overturned.

He noticed this with a tightening stomach. Doubt crept in as he scanned the rest of the apartment. There was a scuff mark on the arm of one couch. Freshly formed. Like someone had clawed it to prevent being dragged away. Discrepancies began to appear. A vase rested on the carpet near the kitchen bench, still in one piece. Like it had been knocked off the bench in a scuffle.

'They're not here, Raul,' King said. 'This doesn't look good.'

Raul gazed around the room, misty-eyed. Probably recalling prior memories.

'How can you be sure?' he said. 'What if they're at the shops or something?'

'They're not.'

'How do you know?'

'I know when things aren't right.'

'Things aren't right here?'

'I'm afraid not.'

Raul crossed to the kitchen and began ruffling through the bills and notices that littered the surface of the bench. Searching for any kind of hint as to what had happened. Or maybe just determined to get his hands on concrete evidence that his mother and sister had gone on living here after he and Luis had been locked away.

King watched with a certain disconnect. He had an idea as to what had happened, but he didn't feel it was the right time to share such information. Especially not after Raul's devastating loss less than an hour ago.

He would be a broken man if King told him that his entire family was likely dead.

Raul shifted a stack of loose documents aside and picked up a small scrap of paper. He studied it hard. An expression of disbelief crossed his face.

'Whoa…' he whispered.

King crossed the room. 'What's that?'

'José Guerra.'

'Huh?'

'An old friend. This is his name and number. It's his handwriting too.'

King snatched the paper from Raul and glanced at it. Sure enough, contact information had been scrawled across the lined paper in freehand.

'Who is he?'

'A small-time arms dealer. We grew up together. He's the one who taught me English — the childhood friend I spoke of. His parents lived in Britain for a few years. They're fluent, so he's fluent. Now I'm almost fluent.'

'How small-time?'

'Well, he *was* small-time. Then I put him in contact with the Movers when I started working for them. They talked. I think they were finalising negotiations when Luis and I were arrested.'

'Negotiations?'

'There were rumours in the pipeline that Rico was looking for a new supplier. That's why I introduced them to José. He'd been expanding for a few years, selling black market weapons to low-level crooks. He'd just started importing higher-quality gear when I told him that the Movers might be looking for a supplier.'

'Lot of money in that.'

'Sure is.'

'How close were you?'

'Very. But he hadn't seen my family in years — I think he was ashamed of what he'd become. He used to live round here. He'd come visit every single day. Mamá would cook us meals, and he'd teach me English. Then that began to fade. We were still close, but we kept our personal lives apart.'

'How long since that went on?'

'Five, six years. Maybe more.'

'So his number shouldn't be here?'

'Maybe he's been helping them. Maybe he knows where they are. We need to find him.'

Just then, the kitchen window shattered into thousands of shards. King recoiled at the noise and ducked his head instinctively, aware that a bullet must have already passed them by. He wrapped an arm around Raul and dove to the kitchen floor, hitting the linoleum hard.

Knowing that more gunfire would follow, he scrambled to the nearest cabinet and pressed his back against the surface. There were several windows in the apartment. He wasn't sure which would bring the next round.

'*Fuck!*' Raul screamed.

King wrapped a hand around the man's collar and held up a finger. 'Quiet.'

Fragments of glass trickled off the pane and into the sink. It created a pitter-patter effect, harshly juxtaposed against the burst of gunfire that had sounded moments earlier. As King held Raul down, another volley of shots broke the silence. These dotted the entranceway, gouging out chunks of plaster, shattering the vase on the coffee table by the front door.

All the gunfire came through the same window. King noted this, and figured that the Movers had yet to surround the apartment entirely. There was a man in the neighbouring building, evident from the direction of the shots. The other windows faced out onto the street. It would take a noteworthy vantage point to cover those.

'There's only one of them,' he told Raul. 'Stay low. Head for the door.'

He swore at his own idiocy. The AK-103 he'd escaped El Infierno with lay useless on the back seat of the stolen hatchback. He hadn't brought it into the building in order to save a panic at the sight of an assault rifle in a residential area. Now, he realised that was the least of his problems. The Movers were fast. Rico must have got the word out instantaneously.

They couldn't have been free from prison for more than an hour.

He noticed a rolling pin on the kitchen counter just above his head. Thick and sturdy and wooden. He reached up and lifted it off, then threw it at an upward diagonal angle like a pitcher hurling a fast ball. The exertion behind the heave sent it shooting out the open window frame, turning end over end. He heard a window shatter in the neighbouring building.

Zero chance of doing any damage.

But maybe enough to make the sharpshooter flinch. Drop his aim for a fraction of a second.

King scrambled to his feet as soon as the rolling pin left his hands, tugging Raul along with him. They fled down the length of the kitchen and reached the front door in a matter of seconds.

He threw it open and hurtled out into the hallway.

And ran directly into two armed men in the process of charging into the apartment.

CHAPTER 30

Most people — no matter how adept in combat — were stunned by rapid bursts of violence. He made use of the confusion, lashing out as soon as he recognised the presence of hostiles.

The guy on the left was tiny, almost an entire foot shorter than King. He had short hair and the shadow of a beard. He gripped a dirty Taurus 24/7 handgun — the same as Tevin's. To compensate for his slight stature it seemed he'd spent half his life in the gym, to the point that he resembled a small round ball of muscle.

It wouldn't do him any good.

Charged with adrenalin, King smashed the man's gun away. He picked him up from the torso and hurled him into the second man, who had been in the process of locking on his aim. He was taller and wielded an identical pistol. The first man crashed into him and they both tumbled to the carpeted floor of the corridor.

King didn't hesitate.

He went through the motions, which were second nature to him. He used the moment of utter panic to crouch down and scoop up the Taurus that the first man had dropped. He got a finger in the trigger guard.

The two hitmen began to scramble to their feet.

King shot the shorter one in the head. He lined it up perfectly and fired, noting the man's death in a spray of gore. The guy had been in the process of getting his feet under him, but the impact killed him instantly and he fell back, trapping his partner under his own deadweight. It took little effort at all for King to send a second bullet through the base of his friend's skull. The second guy went instantly limp. Blood pooled across the floor.

'What the fuck!' Raul said, staring at the two bodies. 'Oh my God.'

King turned to him. 'What? Did you want me to let them live?'

'I don't know, man. Do what you gotta do.'

King held up the Taurus. 'They were here for one reason, Raul. Not my fault they ran into me.'

'Okay, okay. Let's go.'

King retrieved the second Taurus and handed it to Raul. He knew they had to move quickly. The unsuppressed gunshots would have drawn the attention of every resident in the complex. It wouldn't take long for commotion to break out.

The last thing he wanted was to find himself trapped in a mad rush for the stairwell as everyone exited their apartments in unison. He relayed this concern to Raul.

The man laughed. 'Are you crazy?'

King stared at him, confused.

'Look around,' Raul said. 'Gunshots aren't very far from normal. No-one's panicking.'

'Ah. Never mind then.'

They set off down the corridor. King re-entered the stairwell first and descended slowly, Taurus raised, ready for any confrontation that may occur. He didn't imagine that the Movers would send more than three men. He guessed their forces weren't limitless. And the sharpshooter in the adjacent building would take too long to leave his position. He'd missed his first shot, and it had all been downhill from there.

'Do you still have José's number?' he said.

Raul nodded and held up the scrap of paper.

'We might need to chase that up,' King said.

'Now?'

'No, not now. We've barely been out of El Infierno an hour. Every gangster in the city is going to be searching for us. Time to lay low for a while.'

King stepped out into the lobby, not bothering to hide the Taurus. If more Movers came rushing in through the entrance, he needed to be ready. It didn't matter what the receptionist thought. She could wet herself for all he cared.

In the end, she simply gave both men a passing glance. Noted the guns in their hands. Recognised that she was not the object of concern. Turned back to her newspaper and flicked the pages with nonchalance.

He paused by the entranceway, sensing Raul come to a halt behind him. He glanced out into the carport. From what he could see it, the lot was deserted. The neighbouring building that the rifle fire had come from was blocked from view, but it couldn't have been more than a couple of minutes since they left Raul's apartment. He assumed it was safe.

He kept the Taurus raised as he stepped out into open ground. He half-expected a bullet to punch through the back of his head and shut him down forever. If that happened, he would never know. It would simply flick the off-switch.

There were worse ways to die.

Given what had occurred over the course of his life, he wouldn't be surprised in the slightest if his luck finally decided to run out.

They got back in the hatchback and King fired it up and reversed out of the parking space.

'Where to?' Raul said.

'The hotel I was staying at still has a few things I need,' King said. 'My passport, my wallet, a few fresh pairs of clothes.'

'You'd risk going back there for some clothes?'

'Emphasis on the passport, Raul.'

'What if they call the police?'

'I can deal with that. There'll be worse problems than that if I can't leave the country. No offence, but I don't want to stay in Venezuela a moment longer than is absolutely necessary.'

'Oh, believe me, that's understood. Won't they just arrest you at the airport though?'

King paused. 'How would they do that?'

'What do you mean?'

'I had no trial. They threw me in there solely based on Rico's instructions. I wasn't an official prisoner by any means. They didn't even ID me. They just kept me in a holding cell overnight and then transferred me across. The entire thing was off the books.'

'What if they tell airport security to keep a lookout for you? You're fairly noticeable.'

'Then I'll retaliate. You can be sure as shit I won't go willingly this time. I had slight faith in the justice system here a few days ago. That's gone.'

'Then what?'

'Then Plan B.'

'Which is?'

'Old friends. Contacts in the military. Higher-ups. They'll get me out of here. It'll just take longer.'

'Your life sounds like insanity.'

'It is.'

He drove on.

CHAPTER 31

The hatchback crawled through the mid-morning traffic, entering the heart of Maiquetía. King looked around as they drove, admiring the culture — but he didn't want anything to do with the country any longer.

Your whole system can go fuck itself, he thought.

It took ten minutes to reach Diamanté Resort, and in that time their surroundings underwent a dramatic transformation. The dilapidation vanished. The roads became cleaner, the air seemingly fresher, the atmosphere more relaxed. This was the tourist district. Little chance of a war between drug cartels occurring in these parts. He turned the car onto a pristine road running along the beach. Parallel to them, the Caribbean Sea twinkled in the sun.

Raul stared in awe. 'Never used to come to these parts. I look like a local thug. The police would always chase me away.'

King pulled into an enormous parking lot filled with luxury cars. He ignored the questioning glances from the valet. The beat-up hatchback stood out against the other vehicles.

He and Raul got out and made for the lobby. He recalled the high-ceilinged reception area, complete with vast walls of marble and a broad sweeping desk housing more than ten receptionists in pristine uniform.

King drew the attention of everyone in the building as he entered. He knew he was a mess. His clothes were now three days old, covered in dried mud. Blood dotted his collar — not his own. Cuts and bruises littered his exposed skin. Dirt caked his fingernails. His right cheek had swollen from the beatings it had sustained.

For a moment, he felt detached from reality. Two hours ago, he'd been in the midst of a wild brawl between prison inmates and Guardia Nacional, fighting for his life, knocking brutish thugs senseless left and right. Now he stood in utter luxury as a free man.

He took the lead and approached the front desk. Raul followed tentatively. King wasted no time in making his intentions clear. He withdrew the rest of the money in his pocket — probably over twenty thousand bolivares — and slapped it down on the table. Then he looked at the well-groomed man in front of him. The man recognised him. He'd been the one to secure the penthouse suite for King several days ago.

'You probably have a million questions,' King said. 'Like — why was I carried out of here under police escort? Why have I come back looking like I've been through World War Three? What did I do to warrant all of that effort? Why would I return when I made the hotel look bad?'

'You're quite right, sir,' the man said. 'I can't help but find myself curious.'

King pointed at the wad of money littering the unblemished marble surface of the desk. 'That's all yours. I'd like my stuff back that I left in the penthouse. I'd like a room for the night — the cheapest one you have. And I'd like to not have to answer any questions. Can that be arranged?'

'Sir, I may have to contact the authorities before—'

'No need for that.'

'Were you released from the station?'

'You bet. It was all one big misunderstanding.'

The man sighed. He sensed the sardonic nature of the tone, but King had communicated what he wanted clearly, effectively, and decisively. There was no room for interpretation. He wanted to be left alone, and he didn't want to bother anyone else. And money always held some level of influence.

So the receptionist tapped a few keys, clicked a few times with the mouse, withdrew a keycard from a drawer next to him and slid the wad of cash into the same drawer.

'No more trouble, okay?' the guy said.

'You won't hear from me again,' King said. 'Thanks for your co-operation.'

'Third floor. You're in a two-bedroom suite.'

'Appreciated.'

The receptionist retreated into a back room for a moment, then came back with an expensive-looking sports bag.

'Everything should be in here,' he said. 'We cleaned out the room after your hasty departure and put all your belongings in this bag. We hadn't got around to delivering them to the police station yet.'

Lucky you didn't, King thought.

He took the bag, nodded his thanks and led Raul into the same spacious elevator.

'This is crazy, man,' Raul said. 'Some people live like this?'

'This is a luxury resort, so nobody lives here,' King said. 'But yes, people live like this. Elsewhere.'

Raul glanced around. 'You said you were staying here...'

'I was. Until all this happened.'

'Are you rich, Jason?'

King hesitated. Then he decided to tell the truth. 'Yes. I have enough money to not have to work for the rest of my life.'

'From being a soldier?'

'Soldiers don't make that kind of money.'

'But you did?'

'I was one of a handful of men. We were basically thrown to the wolves for ten years straight. And we were compensated as a result.'

'I think I would want to be rich,' Raul said. 'If it means living like this. I would sign up.'

'No you wouldn't, Raul,' King said. 'If you knew what I've done, you definitely wouldn't.'

He recalled times when bullets had shredded his limbs, when third-world dictators had tortured him for days on end, when his life had been nothing but a constant raging battle to simply stay alive. Often — when he looked back on it — he couldn't believe the things he'd achieved. The fact that he was alive today was something of a miracle. But he knew he possessed a gift — the reaction speed that had yet to fail saving him from death. He'd used it to forge a path of destruction through terrorist organisations and drug cartels and hired mercenaries.

Now, he wanted nothing more than to avoid reckless situations.

It was about time to hide from them.

But not yet.

Raul needed him. He'd been nothing but a low-level drug dealer with his heart in the right place. Now he was facing the loss of his brother and the potential loss of the rest of his family.

He'd helped King escape from El Infierno. So King would help him make things right.

Or at least try to.

But there was more to it than that. If that had been the sole motivation keeping him attached to Venezuela, he might have ignored it and fled. It was about time he took his own interests into account instead of desperately battling to help others.

But Rico infuriated him.

He couldn't force the man's expression out of his mind. The way he'd slaughtered Percy and shot Luis. The way he'd thrown King into El Infierno with little regard to his own survival. King clenched his fists as the elevator rode smoothly to the third floor.

He would not stop until the man was dead.

Sometimes, a lifetime of experience in killing proved useful.

They walked down a corridor with antique side tables and plush carpet and exquisitely decorated wallpaper. Raul continued to flick his gaze between each individual object in turn, struggling to comprehend such decadence.

King unlocked the door to a plainly-furnished hotel room, similar to many he'd seen before. The cheapest rooms in luxury hotels all looked the same. Kept clean, freshly maintained, but nothing was there that didn't need to be. Nevertheless, it was probably the nicest place Raul had stayed in. Especially after a year in the hellhole they'd just came from.

'Can we rest for a bit?' Raul said, cautious to sit down on his bed and ruin the pristine sheets. His clothes threatened to fall off him at any moment. They were tattered, torn to shreds, muddy and caked with blood and dirt. 'I can't keep going much longer.'

'You need to help me with one thing first.'

'And that is?'

'I have personal reasons for helping you out.'

'You do?'

King nodded. 'I'm going to find Rico, and kill him.'

Raul scoffed. 'Your best shot was in El Infierno. He made himself vulnerable by acting as a guard. He had none of his usual securities. Now he will.'

'I can deal with securities.'

'No you can't. You don't know the Movers like I do.'

'I'm about to.'

Raul stared at him blankly.

'You need to show me where your old co-workers operate,' King said. 'It's about time I paid one of them a visit.'

CHAPTER 32

At mid-afternoon, the avenue had come alive with activity. It reminded King of the bazaar where his troubles had first begun. There were no stalls. There was no steam rising from hot grills and loud arguments between haggling customers and determined traders. But the pavement was just as populated. Civilians bustled along the strip, darting in and out of shopfronts and carrying bags of produce over their heads.

Raul had led King here after a half-hour nap. They'd showered one after the other, washing away all the filth and degradation of El Infierno. King had stepped out from under the jet of water feeling like a new man.

He ensured the water was ice cold. He hadn't had a warm shower in months. The process gave him a temporary boost of energy by increasing his overall oxygen intake.

Short term discomfort for long term benefits.

King was beyond tired, but he didn't want to sleep. Not just yet. Partially because there was work to be done, and also because he was unsure as to whether he had been concussed during the mayhem of the prison breakout. Going to sleep after a concussion was one of the worst responses. It could lead to death. He knew he had a splitting headache and a shooting pain behind his eyes, and he had yet to determine whether that had come from sleep deprivation or being rattled by a stray punch or kick. Whatever the case, sleep could wait.

Raul had become distant once again.

'You okay?' King said.

Raul looked at him. 'Does it look like it?'

'Not at all.'

'I'm worried, man. What if José's a dead end?'

'Then we can use other methods.'

'Such as?'

'There's always other options, Raul. Let's worry about those later. Don't overthink it. Your family is probably fine.'

'Mamá has her medication. I don't know if Ana can deal with all of this on her own…'

'We'll find them.'

They set off into the crowd. Occasionally, a passerby would rudely bump into King. He ignored it each time. He didn't want to set off another chain of events and wind up locked behind bars by corrupt prison officials and a psychopathic drug lord.

In fact, he never wanted to experience such a situation ever again.

'Me and Luis used to deal along here,' Raul said as they walked. 'In fact, it's where we got arrested.'

'Along here? You never used to go into the tourist district at all?'

'Look at me, man,' Raul said. 'I'm almost your height. I'm imposing. They kept me away from those places. The dealers in that area are pros. They can blend into the tourist crowd. They can look pleasant and approachable. All that shit. I never learnt that.'

'Maybe that's why you two got arrested.'

'Maybe … you know, I thought they would have paid the cops off. Like, don't interfere with any of the Movers.'

'They might not have known you were a Mover. They might have thought you were competition and pounced on you for interfering with the territory your gang was paying them to protect.'

'You think?'

'Then when they realised you were a Mover, they would have approached Rico. And obviously he had no further use for you. So he let them lock you up.'

'Piece of shit.'

'I concur.'

Raul looked ahead and his eyes widened. He changed direction and came to a halt out the front of a food vendor's truck. The pleasant smell of cooking meat wafted from the opening. Raul pretended to study the menu.

'There's one right behind me,' he said. 'Loitering out the front of that alley.'

King turned and scanned the pavement inconspicuously, trying not to draw attention to himself. He saw the man Raul was talking about. A guy in a sleeveless vest showing off his muscular arms. He had a mean scar under his right eye and his head was shaved bald. He looked Spanish, with olive skin and pearly white teeth. Tough, but approachable enough to buy drugs off. He had his hands clasped behind his back and he patrolled slowly between each side of the alleyway.

King saw the unmistakeable bulge of a firearm tucked into the side of his waistband. That might pose a problem.

'You sure?' he said to Raul. 'I don't want to confront the wrong guy.'

'I'm sure,' Raul said. 'He worked for the Movers back when I was around. I saw him every now and then.'

'You think he'll recognise you?'

Raul shook his head. 'Not a chance. I was a nobody. Still am.'

'Well, here goes…'

He turned on his heel and made straight for the guy. Strolling slowly. Non-threatening, simply curious. He stopped in front of him and surveyed the scene, making a point to linger within just enough range to be noticeable.

The guy perked up. He spoke sharply in Spanish. King turned and feigned curiosity.

'English?' he said.

The guy held up a flat palm and tilted it to each side a few times. 'Little bit.'

'I'm looking to get high.'

The guy smiled. 'You come to right place. You tourist?'

King nodded. 'I've got a lot of cash to burn.'

'What you want?'

'Whatever you've got.'

'Cocaine?'

King nodded again. 'Fine by me. How much do you have?'

'You take what I give. I no have much.'

'Wonder why that is…' King muttered, then thundered a fist into the man's gut.

He'd been surreptitiously advancing as the conversation progressed, leading the man just far enough into the lip of the alley to avoid the attention of most passersby. When he found himself in enough of an isolated position to deal with the guy, he shredded the casual, relaxed demeanour that had baited the Mover. The man had received no warning signs from King, and as a result he'd dropped his guard.

The first punch almost took him off his feet. It drove into the guy's stomach with enough power behind it to send him skittering back a few feet, shuffling further into the alley.

King's heart rate skyrocketed. He'd been eager to deliver as much damage as possible with the element of surprise on his side. He'd put everything into the punch. It hadn't hit the vital organs he'd been aiming for. The guy didn't double over. He didn't drop to the ground in a heap. He stayed upright …

… and began reaching for the gun in his waistband.

King had a running start, so he made full use of it. There wasn't time to reach back for the Taurus tucked into his own waistband. By that point, he'd have a bullet buried in his skull. He had a split second to act.

Without hesitation, he took two steps and launched off one foot, using every shred of athleticism he had. With the other leg he bent at the knee and followed through, swinging it in a scything uppercut. His kneecap smashed into the Mover's jaw as the guy was fumbling at his belt.

Hands down. Chin exposed. A perfect shot.

The man crumpled, his legs giving out. King landed with a foot on either side of the guy's motionless body and looked down. The man was now in the throes of unconsciousness. His jaw had cracked under the force of the blow.

King realised he wouldn't be getting any answers from the man.

'Shit,' he whispered.

The plan had been to knock the breath out of the Mover, drag him further into the alley and interrogate him about where Rico was stationed and how exactly to gain access to him. He might have been able to determine the location of Raul's family, if the Movers had them. The reality meant King had over-reacted and created a situation that drew attention. The frantic movement had caused a couple of pedestrians to swivel their heads, noticing the incident.

He couldn't stay here.

Swearing at his own ineptitude, he crouched and searched the man's pockets, moving quickly. He had to get out of here before more eyes reached them. The last thing he wanted was an on-foot police chase through the streets of Maiquetía.

In fact, he didn't want to see another policeman for the rest of his time in Venezuela.

His search turned up a thick roll of cash and a cheap plastic mobile phone. He slotted both items into his pockets, then turned and retreated out of the alley, leaving the Mover to come to in a dazed stupor, wondering exactly what had happened and where his possessions had gone. King knew his memory would be hazy.

He'd experienced his fair share of severe concussions, including one just a few short months ago in Australia.

That brought back memories of a similarly dangerous situation. It truly seemed that wherever he turned, trouble followed. King scurried out of the alley and blended back into the crowd, cursing his bad luck.

But how many times could he find himself in similar situations and still attribute it to coincidence?

Perhaps he was supposed to do this forever. Maybe violence was attracted to him. Maybe his destiny was to travel the world, righting wrongs, helping those who couldn't succeed on their own.

He forced the dumb thought from his mind and headed back to the hotel with Raul trailing quietly in his wake.

CHAPTER 33

'The hell was that?' Raul said as they stepped back into the hotel lobby.

'I got a little too aggressive,' King said.

'I know. Why? I thought you were some kind of superhuman.'

King glanced at him. 'Quite the contrary.'

'You knocked a guy out with a flying knee on your first attempt. That's not exactly normal…'

'Just a lot of practice.'

'Whatever you say, man. You're crazy.'

'I wasn't supposed to do that. He went for a gun and I reacted.'

'Couldn't you get the gun off him at the start? Or do your all-seeing powers not extend that far?'

'I thought I'd incapacitate him with the first punch. Ended up missing the target area.'

'Ah,' Raul said, punching one of the buttons on the panel next to the elevator. 'So you make mistakes after all.'

'We all make mistakes.'

Raul stepped into the elevator as the doors swung open and sighed. 'I've made a few.'

'What will you do after this?' King said.

'No idea, man. Let's just find my family. Then I'll work out what the hell to do with my life.'

King nodded and decided not to press the matter any further. It was time for a proper sleep, even though it was still mid-afternoon. He found his muscles exhausted after a gruelling three days. Fighting exerted enormous physical energy, fatiguing the body faster than almost all other exercise, and King had done his fair share of the stuff over the course of his latest escapade. He knew he needed sleep to recharge for whatever lay ahead.

They burst into the hotel room and headed to separate beds, both large and spotless and inviting. King locked the door behind him, dropped his head onto the mattress and was asleep in a matter of moments.

They slept through the evening and into the night. Again, King didn't dream. He slept soundly, undisturbed. And he knew why. He'd experienced the same sensation in Australia, and it worried him sick.

He seemed to struggle to sleep when his life followed the course of normality. When he wasn't fighting for his life, or being pursued by various members of society looking to kill or torture him, he didn't feel at home. For ten years he'd dashed from one location to the next, always fighting, always in motion. When he tried to live an ordinary civilian's life, he struggled to acclimatise.

It was a habit he knew he needed to break.

A harsh, discordant ringing woke him up in the early hours of the morning. It came from somewhere within his jacket pocket. The sound tore through the silence of the hotel room. Raul's head reared up from his pillow as King sat up to withdraw the source of the noise.

The Mover's phone.

There was no caller ID on the screen. Just a random number. King hesitated, considering letting the call go to voicemail. He hovered a finger over one of the buttons.

'Answer it,' Raul said. 'Just don't say anything. See who it is.'

King nodded silently, and took the call. He switched the phone to loudspeaker and stayed quiet. Wondering if it might be the man's employer checking in on him.

A voice crackled to life, blaring through the quiet of the hotel room. 'Well, if it isn't just the man I wanted to talk to. And Raul, I see you're tagging along with him. That's awfully rebellious of you. Why didn't you do your time like you were supposed to, huh?'

Rico.

King glanced across to Raul, whose face had turned pale. He saw Raul's hands beginning to shake. Utter fear. Not many people could evoke such a reaction.

There was no use staying silent. Rico was onto them.

'How did you know?' King said.

'I run a tightly oiled ship,' Rico said. 'That's how I got to where I am today. By clawing my way up through the disgusting ranks of society and sticking to the game plan. And that game plan involves regular check-ins from every dealer I have out on the streets. This guy missed his. Which must mean he's dead, because I do not tolerate ineptitude.'

'He's not dead. I knocked him out.'

'Oh. Well, when he crawls back here I'll be sure to finish him off.'

'What do you want?'

'You shot me. You broke my arm. You don't do that to someone like me.'

'You put me in prison for something I didn't do.'

'You're fucking right I did. And you should have shut your mouth and done everything I told you to. Yes sir, no sir, of course sir, right away sir. You clearly have no idea who I am.'

'I don't care who you are. Or how powerful you think you are. You know the thing about people like you?'

'What's that?'

'Everything in you breaks just as easily.'

'See, the way you're talking shows how much of an amateur you are. You're out of your depth here.'

'I seem to have gotten away with it.'

'Not really.'

'Oh?'

'Ask Raul how his family's doing.'

An icy atmosphere descended over the hotel room. King felt his heart rate increase as his worst fears were confirmed. Raul's mother and sister hadn't fled. They weren't hiding away somewhere, waiting until all was safe to return to their ordinary lives.

They'd been taken.

Raul began to hyperventilate. It seemed that he'd been suppressing his emotions. Now the sheer panic ripped through him, brought on by the knowledge that his mother and sister were in the hands of a psychopath. He gripped the bedsheets with white knuckles and gnashed his teeth, attempting to disperse some of the rage flowing through his veins.

King stayed level-headed.

'You have them?' he said.

'Of course I do.'

'When did you take them?'

'I got my men to move in as soon as you two left El Infierno. I knew exactly where they were.'

Raul burst to his feet, veins popping in his neck. '*How long have you known about them?*'

'There he is!' Rico said, and laughed cruelly. 'Wondered how long it would take you to rear your head.'

'How long?'

'Since you stepped foot in my office and asked for a job. You must think I'm stupid. Leverage is an important tool in my business. I know where the families of all my employees live. I have a hundred men willing to take anyone out on my command. I was going to do the same to you. Really brutalise their bodies, leave them in place for you to find. Maybe paint the walls with their blood. But — as much as I hate to admit it — your friend is rather talented. If I killed them, it would carry the risk of you escaping. So I've taken them alive, because I want you on a silver platter, Raul. And your friend. I'll show you what happens when you fuck with us.'

'What's stopping me from leaving?' King said. 'This isn't my concern.'

'Because you seem like the type of idiot to try and help. If you wanted to leave, you would have done so already. I'm very interested to see how this plays out.'

'What do you want?'

'You two will meet me at La Guardia Enterprises in exactly three hours. It's a big abandoned warehouse. Just closed down.

You'll come unarmed and you'll both surrender yourself. Then I'll let Raul's mother and sister live.'

'You're insane if you think we'll do that,' King said.

'Your choice. If you don't show, I'll torture his family for a month. And I'll make sure to find where he's holing up and mail him little pieces of them for the rest of his short life. How's that sound?'

'Fuck you,' Raul said.

'I knew you'd come round. Three hours. Or you'll never hear from us again, and I'll make Ana despise you for never showing up.'

A sharp click came from the other end of the line, signifying that Rico had hung up. Raul surged forward, snatched the phone off the bed and hurled it at the wall. It gouged out a sizeable chunk and came to a halt lodged halfway into the plasterboard.

'What do we do?' he said once the initial anger had subsided.

King stared into space, chewing a fingernail, contemplating. The choices were grim. Rico had them both exactly where he wanted them. He sighed and got off the bed.

'I don't know, Raul,' he said. 'I honestly don't know. We have no idea where he's keeping them. We have no firepower. We honestly don't stand a chance.'

'What about all the shit you've got away with?' Raul said. 'Why can't you help me?'

'Punching people has its limits. We're up against an entire gang here. I'm not sure what can be done with what little information we have.'

Raul paused and crossed the room. He took a long hard look out the only window in the room, facing out over the Caribbean Sea. He glanced down at the buildings lining the shore. Then he turned back to King.

'We have some information,' he said. 'Because I know where Rico's keeping them.'

CHAPTER 34

He led King to the window and showed him a stretch of land alongside the ocean. Most of Maiquetía's coastline was home to beautiful beaches, yet there was a small portion on the outskirts of the city that was nothing more than a vast patch of concrete, littered with tiny specks. From this distance, King couldn't quite make out what they were.

'What is it?' he said.

'It's an abandoned shipyard,' Raul explained. 'Those are boats. Some are cruise ships.'

'Big place.'

'Very. It's where the Movers operate out of.'

'Surely the authorities would catch wind of something so large being run by a gang of drug dealers.'

'Trust me, they know.'

'They pay them off?'

'They pay everybody off. No-one even glances at it.'

'You've been there?'

'A few times. Not often. I was low-level. Wasn't granted access to those kinds of places. Most of my instructions were delivered over the phone or at a random location.'

'I'd hazard a guess that they smuggle most of their supply in through the port?'

Raul nodded. 'Mostly cocaine. They import it from Colombia.'

'Smooth operation.'

'For the most part. Rico mentioned something about you ruining their operation?'

'I beat up a few of them who were supposed to attend a very important meeting. It seems there's been a breakdown in communication between the parties. I inadvertently caused that.'

'That's a shame.'

King smiled, then realised the magnitude of the task at hand and lapsed back into concentration. 'So you think your mother and sister are in there somewhere?'

'I'm certain.'

'You can't be sure.'

'It's the only place they have that's heavily fortified. Every other property they own is small-scale production labs and packaging facilities. Rico wouldn't risk keeping prisoners anywhere near his pipeline. They have a small army stationed in the shipyard at all times. Mercenaries, gangsters, you name it.'

King sighed and thought back to Australia. 'Nothing I love more than mercenaries.'

'I don't know why I'm showing you this,' Raul said. 'It's just false hope.'

'Why's that?'

Raul stared at him like he was an idiot. 'I'm just saying, I know where Rico's keeping them. Nothing more than that. There's nothing we can actually do about it. You said it yourself.'

King gazed out at the shipyard far in the distance. From here, the task seemed surmountable. The graveyard looked like any of the other hundreds of strongholds he'd stormed in the past. But that had been in his prime. He was older. Slower. And he'd spent the months since his retirement determined to avoid death.

Charging headlong into a drug gang's headquarters would counter-act that goal.

'Like I said, you can't be sure that they're there,' King said. 'What if the Movers don't even use the shipyard anymore? What if Rico's decided to keep your family somewhere secluded, where we'll never find them?'

'Okay, fine,' Raul said. 'You're right. I can't be sure. But it's my best guess. And I'd rather die trying to get them out than surrender to Rico.'

'He'll kill them either way, won't he?'

Raul nodded. 'So you know what he's like, too.'

'I've seen enough of him. I can't imagine he'd let them go. Even if we turned ourselves in.'

'So that's it,' Raul said, slamming a hand against the window pane hard enough to rattle the sill. 'I'm fucked either way.'

'We both are.'

Raul turned. 'No, we're not. You don't have anything to do with this. Rico wants you to join me in a suicide mission because he wants to make you pay for everything that's happened. He said it himself. You're too stupid to leave when you have the chance.'

'I'm not leaving.'

'You should. I won't let you do this with me. You'll die.'

Images of Rico flashed through King's mind. 'You need me. And there's nothing I'd enjoy more than seeing that piece of shit get what he deserves. I can make that a possibility.'

'King, I'm running into the shipyard to die,' Raul said. 'Dress it up any way you want, but that's it. I'm going to get killed. I don't have any other choice. I couldn't live with myself if I backed out and the rest of my family died too. I will die with them. It would be foolish for you to condemn yourself too.'

'If I leave, then that's exactly what will happen,' King said. 'You'll die. Without a doubt. But with me, there's a possibility. Very slight, but it's there.'

'Why are you willing to do this?'

King paused before responding. Truth was, he had no idea. It's just what he'd done for the last ten years. Help people who needed helping. Kill people who needed killing. Sure, that was an oversimplification for a multi-faceted state of mind, but in the end he felt at home in combat. Despite not wanting to admit it, the time he'd spent in El Infierno had rejuvenated him in a way which was difficult to describe. He felt fresh. He felt peaceful.

'I guess I'm not quite sane,' he said, admitting the truth. 'But this is what I enjoy. I'd rather help you and demolish Rico in the process than flee Venezuela and spend the rest of my life thinking about what I could have done. Who I could have helped.'

'So this is personal too?'

'Of course. I despise Rico. I wouldn't be here if there wasn't something in it for me. Nothing would bring me more satisfaction than seeing him dead. So I'll make sure that happens. If they stop me, bad luck to me. But I'll try.'

Raul held out a hand. King shook it.

'Thank you,' the man said. 'Honestly, thank you so much. You don't know how much this means to me.'

'I do,' King said. 'Trust me.'

Raul paused and surveyed the hotel room. He smiled wryly. 'It took me this long to realise there are levels to this game.'

King cocked his head. 'What do you mean?'

'I used to think some of the Movers I met were the scariest people on the planet. I thought they could break me in half with one hand. When I got thrown into El Infierno, I thought some prisoners were even tougher. Luis and I had to battle to appear strong-willed — so that no-one would bully us. I've been scared to death the whole time. I thought it couldn't possibly get much worse than the men around us.'

'What do I have to do with this?'

'I've never seen anything quite like the two days you spent in the cage with us.'

'How so?'

'You're something else. These men are vicious gangsters and hardened criminals and seasoned killers. And you just strode in there and didn't take shit from anyone. You beat the crap out of half the men in the pavilion. Anyone who antagonised you ... it was like you were scolding toddlers. And these were men who weren't used to resistance in any way, shape or form. They'd bullied their way through life because everyone gets out of their way. I did the same. And all it took was for you to fight back for a couple of days and all hell broke loose.'

'I wouldn't go that far.'

'King, if you'd spent another week in that pavilion you would have been running the place.'

'You think?'

'I've never seen a newcomer react the way you did.'

'I guess I have the nerve to stand up against anyone. Maybe that's why I keep ending up in situations like these.'

'It's not just that. The way you move … I've honestly never seen anything like it. You're so slow and controlled all the time. Then, when you need to act, you go off like a grenade. I haven't seen a single man who's managed to deal with it since I met you.'

'Offence is the best defence,' King said. 'And yes, you're right. The skills that I've learnt over my career are very useful. But it's time to stop fawning over me. I'm just a guy who can punch people faster than they can punch me. We have three hours to do what we need to do.'

'I'm just glad you're on my side.'

'I'm on no-one's side. I happen to dislike Rico with a passion. And I happen to dislike people who mess with innocents. If I didn't have personal motive for this, I'd be out of here. Remember that.'

'Understood.'

'Now,' King said, fetching the scrap of paper off the bedside table and holding it high, 'why don't you give your old friend José a call?'

CHAPTER 35

Ten minutes later they were back in the stolen hatchback. The receptionist had eyed King off from across the marble lobby, noting his purposeful stride and the determined expression on his face. He probably figured that King's troubles had yet to cease. But if business was conducted outside the grounds of his place of employment, it didn't concern him in the slightest.

King started the car, shoved the gearbox into reverse and stamped on the accelerator. The tyres squealed on the asphalt as it peeled out of the parking space. He slammed it back into drive and took off towards the exit.

'You don't fuck around, do you?' Raul said.

'Time is of the essence. What did José say?'

'Not much. I think he was surprised that I was out. He knew the situation around my arrest. Probably figured me and Luis would spend the rest of our lives in El Infierno. Not many people have got on Rico's bad side and lived to tell of it.'

'I'm still hazy on the details as to why Rico hates you so much.'

'He hates incompetence. Luis and I were dumb enough to get arrested. It jeopardised his operation, which is everything to him. He doesn't do anything else. He just works, and pays politicians and policemen off, and kills people he doesn't like. It's his entire life.'

King nodded. 'That explains why I provoked such an insane reaction.'

'If you ruined some kind of business deal, he won't stop until he kills you.'

'So I'll kill him first.'

King lapsed into silence and concentrated on the morning traffic. José had given Raul directions to an industrial zone far from the tourist district. Before long they had re-entered a sprawling maze of congested traffic, shouting locals and general commotion. King breathed in the smell of Maiquetía. The *real* smell. In that moment he convinced himself never to buy into the facade of luxury again. His time in Venezuela had been a trial run of sorts. He'd never strayed into the artificial commerciality of expensive hotels and designer malls before, even though he'd had the funds to for a long time. He'd always thought it wasn't the true way to experience the world.

The brief period of time he'd spent in luxury had done nothing but prove himself right.

This was the real Venezuela. The slight edge of danger, the natural conversing of the locals, the dirtiness and the claustrophobia and the mixture of smells and sounds and sights. If he'd isolated himself solely to the tourist districts, he would never have seen the country for what it really was.

He vowed never to cocoon himself again.

Then his mind began to wander. He thought of Rico, and the mess that he'd become wrapped up in. He flashed back to an earlier time, only just after he'd stepped away from Black Force. To a small-town police officer who had been willing to help a psychopath all because of the lure of financial gain.

'Raul,' he said, breaking the quiet inside the car. 'Did you know Rico well?'

The man shook his head. 'Not at all. But I heard a lot of things. Rumours spread through the ranks, especially with someone so secretive.'

King nodded. 'Why do you think he's doing this?'

'Doing what?'

'He kills people and ruins lives. All for his operation. Does money motivate him that much?'

'Not money. I've seen some of the things he's done, and it wouldn't be solely money driving him. I've seen him murder people based on a whim, just because he felt like they might be a threat down the line. Rico grew up poor as dirt. I think he was abused. I'd say he never wants to feel like that again. He wants to be in such a position of power that he would never go back to what life used to be like.'

'Pretty selfish.'

'He runs a drug gang. What were you expecting?'

King nodded and shrugged. 'The world's full of people like him.'

'You know that from experience?'

He nodded again. 'A hell of a lot of experience.'

'Did you deal with people like that in the past?'

'You bet. I spent ten years killing them.'

'That's why you're doing this.'

King looked across, taking his eyes off the road for a moment. He met Raul's gaze. 'What?'

'You went your whole life being ordered to do shit like this. Maybe that's why you're helping. It's what feels natural. You've been conditioned to do it.'

'Maybe you're right, Raul. Maybe you're right. Where did José say to meet?'

'At his warehouse.'

'As in where he keeps his supply?'

Raul nodded.

'He must trust you,' King said.

'He does. We were like brothers.'

'You think he'll help us?'

'I doubt it. We're planning an attack on his most lucrative client.'

'That did cross my mind,' King said. 'But we don't have any other options. Only thing we can do is try. Let's see if family trumps business.'

'I don't think it will in this instance,' Raul said, gazing out at the passing shops. 'It's a cruel world. Got to fight to stay ahead.'

Raul directed King into the industrial complex on the outskirts of Maiquetía, buried amidst the rolling plains and shanty towns. The area was barren, with wide roads devoid of traffic save for the occasional rumbling lorry. The hatchback ascended a rise in the road and for a moment they could see out over the city. King spotted the shipyard directly ahead, separated from them by a few miles of civilisation. The Caribbean Sea sparkled in the mid-morning sun.

'This is his place,' Raul said, gesturing to a small rusting warehouse buried up the back of a spacious property. It was dwarfed on either side by buildings almost double the size, giant behemoths that catered to the needs of Maiquetía's various industries.

'You sure?' King said.

'I helped him find it when he was just starting out. I'm sure.'

King turned the wheel and passed through an open gate. The cracked pavement leading to the warehouse was overgrown with weeds. The path cut through a field full of litter and discarded plywood, strewn randomly across the empty land.

The warehouse itself looked like it had been abandoned for years. There were no logos or lettering on the exterior whatsoever. There was none of the usual sounds of an operating business; no buzzing of machinery, no hissing of industrial presses, no beeping of heavy vehicles as they reversed into place.

'I'm having doubts, Raul,' King said, studying the compound. 'This doesn't look like an arms dealer's place.'

'Exactly why he bought it.'

'Whatever you say.'

He coasted to a stop at the end of the path and killed the engine. The warehouse's enormous roller door rested shut. As the noise of the hatchback subsided, complete silence descended over the property. Not a peep of noise came from inside the building.

King opened the driver's side door and stepped out, his boots crunching on the gravel. He brought the AK-103 out with him. This far from the bustling heart of the city meant there were few potential witnesses. He could wield a Kalashnikov assault rifle as much as he desired with little fear of police interference.

It also carried with it the risk that he would be seen as hostile and shot from a distance.

He took that risk in full stride and aimed the weapon at the warehouse, resting the stock against his shoulder.

He'd rather be able to fire the opening shot.

'Relax, man,' Raul said. 'No need for that.'

Suddenly a voice exploded out of a loudspeaker, harsh and discordant. 'I agree. Put the weapon down, please.'

King searched for the source of the noise and noted a small megaphone drilled into one corner of the warehouse's exterior, perched high up. He wondered if it had come with the building, or was a custom addition from Raul's old friend.

'That's him,' Raul said, smiling. 'Put the gun down, man.'

It took King a moment of hesitation to figure that he had no other choice. He wasn't one to surrender his chance of survival, but if anyone in the property wanted him dead, he'd be dead. He abandoned his aim and hurled the rifle away into the gravel. Then he raised both palms towards the warehouse.

'I hope José's motivations haven't changed in the time you've been away,' he muttered to Raul.

'I trust him,' Raul said.

A narrow door swung open in the corner of the building and a short man stepped out into the open front yard. His rotund belly strained against his cheap flannel shirt and his thin greasy hair had been combed back over a bald spot. In direct contrast to his stomach, his bare arms were packed with muscle. Veins ran along the surface of his forearms. King smiled. Testosterone replacement therapy had treated the man well. At first glance, he seemed to be in considerable shape, but further scrutiny revealed that he'd simply become wealthy enough to inject a cocktail of growth hormones that allowed him to stay vascular with minimal effort.

Still, it probably had its intended effect.

It certainly afforded him the look of an arms dealer.

'Raul!' the man exclaimed as he approached them, beaming from ear to ear. 'I never thought I'd see you again.'

Raul looked at him, and for a moment his expression was cold and hard. 'You didn't bother to try and talk Rico into letting me out, José?'

'Of course I did,' José said. 'You think I would just give up on you after everything you did for me? But Rico wouldn't hear a word of it. I'm an outsider. I'm not part of them. I just sell them weapons.'

'Pleased to meet you,' King said.

José looked across. 'And you are?'

He spoke with the blunt, reserved nature of someone who hated strangers. He didn't know King, and King was dangerously close to his illegal operation.

'I helped Raul get out of prison,' King said.

'He's a good man,' Raul said.

José extended a hand. King shook it. 'Any friend of Raul's is a friend of mine.'

'What have you been up to since I was put away?' Raul said.

'Keeping busy. The position you put me in took off very quickly. Soon Rico had me outfitting all his men. He fortified the shipyard, too. Most of his supply comes in through there so he wanted to be able to defend it from any sized attack.'

'Fantastic,' King muttered.

José looked his way for a moment, then shrugged it off. 'Come on in, my friends. You sounded like you needed something on the phone, Raul.'

'I do.'

'Anything for a friend.'

The three of them headed into the warehouse.

CHAPTER 36

They stepped into a cramped front office with orderly stacks of paperwork lining a long timber desk. A desktop computer rested in the far corner. José looped around the desk and sat down behind it. King and Raul both took seats facing him across its surface. King's groaned as it adjusted to his bulk.

'Let's cut to the chase,' King said.

José looked at him. 'Okay.'

'I'm ex-Special Forces. I know what I'm talking about. I'm not some lunatic who decided to get wrapped up in all this on a whim. I'm here for a very clear reason and you don't need to question me about that. Let's clear that up first.'

'Got it.'

'Over to you, Raul.'

Raul paused, waiting for José's attention to drift over to him. 'Mamá and Ana are missing.'

José's eyes widened. 'Are you serious?'

'You think I'd joke about that?'

'Fuck. I had it in my diary to check on them this week.'

'You've been doing that?'

José nodded. 'I felt terrible when you two got sent away. I knew you were the household's only income. My relationship with the Movers meant I had a lot of spare income, so I made sure to siphon some off to your family. It's the least I could do, brother.'

Raul leant forward and offered a hand. José clasped it. Raul bowed his head and touched it to the handshake. He sighed. 'Thank you so much.'

'You don't need to thank me. I would be a monster not to help them out.'

'It means the world to me.'

'They are missing...' José said, his voice drifting off. The blood had drained from his face, turning his skin pale.

King piped up. 'Not for long. I managed to briefly get in contact with Rico. He said he had his men take them as soon as he realised we had escaped from El Infierno.'

'When did that occur?'

'Yesterday. He wants us to meet him in a couple of hours and surrender ourselves over.'

'Do not do that.'

'Does it look like we're doing that?'

'If you give yourselves up, he'll kill all of you.'

'We know that,' Raul said. 'So we're thinking of trying an alternative.'

José raised an eyebrow. 'Trust me, Raul, I do not know a man more ruthless than Rico. I still fear the day where I fail to deliver an order, or miscalculate a truck full of firearms. He's not mentally stable. He would kill me if I fuck up, but I'm in too deep. Don't try and mess with him.'

'Remember that part about me being Special Forces?' King said.

José nodded slowly.

'That's an oversimplification,' King said. 'I was something else. Something worse. I'm not going to go into details, but I used to do this type of thing for a living.'

'What type of thing?'

'Tell him,' Raul said. 'No use skirting around it any longer.'

'We're going to infiltrate the shipyard,' King said. 'I'm going to kill anyone who tries to stop me, and I'm going to find Rico and deal with him, and then I'm going to get Raul's family out of there. He's a good friend, and I want to help him.'

'Do you know Rico?' José said.

'Well enough.'

'Then you must know that you will die if you attempt something so stupid.'

'It doesn't matter what you say, José,' King said. 'You're not going to change my mind.'

'You know how many men he has in that shipyard?'

'Over a hundred?'

José paused. 'Uh, no. More like sixty.'

'Then I can handle it.'

'Keep up the badass act all you want,' José said. 'You will still die.'

'I'm simply telling you what I'm capable of,' King said. 'Based on past exploits. I'm not asking you to believe me, because I honestly don't care. But we need guns.'

The man's eyes widened behind the desk, and his tone shifted. 'Wait ... you think—'

'Yes,' King interrupted. 'Yes, you will help me try to destroy your main source of income. And you'll do it because you're not a soulless piece of shit. From what he tells me, Raul's family gave you a home. You won't dishonour that. At least, I hope you won't.'

José looked at Raul. 'You're helping this madman?'

'He's helping me,' Raul said.

The office went quiet as José leant back in his chair, mulling over what had told him. He drummed a hand against the desk, the hollow echo ringing through the office. Then he spoke. 'Nine out of ten times that you came to me with that proposition, I would tell you to get the fuck out of my sight.'

'But?' King said.

'But today is your lucky day.'

'I get the sense this is mutually beneficial to you.'

'And what makes you think that?'

'You're very interested in making money. You wouldn't have fought so hard to get where you are now otherwise.'

'I've been considering something for a while,' José said. He spoke slowly, clearly choosing his words very carefully. 'I think this may be my opportunity to capitalise.'

'You want out, don't you?' King said.

José nodded. 'I have for a while. Rico's paying me exorbitant sums of cash. I have enough to support myself for as long as I want. And frankly, it's not worth fearing for my life anymore. I want to get the hell out of Vargas but I know he'll hunt me down and tear me to shreds while I'm still alive.'

'Give me everything you can,' King said. 'I'll make sure you have the opportunity to get a fresh start.'

'I haven't made up my mind yet.'

'You will soon. This suits everyone.'

José's expression glazed over. The man was deep in thought. He had clearly reached the financial position he was in by making carefully calculated decisions. King knew he would not be brash. But hopefully he would see the advantages.

'I need to make a call,' he said. 'Give me a moment.'

He launched off the chair and scurried through a side door, disappearing into the warehouse. The door clattered shut behind him.

'You think he'll come round?' Raul said.

King nodded. 'I think so. He seemed to believe that I can help.'

'And he hasn't even seen the shit you've done.'

As Raul spoke, his right leg twitched violently, shaking up and down on the spot with the fervour of someone terrified by what lay ahead.

'You okay?' King said.

'To be honest, no. At least there was some kind of structure in El Infierno. This is going to quickly turn into madness. I just know it.'

'I'm the opposite,' King said. 'The prison was madness. Being locked up inside those walls drove me insane. This is more like what I used to do.'

'You're not nervous?'

King shrugged. 'I will be later. Right now — I don't feel anything.'

'Lucky man.'

King looked at him. 'I'd rather be scared. Makes me feel more human.'

With a resounding *crash* the door to the warehouse burst open. King jolted off his seat, reacting to the sudden noise the only way he knew how. He spun. Clenching his fists. Gritting his teeth. Ready for a fight to the death with whoever came charging through into the office.

José stood in the doorway, a confused expression plastered across his face. He held a mobile phone in one hand. The other was empty.

'Fuck me,' he said. 'You react quick.'

King shrugged. 'My life hasn't been relaxing.'

'Evidently.'

'Do we have a deal?'

José extended the hand with the mobile phone in it and shook it back and forth, indicating he had just made a call. 'I spoke to a few business partners. They've given the all-clear. We have a deal.'

'*Shit,*' Raul whispered.

King turned to him. 'Did you just get cold feet?'

'I didn't think this would actually go ahead…' he said. 'I thought it was all ludicrous … fuck, my heart's racing. Okay, let's do this before I back out.'

José beckoned them through into the warehouse. They followed him through, and King's eyes widened as he gazed out at an extraordinary arsenal of firepower.

CHAPTER 37

The cavernous space had been outfitted with symmetrical rows of metal shelving, towering far above them on all sides. A few forklifts were scattered across the warehouse floor. Hundreds of crates littered the shelves, ranging from the size of a man to the size of a tank.

'You weren't kidding,' King said. 'I thought you were an amateur…'

'I was,' José said. 'I learnt quickly. Expanded quickly. That's why I have enough funds. At some point the risk begins to outweigh the reward.'

'Are you worried about arrest?'

The man scoffed. 'Are you kidding? I'm integral to the operation of the largest drug gang in Vargas state. The police probably know exactly where I'm located, and what's in this place. They wouldn't dare do anything about it.'

'So it's solely Rico that's making you want to step away?'

José nodded. 'He's a lunatic. A high-paying one, but a lunatic all the same.'

'If he finds out you supplied me…'

'That's why I'm praying to God that you are who you say you are. I'll give you enough firepower to level a skyscraper. Please use it effectively.'

'I will.'

'I hope so. Because I'm dead otherwise —'

He trailed off mid-sentence, as if a new thought had struck him.

'What is it?' King said.

José turned to Raul. 'You don't expect to rescue them, do you?'

'My family?'

José nodded.

Raul shrugged, his eyes turning wet. 'I can try, right? I can hope.'

José sighed. 'Don't go in there expecting to save them, my friend. In all likelihood they won't be there. Or if they are, Rico will simply see you coming and kill them before you can reach them.'

The spiel hit Raul hard. King watched as he bowed his head towards the ground and blinked hard, struggling to control his emotions. He cleared his throat, composing himself. He looked up. 'It's the only thing we can do. I don't have any other options.'

'I know, my friend,' José said. 'They were dear to me too. It hurts to think about what might have happened to them. But with so many unknowns, please don't charge in expecting for all to end well. It won't.'

Raul nodded. 'I know. Thank you, brother.'

They embraced, pulling each other tight. Raul slapped his childhood friend on the back hard several times, letting out the frustration bubbling to the surface inside him. As they rode out the anger together, King turned away. He let them have their moment. He scanned the nearest shelf, looking over a dozen open crates propped side-by-side, exposing glinting gunmetal within. He studied their contents. His eyes widened.

When Raul and José separated, King thrust out a hand and pointed at the wooden boxes.

'Where the *fuck* did you get these?' he said, his tone incredulous.

José peered past King and noted the crates of weapons intended for delivery to the United States Special Forces.

'Ah,' he said. 'That's right. You're ex-U.S. military.'

'I am. How'd you get them?'

José raised both eyebrows and scoffed. 'You honestly expect me to tell you? You could have me arrested and extradited by dialling a number. I'll spend the rest of my life in Guantanamo Bay for that.'

King let out a wry smile. 'Trust me, I won't be dialling any numbers in the foreseeable future. I've had enough of that life. At least for now.'

'You don't want anything to do with the government?'

King shrugged. 'Not so much that. I just want to move on.'

'You're probably telling the truth,' José said. 'But out of principle, I'd be the worst arms dealer on the planet if I even considered trusting you.'

'Well, do you mind if I make some selections?' King said.

'Rico specifically requested those. He offered me double the asking price.'

King took his time to respond, letting the idiocy of José's statement hang in the air. 'You're sending me to kill him.'

José shrugged. 'Yeah, whatever. Point taken. Choose whatever you want. Fuck, man, I can't believe I'm doing this…'

'I don't understand the hesitation,' King said. 'You just agreed to help us.'

'Because if you take guns out of those crates and head off, it becomes real,' José said. 'I've built a stable business here. As soon as you leave, shit hits the fan. I'm still in disbelief that this is all happening.'

'Where will you go?'

The man checked his watch. 'First flight out of here. I can choose where I'm headed at the airport.'

'Just like that? You'll drop everything and leave?'

'I've been considering it for months. If I don't make my mind up now, it'll never happen. Time to move on.'

King approached the first crate. It contained orderly rows of brand new weaponry, intended for use by elite infantry. He stared at Heckler and Koch HK416 assault rifles, HK MP7 sub-machine guns, and a pristine row of M32 6-shot grenade launchers. Just the sight of the weapons brought back a swarm of memories.

Body parts flying in all directions.

Thousands of rounds of ammunition tearing his cover to shreds.

The *punch* of explosives detonating nearby, resonating through his chest wall, shaking him to his core.

The savage violence of the battlefield.

The lack of mercy.

The flow-state he entered where killing became second nature, something primal and animalistic, when he transformed into a rabid animal demolishing everything in his path.

Those times had killed some part of him. That much he knew. He'd ignored it for years, suppressing the things he'd seen, the things he'd done.

He grimaced and battled the memories away. It took a good few minutes to squash them back down within himself, and by the time he did so a cold sweat had broken out across his brow. His hands shook, suddenly clammy. He rested a palm on the lip of the crate and took a deep breath.

Raul watched with hesitation. 'What's wrong?'

King looked at him, still sweating. 'I might need to go to a dark place soon. I want you to be ready for that. If this goes according to plan, I'm going to kill a lot of people today. It might shock you. I want to warn you before it all kicks off.'

'Obviously…' Raul said. 'We're going there to save—'

King shook his head vigorously. 'No, Raul. You don't get it. You probably have an idea of what this will be like. All noble and honourable. Fighting for the greater good, that sort of thing. It doesn't work that way. You might have seen some shit in El Infierno, but this is going to be on another level. Don't take it lightly.'

Raul nodded. 'Understood.'

King motioned to the crate and turned to José. 'This will be very useful. Thank you.'

José shrugged. 'We're both helping each other. I actually have something to show you. It took me almost three months to secure one. Rico requested it. I think for high-security transportation. You might want to use it. I don't have use for it anymore.'

'What — like an armoured truck?' King said.

José smiled. 'A little better.'

He led King between two rows of shelving, guiding him to a secluded corner of the warehouse.

CHAPTER 38

They rounded a corner and King laid his eyes on the vehicle parked in a designated bay against one wall.

He whistled softly. He knew exactly what it was.

'What kind of an arms dealer are you?' he said. 'How the hell did you manage to get access to that?'

'A contact in the Turkish military,' José said. 'They had a surplus. I paid double what it's worth. Rico's paying double that.'

'Not anymore he's not.'

During his time in Black Force, King had seen a couple of Otokar Cobras. None quite like this.

'Is it a Cobra II?' he said.

José nodded. 'Almost double the weight. Rico said he'd pay me a couple of million for it.'

Another low whistle. 'And you're willing to give it to me?'

'I've made more than a couple of million doing this. I don't need the money. I need the security.'

'And I'd very much like to kill Rico.'

'So we both come out on top.'

'I hope so, José. I hope so.'

The Otokar Cobra was a 25,000-pound armoured vehicle, almost the same size as a tank. Its enormous heavy-duty tyres almost reached King's chest, and its steel hull would protect them from any small-arms fire the Movers could throw at them. They were developed and manufactured by a Turkish firm. He'd used one to storm a compound manufacturing biological weapons in Kuwait almost a year ago. The operation hadn't quite gone according to plan.

'If I use this, it will change my tactics considerably,' King said. 'We'll have to use it as a battering ram.'

'That's what I would advise you to do,' José said. 'Smash the gate in, find cover somewhere in the shipyard, and work your way through from there. There's no way you'll be able to sneak in undetected.'

'Overwhelming force.'

'Yes.'

'That works for me.'

Raul caught up to them and King saw his eyes widen at the sight of the Cobra. 'We can't be using that! We'll draw every Mover in the shipyard to us.'

'That's the point,' King said. 'More effective than trying to carry out a slow burn. I'd rather this.'

'I—'

'You don't have to come with me, Raul. I never said you had to. I'm doing this mainly for myself. It's not your responsibility to get wrapped up in it.'

Raul stared at him. 'You know I can't do that. What if you die? Then I'll have to sit back and watch as Rico slaughters my family.'

'Suit yourself. But it's on you.'

'What are we waiting for? We've got less than an hour.'

With that, the decision was made. King didn't prod the man any further. He was clearly desperate, and King had enough experience to know there was no reasoning with desperate men. It would be against Raul's better judgment to willingly dive into a war, but it seemed that was inevitable. He wanted his family back.

King didn't dare let him know that in all likelihood they would never find them. He'd seen the shipyard from a distance. His mother and sister could be anywhere amongst the desolate shipwrecks. It was a barren wasteland that would take months to search from top to bottom.

They didn't have months.

José helped him cart a trolley full of guns to the Cobra. Four assault rifles, four sub-machine guns and four grenade launchers, along with a few thousand rounds of ammunition. If they needed more than that, they would never make it out of the shipyard alive. He tugged open the rear door, feeling the

313

weight of the frame. José and Raul got to work hauling the weapons into the back of the Cobra, where there was space for four or five soldiers. King glanced into the interior of the vehicle, noting that the gunner's perch had no turret attached. From experience, he knew the Cobra usually came equipped with a 12.7mm machine gun with a mounted shield.

'Where's the turret?' he said. 'That could be useful.'

'Afraid you're out of luck,' José said, hauling the last grenade launcher into the vehicle. 'That was the one condition of the exchange. The Turks kept the big gun. Needed it for their armed forces, or something along those lines.'

'Or had their own self-interests in mind.'

'More than likely,' José said. 'But I'm not one to complain. Especially when Rico couldn't give a shit about the lack of a turret. He just wanted it for intimidation purposes, I assume.'

King nodded. 'I thought so.'

It meant there was nothing but a circular hole in the roof of the Cobra. It left them awfully exposed.

'One of the Movers can lob a grenade straight through that when we slow down,' he said.

'So keep your foot on the accelerator,' José said. 'Throw their aim off.'

'Right.'

'Hey, you asked to do this.'

'And I'm sticking to it.'

Raul slammed the rear door closed. The noise echoed off the aluminium walls. It rang out across the open space. King felt his heart race increase. The sound had a ring of finality to it. They had committed to the task at hand. There was nothing left to wait for. Soon they would be on their way to Rico's stronghold.

Just like that, he found himself in the exact situation that he'd left Black Force to avoid.

He rested a hand against the hull of the Cobra. Breathed deep. Channelling the inner hum that signalled approaching combat. Nothing masked the feeling of complete terror before throwing yourself into the line of fire. Not much could. He'd experienced the same sensation a hundred times over, but it didn't seem to grow any easier.

King turned to José and the two shook hands. He knew it would be the last time they'd ever see him again. Whether they died or not, the man would be halfway across the planet by the time the day had drawn to a close.

Sometimes crime pays, he thought to himself.

'Good luck, my friend,' José said. 'You're not quite right in the head for doing what you're about to do, but you're doing me a favour — so I won't protest.'

'You're doing me a favour, too,' King said. 'Without this we'd still be scurrying from building to building, scrounging whatever we could. We'd probably be dead.'

'You'll be dead in an hour. I think I just hurried the end result along. But that's not my concern.'

'You're right, it's not. And I'll try my hardest not to be.'

He popped open the driver's door of the Cobra and climbed into the seat. It felt like he was sitting in a cockpit. He stared out at the industrial complex ahead through the open warehouse door. A sheet of bulletproof glass gave the view a slight tint. Raul climbed into the passenger's seat, shaking with adrenalin. It would be uncontrollable until they got there — King knew that much. Raul had lived a hard life, with a sizeable chunk of it spent inside the walls of a brutal third-world prison, but that got nowhere close to making him adept at handling this sort of scenario.

King had seen many so-called tough guys break over the years. It didn't take much.

Hopefully the man could preserve his sanity during the chaos that inevitably lay ahead.

'King,' José said as he reached out and snatched the door handle, a second away from pulling it shut.

King looked across.

'I've been supplying the Movers for a year. They're all horrible people. Trust me when I tell you Raul and Luis were a once-off. That's why Rico threw them in jail. Because they're good people. I've seen the Movers rape, torture and kill more innocent people than I can count. Rico especially.'

'And you helped them.'

José shrugged. 'It's a cruel world. But please don't show mercy. They don't deserve it.'

King let the request hang in the air for a moment before responding. 'I never do.'

He swung the Cobra's door closed, sealing them into a vehicular battering ram. Then he fired it up and touched the accelerator.

The gargantuan vehicle rumbled out of the warehouse.

He turned out of the lot and gunned the engine.

They shot off the mark, roaring towards the shipyard.

Towards war.

CHAPTER 39

The sealed interior of the Cobra created a bubble of nervous energy. King had long ago worked out how to control it. He still felt just as terrified as ever, but he'd learnt ways to suppress it, to keep the fear in check, to concentrate on the task at hand with laser focus.

Raul had learnt none of these things.

He shifted every couple of seconds in his seat, unable to stay still. Every now and then he glanced back at the arsenal of weaponry behind them. Perhaps reassuring himself. Perhaps making himself even more terrified.

Whatever the case, the terror would only continue to escalate until conflict broke out.

'I don't think you're ready for this,' King said finally, breaking the silence.

'I am,' he said. 'Just struggling to process it.'

'So am I.'

'Bullshit. You look completely calm. This is second nature to you.'

'I'm scared out of my mind. I just know how to hide it.'

'You enjoy this, don't you?'

King looked across. 'Enjoy what? Killing?'

Gunfights and fighting and violence. You thrive on it. I can tell.'

'I don't enjoy it,' King said. 'But it makes me feel normal.'

'There's still time for you to leave.'

'Yeah, right.'

'I'm serious.'

'Every decision I've ever made has been final,' King said. 'I don't change my mind. When I told you I would help in the hotel, I'd spent a long period of time weighing everything up. Nothing you say is going to stop me entering that shipyard. Okay?'

'Okay.'

King gripped the wheel and looked around at the Cobra's interior. 'Something's not right here, Raul.'

'What do you mean?'

'How well do you know José?'

'I told you. Like a brother.'

'He's a good man?'

'I think so. I mean, he's an arms dealer … but I think he has good intentions.'

'I don't know,' King said. 'Something's off.'

'You keep saying that.'

'When I have a hunch, I'm not wrong often.'

'What makes you so sure?'

'He didn't hesitate to give us all of this shit. This is millions of dollars worth of equipment. And he just threw it away, and told us he was leaving this life behind. We were there for less than twenty minutes.'

'That's what he's like. He doesn't spend much time considering his actions. He just does things … and thinks about them later.'

'You sure? It doesn't feel right.'

'I'm sure.'

King shrugged. 'Whatever. His intentions aren't our concern any longer. We have all of this. I'll forget he ever existed.'

'You don't like him.'

'He seems slimy. Like he had ulterior motives.'

'I won't bother trying to convince you,' Raul said. 'Like you said, it seems you've made up your mind. I won't change your opinion.'

King smiled. 'You're catching on.'

He turned the Cobra out of the industrial zone and onto a long, twisting road that descended down to the ocean. Now surrounded by traffic, he kept his gaze fixed firmly ahead and tried to draw the least amount of attention he could. It proved useless, given the fact that he was behind the wheel of an enormous armoured vehicle.

They were both still wanted men.

'You think the police will catch us on the way there?' Raul said, seemingly reading his mind.

'I hope not. If they do, I'm not stopping.'

'That'll cause more problems than it solves.'

'If we get arrested again, they'll either execute us and bury the bodies or lock us in solitary confinement for the rest of our lives. We had one chance to get out, and we took it. There won't be another one.'

Raul breathed out. 'Okay. So between law enforcement and the Movers, I'd say most of Maiquetía's population wants us dead.'

'You're probably right.'

'Where do I go from here? I mean, if I'm alive in an hour...'

'Wherever you want,' King said. 'I can give you money.'

'What if my family die...?' He trailed off.

King didn't answer that, for he had no magical solution to that question. If they stumbled upon the corpses of Raul's mother and sister, he feared the man would never recover from such a brutal and unforgiving chain of events. And as the seconds ticked away he found it increasingly likely that said outcome was inevitable.

'You said you've been in the shipyard?' King said.

'Yes. A few times. But it was a while ago.'

'Where is Rico likely to be? I'd like at least a little intel before we do this.'

'The cruise ship,' Raul said. 'The one in the port, resting in the water. Did you see it from our window?'

King recalled the ominous structure looming in an inlet. It had been one of the only distinguishable features in the place from their vantage point in the hotel. He nodded.

'How confident are you?'

'Everything of any importance takes place in that ship,' he said. 'I've never been inside. I was too low in the ranks. But that's where all the supply is kept, it's where most of the guards are stationed around, it's where Rico does business. Mamá and Ana are in there somewhere. I know it.'

King brought up the layout of the shipyard in his head, recalling the view from Diamanté Resort. He remembered an open expanse of concrete that cut through the wreckages, leading to the ocean. A straight path cutting through to Rico's stronghold. Once inside the cruise ship, he could utilise his skills more effectively. Raul had seen enough of King in action to recognise his talent in close quarters.

It was reaching the cruise ship that seemed to be the major hurdle.

King turned the wheel and brought the Cobra off the main road as they grew closer to the shipyard. He entered a claustrophobic neighbourhood where houses had been seemingly squashed together to ensure maximum occupancy. Every local they passed stopped what they were doing and stared in surprise at the armoured vehicle rumbling through the tiny streets.

Raul directed him left, then right, then left again, and finally raised a hand. King pressed on the brake and the Cobra's enormous tyres ground to a halt on the gravel. They had stopped just before the street opened out into a wider main road. The road trailed downhill towards the Caribbean Sea.

'Don't go any further,' Raul said, his eyes wide.

'Why?'

'It's been a while since I navigated these streets. I was rusty. Turn right here and the road runs right up to the main gate of the shipyard.'

'There's guards stationed there?'

Raul nodded. 'Rico always keeps half a dozen of his thugs patrolling the entrance.'

'Describe the gate.'

'It's big. It's some kind of steel mesh.'

'You think we could break through it?'

Raul's eyes darted over the interior of the Cobra, taking in the bulk of the vehicle. 'Yeah, probably. There's no other way in. Big steel walls running around the rest of the shipyard.'

'Could we climb over them?'

Raul looked at him. 'Maybe. But then we don't have a tank.'

King opened his door and let the humid Venezuelan air flow into the Cobra. 'Let's take a look.'

They got out and scurried to the footpath beside an abandoned apartment complex. Scaffolding and building tools lay scattered across the structure, indicating it had been in the process of construction before either financiers or workers had given up on the project. Whatever the case, it blocked the Cobra from the view of whoever was looking up the hill from the bottom of the main road.

King moved slowly along one wall of the complex, feeling the heat of the day drawing sweat from his pores. Raul stayed back. King crouched low as he approached the corner of the building, then peeked around the bend, taking care to expose as little of his frame as possible to whoever may be watching.

Raul was right.

The cracked asphalt descended the rest of the slope, where it ended at a steel wall running the length of the road. The wall had been thrown together haphazardly, probably by Rico and his men when they moved in. Large slabs of concrete and metal and barbed wire had been slapped together at random. Just high enough to prevent intruders. He couldn't imagine who would want to enter the shipyard anyway, save for having a death wish.

Like he did.

He counted four men loitering at a chain-link gate in the middle of the wall. All tough-looking types, most smoking cigarettes. Each man had a sub-machine gun dangling from a shoulder strap, the gunmetal glinting in the sun. King couldn't make out their type from such a distance, but the weapons looked fearsome. Supplied by José, no doubt. The four of them strolled about with a sense of brash confidence, openly brandishing illegal firearms, aware that all the proper authorities had been paid off and as a result they ran no risk of being arrested.

They were on top of the world.

King would soon change that.

He shrank back into the side-street and met Raul's gaze. 'Four men on the gate.'

'Used to be two. He's doubled security.'

'Is that unusual?'

'I think so.'

'I don't like this, Raul.'

'I don't have any other options. I'll take the Cobra and the guns if you don't want to continue.'

King shook his head. 'We have the element of surprise. I like that. And they look like amateurs. Street thugs. I can deal with them.'

'You sure?'

'I'm never sure. But I'm confident.'

King headed back to the Cobra, gnashing his teeth together as he rode out waves of anxiety. His head began to pound, either an effect of the blows he'd sustained over the last few days or because of the rush of adrenalin. He clambered back into the driver's seat and gripped the wheel until his fingers turned white and his forearms swelled under the exertion. Raul got into the passenger's seat beside him and watched him silently.

King didn't bother to check whether Raul was scared. He knew the man would be. Right now, he had to focus on himself. It would take extraordinary focus to achieve what he wanted in the coming storm. But he'd done it before. He could do it again.

He gazed out at the T-junction ahead and zoned in. He touched his foot against the accelerator — ready to press it down. When they turned the corner, it would be full speed ahead. The element of surprise would lend a sizeable advantage that he knew how to exploit. They'd have to hit the shipyard fast and hard. There was no time for hesitation, which meant a single mistake would end them.

A lot of pressure to handle.

He began to put weight on the pedal when a flash of movement in his peripheral vision caught his eye. Something ordinarily forgettable, but in his heightened state of mental alertness he paid attention to every shred of movement. He glanced out the side window.

Shit.

Two men, decked out in combat gear from head to toe, brandishing automatic weapons on the third floor of the adjacent apartment complex. He saw them. They saw him.

The pair shrank back into the shadows of the construction site, disappearing from view.

And just like that, King knew he and Raul had been compromised.

CHAPTER 40

'Fuck,' he whispered, reaching back and snatching an MP7 off the floor. He checked the gun was loaded and racked the safety off.

'What is it?' Raul said. He hadn't seen them.

'They saw us.'

'Who saw us?'

King didn't respond, because by that point he'd thrown the door open and dropped to the ground outside. He set off in a full-paced sprint into the construction site. He hurdled a low fence and pushed himself faster, legs pounding across the concrete. The complex loomed overhead. He ducked through an open doorway and found himself in a dusty open-plan layout, faintly illuminated by the sunlight dipping in through open windows along the perimeter.

The place had been abandoned long ago. Water dripped from the ceiling. Crude graffiti covered all exposed surfaces, and the floor was littered with empty cans and dirty rags. King's own panicked breathing was the only audible noise.

There was no sign of the two men. He stayed still for a moment as he took in every inch of his surroundings, making sure that they hadn't made it to the ground floor before he'd entered the building. But the lower level was desolate. It felt like no-one had stepped foot in the complex for years.

He spotted a half-finished concrete stairwell in the corner, ascending into darkness. It seemed to be the only way to reach the higher levels. A dilapidated elevator shaft sat in a far wall, abandoned halfway through construction. It served no purpose.

The stairwell it is.

King powered across the room and took the stairs three at a time, keeping one finger slotted inside the trigger guard of his sub-machine gun. He knew the odds were in his favour. Not many people on the planet could react faster than he could — but it only took one bullet from behind to shut the lights out.

He cleared the second floor, keeping one eye on the stairwell at all times to make sure the two men didn't pass him by. He could search the entire building this way. At some point, he had to run into the duo. It was paramount that he did. If either of them made it back into the shipyard, the Movers would be prepared for an attack.

He swore as the second floor turned out empty. Every second that ticked away created a higher likelihood that their cover had been blown. He darted back to the stairwell and made it to the third floor in seconds. He kept the MP7 raised, ready to react to the slightest unnatural movement. He looked past dusty columns and through the skeleton frames of half-erected plaster walls. Nothing. Completely empty.

Heart pounding in his chest, King took a deep breath and prepared for a trip to the fourth floor. Then he glanced at the elevator shaft and went pale.

A thick hessian rope had been fixed to the side of the shaft, dangling down to the lower floors. It swayed softly from side to side without any kind of draught. Which only meant one thing.

It had been used recently.

Very recently.

King swung the MP7's leather strap over his shoulder and let go of the weapon as he ran back towards the stairwell. He knew he would not need it. It dangled by his side as he ran.

The two mercenaries would be long gone, high-tailing it back to the shipyard to inform their comrades of an approaching Otokar Cobra. He no longer had any advantages except for his experience in the heat of combat.

He doubted that would get them through the coming battle.

But every second that ticked away signalled another moment that Rico could spend getting ready for an attack.

So he tore down three flights of stairs. He burst back onto the ground floor and flew through the complex. His lungs pounded and the blood rushed to his head. He saw Raul peering out the windscreen of the Cobra. When the man saw

King tearing towards the Cobra at breakneck speed his eyes widened and he opened the driver's side door.

King dove in.

'What's going on?' he demanded.

'We're compromised,' King said, slamming the door shut behind him. 'Two Movers saw us and got away. They've probably already raised the alarm.'

'*What?!*' Raul said with panicked urgency. King realised he should have just kept his mouth shut. The man was nervous enough.

'We need to move,' he said. 'Right now.'

'Fuck,' Raul said, eyes widening. 'I don't know about this. Are you sure that—'

King leant over and gripped his shoulder tight, his own blood rushing. 'Raul, I know instinct is telling you to back out. But we either go right now or we never go at all. There's no other option. You can get out if you want to.'

With a determined nod of the head, Raul grit his teeth and nodded acceptance.

'We're going?' King said.

'We're going.'

Adrenalin ran high as King seized the wheel and slammed the Cobra's accelerator. It took off with surprising power given its extraordinary weight. The tyres spun on the gravel for a moment before finding purchase. The tank-on-wheels rocketed out onto the main road, coming into full view of the guards.

In King's heightened state he noted each wave of reaction in the gangsters' expressions.

First came shock. The sight of such an enormous vehicle made them hesitate. For a moment no-one moved. Their weapons hung at their sides as they stared at the scene with utter disbelief. King imagined they were fully unprepared for an actual attack. With absolute control over the city of Maiquetía and dominance over all competition, he didn't imagine they faced threats very often. They were stationed at the gate for nothing more than deterrence. They looked imposing, even though Rico probably knew a full-scale invasion would never come.

But now it was happening — and they had been thrown into the midst of it — and they needed to react in the next few seconds or they would be rendered useless. It was too much for them to process. King grinned and ground his foot into the pedal, pushing the engine as hard as it could take. The guards stood frozen, locked in bouts of mental paralysis as their brains turned over at a million miles an hour.

The Cobra roared towards the gate, descending the slope at a lightning pace.

He didn't even think about moving his foot over to the brakes. He and Raul had committed to the attack. By now there was no turning back.

The guards came to this realisation shortly after. Then came the next phase of reactions.

Sheer panic.

Mouths open, eyes boggling, they snatched for their guns with shaky hands. The four of them were unable to rip their gaze away from the battering ram headed their way. King knew they would get a few shots off before they reached the gate. That was inevitable.

Not that it mattered.

The Cobra went airborne as it crossed from the smooth asphalt to the dirty patch of land in front of the gate. Its massive wheels bounced once, then found purchase and surged forward. King felt the vibration deep in his core. The impact smashed him against his seat, jolting him hard. He kept his grip on the wheel.

A scattering of bullets chipped against the front windscreen. The first guard to gather his wits had unloaded his magazine at the vehicle. It had no effect whatsoever. The Cobra had been built specifically to withstand small-arms fire.

He turned out to be the only man that reacted fast enough to hit them.

The Cobra surged past the four of them — two on each side — and charged at the gate.

'*Brace!*' King roared.

Rico wrapped one hand around his door handle and covered his face with the other. King tightened his grip on the wheel and tensed every muscle in his body at once, ready for the impact.

They smashed into the steel mesh amidst the shriek of tearing metal.

CHAPTER 41

The gate was sturdier than King anticipated.

He'd expected to demolish it with barely any resistance, given the sheer weight and size of the Cobra. But the collision knocked the breath from his lungs and they slowed considerably. He slammed against his seatbelt, coughing as he did so. In the passenger's seat, Raul jolted similarly against his own restraints. They both let out twin grunts of surprise.

The gate tore off its supports as it bore the full brunt of the Cobra's momentum. Metal roared and steel bent and the structure collapsed. Despite the intensity of the crash, King kept his foot down. They stalled momentarily, then gained an extra burst of momentum and bounced over the destroyed frame.

'Holy *shit*,' Raul gasped, wheezing for breath.

The Cobra rattled to a halt inside the shipyard. They had entered the same stretch of bare ground that King had seen from the hotel window, running all the way from the entrance to the port. Carcasses of long-retired cargo ships had been cast across the space seemingly at random. They looked like enormous boulders amidst a concrete wasteland. The shipyard was deserted for as far as the eye could see. It seemed all the important activity took place in and around the cruise ship.

Raul had been right.

In one fluid movement King undid his belt and launched out of the driver's seat.

'Where the fuck are you going?!' Raul yelled.

'Gotta deter them from following.'

He snatched up a HK416 assault rifle from the steel floor and vaulted onto one of the seats, giving him enough room to stick his top half out the open hole in the roof. As he did so, he took a brief glance at the weapon in his hands.

No, not a HK416.

A HK417.

He hadn't seen many of the variants in his time, which was why it had taken him a while to notice the slight differences. This version was a slightly larger version of the standard HK416, which made room for 7.62x51mm NATO rounds. He only remembered those facts because of intrigue at the time. In reality, they all killed just the same.

Except this model caused slightly more grievous wounds.

Perfect.

He brought the red dot sight to his eye and locked his aim onto the gaping hole in the shipyard's perimeter. He knew how their minds worked. The four guards were stationed at the gate to prevent one thing — intruders. They had failed miserably, and now they would come storming through into the shipyard, recklessly exposing themselves, curious to catch a glimpse of what their shortcomings had resulted in.

One man came into view on each side of the gap. Both had their guns pointed at the ground, expecting King to have continued his rampage with the Cobra. They saw the huge vehicle stopped just inside the grounds of the shipyard.

Both froze in shock.

Too late.

King fired two clusters, separated by a second's hesitation as he moved from one target to the next. He aimed for their torsos — the largest surface area and as such the easiest to hit. All six rounds thudded home. He didn't see the impacts. The exchange happened too fast to fully take in the placement of each individual bullet.

He saw both men crumple like all the energy had been sucked out of them at once, and he knew his work was done. With the added size of the HK's rounds, death would be inevitable. Vital organs had been destroyed.

The brutality of the violence would cause the other two men to pause. They would more than likely suffer shock from seeing their partners die so suddenly. King wasn't interested in needlessly killing them too. If they decided to put up a fight when he returned, he would deal with them accordingly.

But for now, they would be preoccupied with aiding their dying comrades.

He ducked back inside. He dropped the rifle. He dove into the driver's seat and squashed his boot into the footwell. The Cobra took off again, roaring away from the scene at the gate.

'Are they following?' Raul said.

'Not anymore.'

The man inhaled, sucking air into his lungs. 'I don't know what to do…'

'Stop overthinking things,' King said as shipwrecks flashed past on either side. 'Just follow me. I'll get this done.'

'You're awfully confident.'

'Have to be. I'd be shitting my pants otherwise.'

Up ahead, the ocean twinkled under the sun, which had just reached its apex in the sky. The edge of the shipyard came into view as they drew closer to the water. The Cobra flew past a final shipwreck obscuring the way and he finally saw the layout of Rico's stronghold.

The cruise ship rested in an inlet just large enough to fit its gargantuan frame. It seemed to dwarf everything else in proximity. Previously white, most of the paint on its exterior had peeled off, revealing the dirty foundations underneath. In various places, the framework had collapsed, to the point where it looked like a giant beast had gouged chunks out of the ship.

King took in the sight of the behemoth, and then he noted the rest of the scene. His stomach fell into a deep pit.

He needn't have bothered chasing the two Movers into the apartment complex. Because Rico had known an attack was imminent for some time.

And he'd prepared accordingly.

King stared out the windscreen at a barricade that had been erected in front of the cruise ship, made up of dozens of heavy-duty vehicles parked nose-to-end. Behind the trucks and sedans and pick-ups, more than thirty armed men stood in wait, barrels raised. They'd been simply waiting for the moment that King and Raul would come tearing around the corner.

Someone had tipped them off. Not the two scouts in the apartment complex. Sometime before that…

They unloaded their weapons simultaneously.

King slammed on the brakes, partially due to shock at the sudden turn of events, mostly due to the realisation that a head-on approach would accomplish nothing against such a well-prepared force. A hailstorm of bullets slammed against the front of the Cobra, hundreds and hundreds of rounds smashing into the steel and bulletproof glass at an overwhelming pace.

The resulting cacophony of noise made King flinch. The din roared all around them.

'*What the hell!*' Raul screamed above the racket. 'They knew we were coming!'

King grit his teeth. 'Looks like your friend José might be Rico's friend José.'

'Then why would he give us all this shit? He would have just killed us at the warehouse.'

King paused. 'Good question. What the fuck's going on?'

Whatever the case, he knew one of the Movers would eventually get their hands on anti-tank weaponry if they stayed stationary in no man's land. There was nothing they could do against Rico's forces, especially when every man in the shipyard had been prepared for an assault.

King slammed the gearbox into reverse. He spun the wheel and punched the accelerator at the same time. In a scream of smoking rubber, the Cobra spun in a hundred-and-eighty-degree arc, bullets bouncing off its hull the entire time.

'What are you doing?!' Raul said.

'Retreating.'

'My family's in that ship…'

'We'll be no use to them dead.'

'Rico will kill them now that he knows we're here.'

'I *know*, Raul!' King roared. 'Give me a moment.'

But he didn't have a moment, because just as he prepared to round the corner of the nearest shipwreck and take cover behind its massive frame, a frenetic explosion of movement broke out ahead. King jolted in shock. The sight took a second to process.

'What the—'

A convoy of vehicles tore into sight, all beat-up and rusting but armoured with steel plates and other forms of amateur work. Several of them were pick-up trucks complete with pairs and trios of men perched in the rear trays, brandishing all kinds of shiny assault rifles. King spotted a couple of M32 grenade launchers identical to the haul littered across the Cobra's floor.

Armed by José, without a doubt.

'What have we stumbled into?' King said, in awe at the sudden surge of armed forces.

'Oh my God,' Raul whispered. 'That's not good.'

King quickly realised that Rico's forces hadn't been preparing for him and Raul. They'd been bracing themselves for a skirmish with these new arrivals. It seemed that some kind of gang in competition with the Movers had chosen today to launch an assault on their compound.

The Otokar Cobra rested directly in the middle of an all-out war.

CHAPTER 42

The Cobra screeched to a halt once again as King hit the brakes. Chaos raged all around them as both sides exchanged bullets. He heard the familiar *whump* of a discharged M32 and clenched all his muscles simultaneously. If that grenade launcher had been aimed in their direction, it may be the last noise he ever heard.

The distant noise of an explosion ripped through the shipyard, overpowering the storm of gunfire. It came from behind them, somewhere in the midst of Rico's ranks. King breathed a momentary sigh of relief and assessed the situation.

It didn't look good. They were boxed in by shipwrecks, trapped in the middle of the carnage. If they pressed onwards into the hostile forces, he didn't doubt that a stray round from one of the M32s would find its way into their vehicle's hull. Survival was highly questionable. He thought back to the brief glimpse he'd got of Rico's forces, and couldn't recall whether they had been armed with high explosives.

It was all he had to go off. A wild guess.

He could antagonise these new enemies, or charge headlong into Rico's forces. Little good was likely to come from either option. But he had to make a decision, right now. Stalling in the dead space between the two forces would get them killed without question. So he spun the wheel again, aiming back in the same direction they'd just come from.

'King?' Raul said.

King pressed the Cobra forward with a surge of acceleration. It swung in a wide arc, its hull screaming under the impact of hundreds of stray rounds. The deafening rattle made his eardrums ring, but he grit his teeth and ignored it. Now was not the time to get cold feet.

'*King,*' Raul said, a little more urgently.

He completed the one-hundred-and-eighty degree turn. Rico's forces remained behind the crude barricade, firing indiscriminately at both the Cobra and the approaching convoy. The side of the cruise ship loomed behind them, resting in the inlet, separated from the dock by a dozen feet of empty space. He assumed that a drawbridge usually connected the two sections together. Now it had been removed, to prevent enemy forces reaching the ship.

No matter.

Pick up enough speed and momentum would carry them across.

'*King!*' Raul roared.

'We need to get inside the cruise ship,' he said. 'Once we're in there, I can find Rico. I can kill him. I can find your family.'

'How do you propose we do that?'

'Hold onto something.'

With a roar of recognition, the Cobra's engine responded to a press on the accelerator. King's stomach dropped as the massive armoured vehicle roared towards the barricade, travelling faster with each passing second.

He guessed they would hit the parked vehicles at close to sixty miles an hour.

Raul baulked as he realised what was about to happen. The man reached over with the verve of someone terrified beyond belief, fumbling frantically for the steering wheel, desperate to correct the Cobra's course.

King battered his hand away. 'You want to see your mother and sister again?'

'Yes. But we'll die if we do this.'

'We might. But we've got more of a chance than any other option.'

They got close enough for King to make out individual faces in the blockade. The Movers were either reloading or firing, their gaze fixed on the armoured behemoth charging straight at them. Their small-arms fire did nothing to penetrate the Cobra's hull. King flicked his vision across the ranks, searching for any kind of weapon that posed a threat.

He saw it.

An old-school RPG-7 shoulder launcher resting on the collar bone of a skinny thug crouched behind a battered pick-up truck.

The guy rose from his position and took aim, pointing a bulky warhead directly at King. King locked eyes with him through the windscreen and knew he was staring death in the face. The warhead was a PG-7VR, designed specifically with armoured vehicles in mind. Shaped like a miniature space shuttle, the huge explosive contained two separate warheads — one for crippling the exterior and then a second delayed explosive that would pass through the newly created gap and detonate further inside the hull in spectacular fashion. If it hit the Cobra, he and Raul would die instantaneously.

He had to do something to deter the Mover's aim in the next few seconds.

In one fluid motion he unbuckled his seatbelt and scrambled further back inside the Cobra, leaving the vehicle driverless. Raul screamed, a cry of surprise that ripped through the cabin. King snatched up the closest pair of M32 launchers and dove for the porthole. No further action was necessary other than looping a finger in each trigger guard and firing. He'd made sure the launchers were primed and ready for use back at José's compound.

There were six 40mm grenades in each launcher.

He stuck both barrels out the top of the Cobra, aimed in the general direction of the Movers' barricade, and pumped each trigger until both weapons clicked empty.

Twelve total rounds, fired in the space of a couple of seconds. It was highly unlikely that all would hit their mark, but that wasn't King's intention.

Hopefully, enough chaos had been caused by the sudden barrage of explosives that the Mover with the RPG would hesitate.

King made it back into the driver's seat mere seconds after leaving it, discarding both empty launchers on the way through. He felt his chest vibrate as the grenades hit home, detonating against the sides of cars and thunking into the concrete dock. Raul's eyes boggled in his skull at the sight.

King had no time to admire his handiwork.

They were a few dozen feet away from impact.

He saw the cluster of vehicles ahead rushing up to meet them. The Cobra would crush through the blockade at any moment. After that, there was no telling what would happen. King lurched to get his seatbelt back on, at the same time realising he had miscalculated a few things. The impact would be beyond devastating. But there was no time to back out now.

'No, no, no,' Raul whispered, gripping the sides of his seat as tight as he could, knuckles white, sweat dripping off his brow.

'*Fuck*,' was all King had time to say before the Cobra obliterated the vehicles in its wake.

The collision shook him far worse than the impact with the gate. His whole world spun. His vision blurred. The leather over his shoulder bit into his skin with incredible force, sending pain flaring through his chest. The sensory overload incapacitated him, making him unable to work out where they were, whether they were still travelling forward, if they had passed through the barricade or not.

When he got a grip on reality, he instantly realised they were no longer on flat ground.

The Cobra had overturned.

He felt the power behind its enormous bulk as the wheels on the left-hand-side lifted off the concrete. The Cobra had been thrown off-balance by the jarring collision. Carried by its own momentum, the vehicle entered an unstoppable barrel-roll, bursting through the barrier of vehicles. Tearing metal and flying car parts raged all around them. King reached out for any kind of handhold he could find.

His heart thumped hard in his chest. He had no idea whether he would survive the next few seconds. A certain acceptance occurred when a situation was thrown into the hands of fate. There was nothing he could do but hold on for dear life and hope that the Cobra came to rest somewhere safe.

He saw nothing but a blur as the vehicle rolled. Its ceiling slammed into the dock, sending all the loose weapons in the cabin flying. Then it rolled again. King managed a single fleeting glance out the windscreen and bit his tongue out of shock.

They would roll over the lip of the dock.

'Come on!' he screamed, urging the Cobra to carry enough momentum to bridge the gap. If it dropped into the space between the port and the cruise ship, they would be trapped in a watery grave.

'Oh my God,' Raul said.

There came the familiar stomach drop as the Cobra rolled off the dock and became airborne. Raul screamed. King grit his teeth. Both scenarios that could possibly unfold would carry consequences with them. He hadn't expected them to end up in this situation. Either they would fall into the ocean, or hit the side of the cruise ship still upside-down.

Accompanied by a sound similar to a bomb going off in his ears, King felt the Cobra plough into the ship's exterior.

With twenty-six thousand pounds of weight behind it, the vehicle simply demolished the wall. It tumbled inside the ship, buckling steel and destroying plaster and wood and furniture. Under its bulk, the floor of the room they entered gave out. King's stomach dropped for the second time in the space of the minute as the Cobra fell a storey.

It came to rest on its side, surrounded by debris and destruction.

King slammed against his seatbelt. His neck whipped back. He struck the back of his head against the hard plastic casing of the driver's seat and his vision blurred. He let his arms dangle as he struggled to bring his heart rate under control, still suspended by the leather across his chest.

He coughed hard and took a deep breath.

They were alive.

He glanced across and saw Raul still straining to hold onto his seat. His eyes were squeezed firmly shut. His face was a pale, sweaty mask.

'We're okay,' King said, more to reassure himself than Raul.

Raul opened his eyes and looked around. 'What the hell…'

'Are you hurt?'

'I don't know.'

'Adrenalin?'

Raul nodded. King understood the feeling. Seconds after preparing to meet death, the man was so hopped up with nervous energy that it made assessing his wellbeing next to impossible. He could have a plethora of broken bones and still feel fine for the next few minutes.

'But you can move?'

'I think so.'

'Let's get the hell out of this thing. We're nowhere near out of this.'

Compared to the insanity of the port, the eerie silence inside the cruise ship unnerved King. He unbuckled his belt and dropped against the side of the interior, resting one foot against the cracked windscreen. Then he helped Raul out of his seat. The man's hands shook uncontrollably. King didn't blame him.

From somewhere outside, he heard the muffled din of conflict raging. The exchanging of gunfire. The reverberations of grenade blasts.

'What's happening out there?' Raul said as they clambered along the Cobra's interior. 'Who's attacking Rico?'

'I'm just as confused as you are,' King said. 'But let's focus on what we need to do. We have all the time in the world to work that out later.'

'It's a convenient distraction, at least,' Raul said.

King sifted through the mess of objects scattered across the floor of the Cobra. All the loose items had been churned around the interior like a washing machine during the roll. He found a fully loaded HK417. He looped the strap over his shoulder and slotted a finger into the trigger guard. For extra caution, he stuck a couple of spare magazines into his rear pockets.

That would do.

Overloading himself with an arsenal of weaponry would be ineffective at such close quarters. A single high-powered assault rifle was adequate.

Raul picked up an identical gun with a curious look on his face. King assumed the man had zero training with modern weaponry and counted him out of whatever lay ahead. If he wanted to eliminate Rico, he would have to do it himself.

They clambered out of the hole in the Cobra's ceiling, which now rested on its side. King observed the scene around them.

Their entrance had caused substantial damage. The roof over their heads had been mangled beyond belief, taking the full brunt of an armoured vehicle before giving way. They had come to rest in what appeared to be one of the dining rooms, a long low space with tiles the colour of oatmeal and walls the colour of mahogany. Identical circular tables covered in white cloths spanned all the way up to a deserted dance floor and bar. The furniture within a dozen-foot radius of the Cobra had either been smashed into oblivion or thrown across the room with considerable force. The vehicle had left a trail of destruction in its wake.

Meals hadn't been served in the premises for what looked to be years. Dust lay over everything. King felt the structure groan around him and began to get a sense of just how large the ship truly was. Simply finding a Mover in this gargantuan maze would be a sizeable task.

He searched for an exit door and found one. An empty doorway, leading into a narrow corridor that spiralled away into the bowels of the ship. It was as good a place to start as any. He took a step in that direction.

Then he looked again and realised the doorway was occupied after all.

Rico stood in the lee of the hallway outside, staring at them with unmasked surprise on his face. He must have seen their catastrophic entrance with his own eyes. The coincidental nature of his location hadn't given King enough time to react properly. He found himself a beat slower than usual. Which put him in a messy situation.

Rico levelled a pistol at his head at the same time that he brought the own barrel of his HK417 up. No-one fired. Both men had a subtle awareness of each other's talent, an unspoken recognition that each of their reflexes were honed enough to ensure two deaths if either one fired.

'Well, that was a coincidence, wasn't it?' Rico said, his voice echoing through the empty room.

CHAPTER 43

King didn't respond. Raul had frozen with his barrel aimed at the floor, not fast enough to be involved in the stand-off. He observed the situation with shaky hands — aware that one wrong move would set off a chain reaction that would kill all three of them in a hail of bullets.

Rico smiled devilishly. His teeth were still blood-stained. A filthy bandage had been wrapped tight around one of his trouser legs. He was visibly keeping his weight off it. Heavy bags rested under the man's eyes. It seemed like he hadn't slept since King had seen him last. The stress was leeching from his bones.

Something was off.

'I see José got you to deliver my truck for him,' Rico noted, keeping up the facade of superiority. 'Awfully kind of you.'

'It's not much use now,' King said. 'What are you doing down here?'

'We keep some heavy weapons down in these rooms,' Rico said. 'Looks like we need them.'

King flicked his head back, motioning to the dock outside. 'Seems like we got here just ahead of someone else. Who's attacking you?'

'From what I saw, it seems to be our closest competitors.'

'Is that a surprise?'

'It is,' he admitted. 'We will crush them, though.'

'Timing's awfully convenient.'

'Exactly what I was thinking,' Rico said. 'It seems they've paid you a healthy sum to be the spearhead.'

'We haven't been paid anything.'

'I'm sure…'

'Can we reach a truce?' King said. 'My friend here wants his mother and sister back. Give them to us, and we'll leave you alone. Then you can deal with whatever the hell just happened out there.'

Rico laughed cruelly. 'Really? You think I'd do that? The second I lower this gun you'll shoot me in the head. I don't blame you. I'd do the exact same to you.'

'I—'

With his free hand Rico raised a finger. 'No. Don't even try. I know exactly what's going on in your head. You're furious that I killed your friend in El Infierno. You're hiding it very well, but you hate me with a passion. I'm dead the second I consider trusting you.'

King didn't say anything in return, because the man was right. 'So what happens now?'

'We're in a bit of a situation, aren't we?'

'We are.'

'I have other matters to tend to.'

'You're not going anywhere.'

'You sure about that?'

'Pretty sure. Tell me one thing.'

'What's that?'

King paused for a moment, trying to wrap his head around how much chaos had unfolded over the last few days. 'Why put me through all this shit?'

Rico cocked his head.

'Why bother?' King said. 'You could have just shot me in the head back before any of this took place. Why'd you throw me in El Infierno to try and get answers out of me? I ruined your whole operation. Now you're under attack. You're injured. Everything's scrambled. You could have killed me quickly and moved on.'

Rico nodded along, as if agreeing with everything King was saying. 'I needed to let out a little rage. I wanted to watch you suffer.'

'That didn't go so well for you.'

'I underestimated you. Truth is — you weren't the sole cause of the breakdown of communications with our supplier.

They were offended that we didn't show up to the meeting. They threw insults at how we operate. So I slaughtered the pair they sent to meet us. That's why everything's gone to shit. Because I can't control my temper.'

'Wait,' King said. 'So it's your own fault?'

Rico nodded and grinned. 'Still, you were the perfect fall-back to take out my frustrations on. I would have imploded otherwise.'

'Because I was in the wrong place at the wrong time?'

'I thought you might be working for one of my competitors for a while. But even when I started to realise that it was an almighty coincidence, I kept you in there. Just for fun. Degrading you gave me that release.'

'Guess you didn't expect me to adapt as well as I did.'

'I can't say I did,' Rico said, and shrugged. 'But you didn't adapt to this very well. What's the plan after you kill me?'

'Find Raul's family. Get out of here.'

'Good luck. You'll never make it out of this shipyard. Either we'll kill you, or our competitors will.'

'You seem pretty sure of yourself.'

'And before either of those scenarios unfold—' Rico said, '—I'll kill your family anyway, Raul.'

As he finished the sentence, he spun on his heel and pushed off with his good leg, taking off down the corridor. King had half a second to get a shot off, but he wasn't fast enough. He fired twice. The bullets thudded into the hallway's far wall, hitting nothing but wood.

And then Rico was gone.

CHAPTER 44

King took off across the empty dining room, determined to stop Rico before any harm could be done. He heard Raul puffing behind him, following close. If Raul happened upon any more dead family members...

King couldn't imagine the emotional consequences.

He let anger spur him forward. He kept a double-handed grip on the HK417, knowing that there was every chance Rico would be waiting on the other side of the doorway. It would only take one brash step too far to have his brains blown across the opposite wall.

Raul took the bait. He brushed past King, moving with the urgency of a man desperate to keep his family alive.

Exactly what Rico wanted.

King snatched him by the collar and tugged him back, stopping him from hurtling to certain death. As he did so, Raul reacted viciously, turning and swinging a fist in King's direction. Furious that someone was preventing him from rescuing his mother and sister.

King dodged the wild outburst with ease and tightened his grip. He kept Raul locked in place, despite the man's best efforts to break free.

'Are you that fucking stupid?' King snarled. 'You'll get yourself killed.'

He saw the raw emotion in Raul's eyes and grimaced. The guy was in a bad place. King wasn't sure if he could control him, even if he had the man's best interests at heart.

'Let me go,' Raul spat. 'Mamá's up there. Ana's up there.'

'He'll shoot you dead if you stay this reckless. I will do everything I can to get them back. But stay behind me. Okay?'

The tension dissipated and Raul nodded, overcoming the brief flood of urgency. King shoved the man behind him and re-adjusted his grip on the assault rifle.

He pressed forward.

The corridor was silent as they approached it. Either Rico was long gone, or he lay in wait just within the entrance, barrel aimed at the doorway. King tip-toed up to the gap until he could see a narrow sliver of the floor on each side, shrouded in shadow. He guessed the power had been cut years ago. Faint glimmers of natural light crept their way in, but apart from that the decrepit hallway was dark.

King took a deep breath, then fired a ten-round burst into the corridor. The muzzle flash lit up the space like a fireworks display. A violent outburst of sound ripped through the space.

359

It would make anyone flinch. He charged in after the shots, using the shock value to advantage. His reflexes would never be sharper than they were now. He took in the length of the corridor in a single glance. Knowing he had the speed advantage on anyone. Knowledge acquired through countless scenarios identical to the one King currently found himself in. Scenarios where he always managed to come out on top.

But no targets presented themselves.

The corridor lay empty. It stretched into the distance, descending into total darkness until the very end, where a beacon of artificial light illuminated what seemed to be a large stairwell. He narrowed his eyes, squinting at the blurry sight. A shadow briefly passed over the light, dimming it for a moment.

Shit.

Rico hadn't been bluffing. He'd made it to the stairwell despite his injuries. He would be en route to Raul's mother and sister, ascending the steps as fast as his wounded leg would allow. If King had simply charged headlong into the corridor, he probably would have caught the man by now.

'You were right, Raul,' he said, and took off at a breakneck pace.

He knew with each step he was gaining ground on the injured Rico. It all came down to whether he could close the distance before the man reached Raul's family.

He heard Raul's panicked breathing behind him as he tried to keep pace. The noise quickly shrank into the distance. Not many men could match King's speed when he put everything he had into it.

The benefit of having long legs, he thought.

Which proved disastrous as he burst out into the stairwell.

He entered a rusting, winding stairway with a gaping hole in the centre, drilling through the ship's mass all the way to the basement. The stairs themselves curved around the exterior of the space, ascending past dozens of different floors home to cabins, entertainment centres and supply areas. The stairwell seemed to be the hub of activity in the cruise ship, connecting all its various parts together. King burst onto the wide staircase at full pelt, and instantly realised his mistake.

A long metal object flashed across his vision. Before he could react, it powered into his ribs. The blow cracked across his sternum with enough weight behind it to cause serious damage. He ran straight into it like a fool, adding power to its impact.

He coughed and groaned at the same time that he was thrown off his feet. He landed on his side, hard. Rolled once. Slammed into the stairwell's banister — the only thing separating him from a twenty-storey fall to inevitable death. The HK417 fell off his shoulder and skittered away. He watched it disappear under the banister and cascade into oblivion. Just like that, he'd been disarmed.

He came to rest against the wooden railing with burning pain flaring through his abdomen. He looked up, expecting to see Rico standing over him, snarling in victory, aiming a pistol at his forehead, ready to fire the kill shot.

But it wasn't Rico.

It was Roman.

The man from the police station, who had grilled him on his intentions and then vanished when his cover had been blown. King had assumed he worked for Rico in some capacity. This confirmed it. He'd cleaned himself up since departing the holding cells. He was dressed in a tight-fitting long-sleeved shirt and khaki combat trousers. His long hair remained tied back. He held a steel crowbar in one hand. A Zamorana pistol rested in a leather holster at his waist.

King pointed to it, and spoke softly. Still in incredible pain from the rib shot. 'You should probably use that.'

Roman smiled and raised the crowbar, its jagged metal tip gleaming under the stairwell's spotlights. 'No need. This will do.'

'Do you know what's going on out in the shipyard?' King said. 'Killing me won't achieve anything. You won't make it off this ship.'

'Of course I know what's going on out there,' Roman said. 'And it's the only reason I'm going to make it off this ship.'

'What?'

'Who do you think I am?'

King cocked his head. 'You work for Rico. You're a Mover. That's why you interrogated me in the holding cells. You needed to know if I was working for your competition.'

Roman let out a harsh laugh. It echoed through the stairwell. He crouched down until his face rested a few inches from King's.

'I am the competition,' he snarled.

'Oh.'

'Those men out there are my men.'

'You're attacking Rico?'

'I am.'

'How'd you get in here?'

'Very carefully. Something you clearly know little about. I guess I never considered driving an armoured truck through the wall.'

Something clicked in King's mind. 'Ah. That would explain the scouts.'

'Scouts?'

'We were spotted on the way in by a couple of men decked out in tactical gear. In an apartment complex. I thought they were Movers, but they were yours, weren't they? Assessing the situation before attacking?'

Roman nodded.

King flashed back to the holding cells, where Roman had revealed a shred of his true identity. 'You said you were in the import-export business?'

Roman got back to his feet and held his arms out wide, gesturing to their surroundings, to the cruise ship itself. 'Business is booming. At least, it will be. When we have control of this place.'

King made to get to his feet but his ribs flared, buckling his knees. The pain sent him straight back to the floor. Roman noticed the gesture and whipped forward like a cheetah, moving faster than King thought possible. He lashed out with the crowbar, then stopped the blow short. The tip came to rest an inch from King's throat. Another ounce of movement and Roman would sever arteries. King understood the message and stayed put.

'How'd it feel to be played?' Roman said.

'What?'

'We used you.'

'Who used me?'

'I got a call from my business partner before,' he said. 'Asking if we should send you in before we made our move.'

King grimaced. 'Oh, shit.'

Suddenly, the mad situation began to make a little more sense. He'd wondered why José had been so open to handing across most of his expensive arsenal. The Cobra had never been intended for Rico. It had been ordered and primed to carry out an assault on the Movers' compound. The tales José had told them of fleeing the country, of being sick of the life of an arms dealer and deciding to retire.

All bullshit.

He and Roman had been amassing their forces to launch the attack when King and Raul had broken out of prison and stepped willingly into their warehouse. José had seen an opportunity to use two martyrs free of charge, desperate men willing to act as a spearhead for the assault which now raged outside.

Roman saw him thinking hard, and didn't speak. He knew King would be piecing together what had happened.

'You're drug dealers?' King said.

'Small time,' Roman said. 'Movers were shutting us down at every corner. This is the endgame. We win this, and we take over.'

'If I'm not mistaken,' King said. 'It appears that we both have the same short-term goals.'

'Kill Rico?'

King nodded.

'We do indeed,' Roman said. 'But then what?'

'What do you mean?'

'Say we work together to clear this cruise ship,' Roman said. 'And we succeed. What will you do after?'

'Get the next flight out of here.'

'You sure? I thought you hated drug dealers.'

'Is that what you think this is? Me being here?'

'You seem to be some kind of vigilante warrior. What else would you be doing here?'

'If this was a crusade against organised crime I would never sleep,' King said. 'I just don't like it when people fuck with me.'

'So you don't care that I'm just going to carry on the drug trade after we're done here?'

'Not in the slightest,' King said.

'Then I think we have a deal.'

Roman extended a hand. He tucked the crowbar behind his back as a gesture of camaraderie. Probably to show that he meant no harm. King seized the grip and rose tentatively to his feet. He placed a hand on his ribs and took a deep breath. Agony flared. A few were likely broken. Not good. But it wasn't on the level of crippling incapacitation that meant he couldn't continue. The adrenalin dump was still powering through his system. It numbed the pain just enough to press forward for a few more minutes.

That was all he had.

Then he thought back to the last few days, and met Roman's eyes. 'What were you doing in the police station, then?'

Roman smiled. 'We have connections too. José still supplies the Movers. They had no idea he'd embedded himself in a rival organisation. When he found out that the internal mechanisms of their operation had gone to shit, he did some digging. Found out that you had something to do with it. So I went in to try and find out just exactly what was going on.'

'And you realised I was a nobody?'

Roman nodded. 'I did.'

'And you left me there to be transferred to El Infierno and killed by either Rico or the prisoners?'

Roman hesitated. 'I—'

'On second thought,' King said, 'I don't need your help.'

CHAPTER 45

He seized Roman by the collar with one hand and battered the crowbar away with the other. His ribs burned with every action, but he held an uncanny ability to bury pain away for brief spurts of violent explosive action. His brain released neurotransmitters — called endogenous opioids — into his system, suppressing the emotional response to his aching torso. He battled through the physical sensation and continued with his actions, his brain an impenetrable fortress.

Roman's eyes widened as he noted the change in atmosphere. He'd been disarmed in a matter of seconds. He recognised that King had been holding back, refraining from retaliation over the course of their conversation.

The drug boss had underestimated him.

King reached down and undid the holster at the man's waist and ripped the Zamorana free. He touched a finger to the trigger, slotting it inside the guard. One shot was all it took. The bullet entered the side of Roman's skull just above his ear. Compared to the intensity of assault-rifle and sub-machine gun fire that King had grown used to, the round from the pistol felt surprisingly subdued. Roman died quietly, blood spurting from the exit wound on the other side of his head. An instantaneous passing. Probably what the man deserved, considering how little he had provoked King.

Still…

One less crime boss in the world.

King kept the corpse on its feet with the hand he had wrapped around its collar. He took one look at the dead man, and felt no emotion. Roman had said it himself. If he took over the shipyard, nothing would change. Maybe this would do something. Probably not. But King was only a single man.

And he didn't like to be fucked with.

He wound up and tossed the dead body over the banister. It fell into the empty space in the centre of the stairwell and soared away, legs and arms splayed. King turned back to the corridor he'd come from and ignored the brutal *squelch* of the body slapping the ground floor that echoed up through the space.

Raul had emerged from one of the side rooms, still brandishing his own rifle. The HK417's stock rested on his shoulder. His eyes were wide. He'd been ready to fire.

'All clear,' King said.

'I wasn't sure if he saw me,' Raul said. 'I ducked into the room. I was about to shoot him when I heard you two speaking. Some kind of truce?'

'Not anymore.'

Raul glanced at the railing that the body had disappeared over. 'Clearly not.'

'Where is Rico likely to be?'

Raul's face paled. 'I … I don't know. Upstairs. I know he has an office up there somewhere.' He trailed off, staring into space, eyes tearing. 'Fuck, man … what if we don't find him? What if they're dead?'

King slapped him across the face — distracting him from *what-ifs* — and took his rifle. 'We don't know that yet. Until we do, pull yourself together. He could be anywhere.'

The pair took off running, taking the stairs three at a time, ascending the gargantuan stairwell. Around them, the structure groaned. The opioids still flooding into King masked the pain in his ribs just enough to enable full function. They would wear off eventually, and then the waves of agony would begin. He would have to move fast.

As they ran, King felt a sense of dread creeping into his chest. Whether from the eerie sounds of the long-dormant cruise ship and the unnerving nature of their surroundings, or the fact that they were likely heading for a pair of dead bodies that would change Raul's life. King hoped to hell that there would be a different outcome. He couldn't imagine losing everyone dear to him in the course of a single day.

Their rasping breath echoed off the steel walls. There were no other sounds except for the clanging of their feet against the steps. If Rico was around, he would hear them coming from a mile away, but they had no time to employ the benefits of a stealthy approach. Roman's interference had cost them what little time they had.

It had also raised a dozen new questions.

If José is running a rival gang, then what on earth was he doing visiting Raul's family?

There wasn't time to mull over the technicalities. They could do that later. King shot a glance down one of the many corridors branching off the stairwell, just as he had done for the last dozen. All were entirely unoccupied. The sheer size of the ship began to dawn on him. There could be an army of Movers living within and there would be little chance of him stumbling upon one of them.

Then he noticed a flash of movement heading through a doorway. It occurred at the edge of his peripheral vision. Someone darting into a room. A leg disappearing from sight.

'There,' King said quietly, and exited the stairwell into a corridor that was well into the process of falling apart. There was much more natural light up here. It poured in through the windows in each room, which he guessed faced out over the shipyard. He assumed the movement he'd seen had been Rico, darting into his office or personal living quarters.

He kept the HK417 trained on the space in front of him. Any sudden movements would warrant a reaction the instant he recognised them as hostile. He approached the doorway very slowly. Raul stayed behind him, quiet as a mouse, his heart more than likely pounding in his chest. The next few seconds would answer a lot.

King tapped into his reflexes, recalling memories of hundreds of hostage rescue situations he'd been through in the past. He knew how shaky the situations were. One stray bullet would spell complete failure. Raul would be even more devastated if King accidentally shot a loved one in the process of trying to save them.

He would not let that happen.

He paused by the doorway and listened for any sounds from within.

Nothing.

He took a deep breath. Employed tunnel vision. Checked Raul's position, verifying that he was out of the line of fire. Then he spun into the room as fast as he could, taking in all his surroundings in the blink of an eye, sizing up the threats…

… of which there were none.

Rico sat on the surface of an enormous oak desk in the middle of the large room. Behind him, floor-to-ceiling windows revealed a balcony that faced out over the shipyard. Far below, battle raged. King heard it in the form of relentless gunfire and saw a few dozen muzzle flashes, flaring over the dock. Small figures darted to and fro amidst the haphazard cover that had been erected in the form of spare vehicles.

No battle raged in the room.

Because Rico was unarmed.

He sat cross-legged, staring at them with a resigned smile of acceptance.

'What?' he said as the two of them entered the room.

He was the room's sole occupant. There was no sign of Raul's mother, or his sister. No sign of other Movers.

Rico noticed them searching the room for signs of life and laughed cruelly.

'Oh,' he said, and raised a finger in Raul's direction, pointing at him. 'That's right. Your dearest loved ones. Did you really think I ever had them?'

Cold silence descended over the room.

CHAPTER 46

'Where are they?' Raul whispered, his voice cold.

Rico waved a hand around the room. 'Not here. They never were.'

'Where are they?' Raul repeated.

Rico made to answer, and then noticed something. He stared long and hard at the HK417 King had trained on him, barrel pointed directly at the drug lord's face. He paused, thinking. Then his eyes widened. 'José sold you that?'

'He didn't sell us anything,' King said. 'He used us to front the assault out there. Turns out he's in bed with your competition. He was never loyal to you.'

Rico turned and looked out the window at the carnage below. He shook his head, almost in disbelief. 'No shit. So that's what brought me down. Crazy world.'

'It's over, Rico,' King said. 'Just tell us where you're keeping them.'

Rico turned back to them. 'Oh — you don't get it?'

'Get what?'

'José isn't loyal to anyone. Especially not you.'

'How so?' King said.

Rico looked past him, locking eyes with Raul, speaking directly to him. 'Who do you think I sent to kill your mother and sister yesterday? The man who knew them. Who trusted them. That way it was easy. They just went along with everything he told them to do. They happily followed him to the middle of nowhere. Then he shot them. And I paid him well for it.'

Before King could process the new information, he heard a thump behind him. He turned, keeping Rico in his sight the entire time. He saw Raul on the floor, his legs buckled, his face whiter than King had ever seen it before.

The man's feet had given out from underneath him as he heard the news.

Raul stared at Rico with more hate than King thought humanly possible. The man had been clinging to a shred of hope the entire time. Now it was gone. He'd lost everyone close to him. He was struggling to process it.

He would be for a while.

King's stomach sank and he turned back to Rico, who leered at the utter hopelessness of their situation. He relished their failure. Even though his operation had been destroyed, he'd still had the last laugh.

'Why don't you put the gun down?' he said to King. 'Why don't we settle this man to man? You seem eager to hurt me. Do it with your fists. I didn't get the opportunity to prove myself in El Infierno. You caught me by surprise. Let's see who really would come out on top.'

'You'd like that, wouldn't you?' King said.

'I would.'

'The two of us settling our score the old-fashioned way?'

'Exactly.'

'Shame this isn't the movies.'

He unloaded thirty rounds into Rico's skull and chest and stomach and legs. The man was dead within three shots, but King continued to hold the trigger down, letting out the anger flooding his veins. The shots tore through soft skin and sent geysers of blood arcing across the room. As Rico fell back over the desk, carried by the momentum of the shots, an automatic pistol spilled out of his belt. He'd had a hand around the weapon. Even in his last moments, he'd tried to manipulate King.

King had decided he wouldn't give him the chance.

Blood swished over the surface of the desk, spilling across the oak. Emptying the clip of such a powerful weapon in the confined space would normally result in temporary hearing loss, but King had found himself in the midst of such an incomprehensible amount of automatic weapons fire over the last hour that for a moment he wasn't sure if his hearing would ever properly return.

With Rico dead, the only sound in the room came from Raul. A helpless sobbing, racked with pain and dread. King turned and crouched and rested a hand on the man's shoulder.

'Hey.'

The man was inconsolable. He stared vacantly at the ground, completely tuned out. King gripped his shoulder a little harder.

'*Hey,*' he said again.

Raul looked up, his eyes bloodshot, his lip quivering. He was a mess.

'It's going to feel like your whole world has ended,' King said. 'But it hasn't. It's going to be hell for months. I've seen almost all of my close friends die on the battlefield. It feels like everything is pointless and that you'll never recover and that there's no point to living anymore, so why not just join them? I've had the same exact thoughts. And I'm telling you … it gets better. Okay?'

Raul said nothing. King didn't expect him to. In this moment there would be absolutely nothing that would change the way he felt. But hopefully, somewhere down the line, he could begin to move on.

King knew he could.

He was tough. Tough enough to survive a gruelling spell in one of Venezuela's toughest prisons. He would get through this. Some way. Somehow.

King scooped a hand under Raul's arm and hauled him to his feet. The man could grieve when they were safe. Right now, they were still in a warzone.

He started to reach for Raul's pants leg with his other hand, about to switch to a fireman's carry, unsure if he could support himself.

'I can walk,' Raul whispered.

King nodded and let go of him. He needed his space.

King gathered the empty HK417 and pulled a fresh round of his rear pocket. He ejected the old magazine and slammed another thirty-round clip home.

They'd need it if they hoped to make it through a gang war alive.

Before they left the room, he took one last look out Rico's office window at the shootout still unfolding on the shipyard's dock. If José was down there somewhere, King would make sure he ripped the man's throat out for what he'd done. He'd slaughtered Raul's family in cold-blood at the request of a man who he planned to usurp, and then used Raul and King like pawns to ensure he achieved his own self-interests.

King tightened a finger around the HK's trigger and made for the stairwell.

The corridor was desolate. It seemed every Mover in the vicinity was out on the dock, attempting to stem the wave of attackers. Likely failing, given Roman and José's effective strategy. Even King hadn't wised up to how he was being manipulated.

Raul followed him down the corridor and out into the stairwell. As King stepped into the space, he turned to descend.

And found three automatic weapons aimed his way.

All three men were Spanish. Two were thugs, sporting similar neck tattoos and wearing sleeveless vests that exposed muscular arms devoid of fat. The veins running along their forearms bulged as they clutched their weapons. They were high off the thrill of combat.

King wondered if they were Movers, and considered the possibility that their gun barrels might be the last sight he ever saw.

Then his gaze drifted to the third man, who noted King and Raul's presence with a satisfied nod of acknowledgement.

José.

CHAPTER 47

'Nice to see you two again,' he said. Then he noted the expression on Raul's face, and paused. 'What happened?'

'What the hell do you think happened?' King said.

He kept his rifle remained pointed at the ground, and there it would stay. If he tried to raise it in the midst of such a tense standoff, he would wind up dotted with lead. That was an outcome he would prefer to avoid.

'We made it through the Movers' forces,' José said. 'We came up here to kill Rico.'

'Way ahead of you,' King said.

He screamed internally. He'd never been so determined to make an attempt on a man's life until now. José deserved nothing more than a shallow grave.

'Are you surprised I'm still here?' José said. His voice stayed composed. Calm. Rational.

'Things clicked a while ago,' King said. 'Your partner is dead.'

'Roman's dead?' José said, and for a moment he bowed his head. 'We knew the risks trying something like this. Casualties were inevitable.'

'Was he close to you?'

'We were close, yes.'

'Good. I threw him over a railing. If you go down twenty storeys you might see what's left of his body.'

José paused. Blood rushed to his face. A vein protruded from his forehead. 'Why the fuck would you do that?'

'That's rich coming from you.'

'What do you mean?'

'We know what you did,' King said. 'Raul's family. You piece of shit.'

José's eyes widened as he recognised what was causing Raul such distress. 'Oh, of course... I assume Rico told you I killed them?'

King heard a noise behind him, like a foot scuffing along the ground. He realised that Raul was about to explode off his feet, making a suicidal charge. King held out a hand, open-palmed, urging the man to stay put. It would be no use killing himself while trying to avenge his family.

Raul stayed put.

At least for now.

'I'm not the monster you think I am,' José said.

'Oh?' King said.

'It's true that I used you,' José said. 'I saw an opportunity to create a distraction that would help us in our attack. So if you want to argue that I recklessly threw you into the firing line, then fine. But it was your choice to come here. You were going to do it, no matter what I said. If I'd turned you away, you would have found another way to carry out an attack. I could see it in your eyes the second you stepped foot on my property. So yes, I lied to you. And yes, I deal drugs. I enjoy money. I provide a service to the addicts of Maiquetía that a million other people just like me would be happy to do. And I lied to my main client and used the inside knowledge he provided of his operation to approach the competition and plan a takeover of his business. If you have a problem with that, then go right ahead and kill me. I'll give you my own gun to do so. But I'm not a heartless fiend.'

'You took his family away and shot them in cold blood,' King said. 'How can you possibly be trying to defend yourself?'

'Because that's not what happened.'

'That's what Rico said.'

'Of course it is. That's the story I told him.'

King paused. 'What?'

'Why do you think my number was in their apartment?'

'Because you were helping them. And they trusted you. Which is why Rico told you to kill them. Because it would be easy.'

'You're right. It would have been, if I'd decided to.'

Raul let out a whimper. It was a guttural noise filled with confusion and an underlying tone of hope. Maybe there was a possibility that...

'I swear to fucking God,' King said, 'that if you're lying to us, I'll personally rip your head off.'

'Use common sense,' José said. 'If I really was the person you think I am, I'd have shot you the second I saw you. It wouldn't have taken much effort. In fact, I'm still tempted to. You killed my business partner. And a close friend.'

'A close friend who left me to die in the worst prison in the country.'

'Noted,' José said. 'Which is why I'm letting you live. All's fair in war. But now the war's over. Most of the Movers are dead. We control the shipyard. We'll comb the city over the next few weeks and pick off the rest. But that's none of your concern. If you want to wage a war against drug gangs in Venezuela, you'll be here for the rest of your life.'

'That's not my concern,' King said.

'Good,' José said. 'Rico was your concern. Now he's dead. Raul's family was your concern. So here you are...'

He reached into his back pocket. King hesitated, tensing up. If José came out with a gun, he would raise his own HK417 and unload. It would create a blazing roar of gunfire from all sides and every man in the stairwell would die in the crossfire.

But it was better than José having the last laugh. This way, his forces would be leaderless. They would fall apart. Their meticulous planning would have all been for nothing.

King would die, but he would die satisfied.

But José did not produce a weapon. He produced a keychain. Four indistinguishable gold keys were attached to it alongside a plastic replica bullet.

'What is this?' King said.

José looked at him long and hard. 'I trust you.'

'You shouldn't.'

'I know I shouldn't. But I do. Which is why I'm giving you these.'

He tossed the set of keys over. King took a hand off the HK417 — foolish in hindsight — and caught them. José could have shot him right then. Caught him off guard. Put a round through his skull. Finish the job.

But he didn't.

'Once again,' King said. 'What is this?'

'Those are the keys to my house.'

'Why the hell are you giving me the keys to your house?'

'There's a couple of people staying there that Raul needs to see.'

King's eyes widened. He made to respond, then thought better of it. He simply nodded. If what José told him was true, then King could most definitely see the situation from his perspective. In fact, most of his actions were entirely forgivable if Raul's family were indeed unharmed.

'Now,' José said. 'You saw what happened downstairs. There's a lot of clean-up to do. There's a lot of connections to make. The hard work's just beginning for me. But you two get out of here. I don't want any trouble from you, and you don't want any trouble from me. Understood?'

King didn't bother trying to wrap his head around the allegiances and power plays and double-crossings and gang wars. He couldn't care less. If Raul's family were truly safe, then his work was done. The gangsters who'd thrown him around a corrupt prison system were dead. He'd found his revenge.

It was over.

He lowered his weapon, and José's thugs did the same.

'You have my number?' José said.

King nodded.

'Give me a call when you get there. We can straighten things out. Gate code is "8380".'

King nodded again.

José produced a scrap of paper from one of the deep pockets in his khaki trousers. He handed it over. An address was scrawled in ballpoint pen on its surface.

'Let's go, Raul,' King said.

He brushed past the three men in front of him and began the descent. Raul followed swiftly behind. He hurried after King, his pace fast. Probably reinvigorated with newfound hope and promise.

'King,' he whispered. 'Do you really think…?'

'We'll find out,' King said.

CHAPTER 48

They made it out of the shipyard without a shred of protest.

José had clearly informed his forces that King and Raul were not to be interfered with. King kept his HK417 looped over his shoulder just in case any of the gangsters hadn't received the message, yet they were met with no resistance whatsoever. In fact, none of José's forces even bothered to acknowledge their existence. They were busy dealing with the aftermath of the gunfight.

As King crossed the newly erected drawbridge connecting the cruise ship to the port, he surveyed the dock and noted the result of the conflict.

The Movers had lost.

Badly.

José's forces had taken casualties, but that was inevitable. A few of their men lay injured or dead, in the process of being tended to by their comrades. Stress and worry plagued the faces of the gangsters.

King imagined it had been a tense morning for them.

As they passed through a surreal scene littered with the bodies of dead gangsters, some completely torn to shreds by bullets, he pondered what an unbelievable sight it would be to a common civilian. Even a man like Raul — raised on the streets and wise to combat and the brutal conditions of a no-holds-barred prison — struggled to process the swathes of destruction across the port.

King knew it was bad that he felt right at home amongst the carnage.

His pulse barely rose as he glanced from body to body. He simply assessed the dead with cold calculation, scanning for threats. There were none. Every man still alive was preoccupied with other tasks. They would leave undisturbed.

He led Raul to one of the pick-up trucks on the very edge of the Movers' barricade. It had taken the least amount of gunfire. Its rusting chassis had been dotted with only a few stray rounds. He hoped it still worked. He climbed into the driver's seat and checked the ignition. The keys were there, jammed into the slot. Clearly the Movers had figured that there was no use securing the cars. If enemy forces managed to hijack them, then they would probably be dead by that point anyway.

Raul got in next to him and tugged the passenger's seatbelt across his chest. He stared straight ahead. Muted. Untalkative. King guessed all his energy was focused on the thought of his mother and sister greeting him with open arms.

He hoped that the man's wishes would come true.

He started the truck and drove it slowly through the chaos, avoiding living and dead bodies alike. He didn't care what José would do with the shipyard. Like he'd told the man earlier, if drug operations bothered him enough to wage a vigilante crusade, then he would never sleep.

And he needed sleep.

He'd devoted a career to battling injustice. In retirement he'd made the decision to leave those problems to his successors.

That's worked out so well for you so far, he thought.

They exited the shipyard the way they'd come in. The mangled gate had been battered aside by José's forces following them in. They mounted the gravel road and began the slow climb into the hills of Maiquetía.

King held out the scrap of paper. 'You been here before?'

Raul shook his head. 'That's a wealthy neighbourhood. Buried in the hills somewhere. He must have bought the place when he made his fortune. While Luis and I were locked up.'

Talk of his brother clearly drifted his mind onto traumatic thoughts. King saw him shrink up. He turned away to hide his eyes growing damp.

'Your brother was a good man,' King said.

'I know.'

'At least Rico is dead.'

Raul shook his head. 'Doesn't change a thing.'

'I know it doesn't,' King said. 'But it's peace of mind. He won't hurt anyone else.'

'José will just take his place,' Raul said, sounding entirely disillusioned.

'If your old friend is telling us the truth,' King said, 'then maybe he has some humanity. Maybe things will unfold differently with him in charge.'

'We'll see…'

Raul directed him through shanty towns and cramped neighbourhoods and onto a winding road that looped between craggy cliffs of rock dotted with tufts of dead grass. They continued up into the hills, the pick-up's engine chugging as it battled the steep gradient. Finally they entered a neighbourhood that King instantly recognised as upper-class.

Well, at least in comparison to the rest of Maiquetía.

These houses had yards. Most were two-storey, big and sprawling and well-built. King saw sloping terracotta roofs and gated properties complete with security cameras at every turn. He guessed that security systems were paramount in these parts. Anyone with a semblance of fortune would be a target.

According to the address listed, José's property was at the very end of a wide court paved with smooth asphalt. King stopped the pick-up in front of a spacious property complete with a four-car garage and a guesthouse. He let out a low whistle as they got out and approached the steel fence.

'Crime pays,' King said.

'Around here, it sure does,' Raul said.

The man took a deep breath. King rested a hand on his shoulder.

'I just want you to know,' King said. 'Whatever we find … I'm here for you. I'm hesitant to believe José just yet.'

Raul nodded. 'Don't worry. I'm prepared. As prepared as I can be.'

King nodded and punched the code José had given him into a steel panel next to the gate. With a mechanical whir that broke the quiet residential silence the gate swung open. He stepped through into the driveway.

The house seemed deserted. All the windows were drawn. A bird shrieked from a nearby tree. The silence unnerved him. On second thought, he ducked back to the car and retrieved the sole HK417, still fully loaded. Raul watched him move with reserved panic on his face.

'King, what are you doing?'

'Just making sure…' King said. 'José lied to us once already. Better safe than sorry.'

He re-approached the house, mentally alert. He flicked his gaze from window to window, watching for any sign of movement. It was tough. The small mansion had at least a dozen floor-to-ceiling windows facing the wide front yard.

'José's come far from the slums he grew up in,' King said.

'Tell me about it.'

'If he really is a good man,' King said, 'then perhaps he can help you get on your feet.'

'Maybe…'

They approached the front door silently, a huge wooden slab set into a polished stone exterior. King tried every key in the set until one slotted home inside the lock. He twisted and pushed the door open. It groaned on its hinges, cutting through the silence. King grimaced and tip-toed into a marble foyer. He held out a palm, signalling for Raul to stay back. At least for now.

Any element of surprise had just been ruined. If there were hostile forces in the house waiting for them to arrive, they would know exactly where to go.

The foyer was enormous. Its ceiling stretched far overhead, making King feel small. Antique coffee tables lined the walls, adorned with polished vases and exquisite mirrors. It seemed that in his newfound wealth, José had developed fine taste in interior decoration.

Hurried footsteps sounded from an adjacent room. Heading straight for the foyer. Two people, King figured. Possibly

Raul's family. Possibly hired killers. Whatever the case, he couldn't take the chance.

He raised the barrel of his rifle.

A pair of women burst into sight, hurrying through an open set of double doors. Their eyes were wide. They hadn't been expecting visitors. The woman in front had to be in her late twenties. She was beautiful. She kept her long silky hair tied back in a ponytail. She had olive skin and pearly white teeth and a slender figure.

Must be Ana.

The other woman was much older. She was short and mousy with deep wrinkles in her cheekbones signifying a struggle through years of hardship. She stared at King with terror in her eyes. He knew what she was feeling. She had worked so hard to escape her chaotic life. And now there was a tall stranger aiming an automatic weapon at her and her daughter.

King saw the two of them and felt an enormous weight lift off his chest. The constant unease and worry and questioning was gone. The two of them were safe. José had been telling the truth.

He couldn't help but smile with joy. He opened his mouth to speak.

They saw the gun and screamed in unison.

CHAPTER 49

Raul's mother had an instinctual response to the firearm. She first spread her arms out wide, acting as a human shield for her daughter. Even in the tense situation, King admired her courage. Next she charged at him. Her face balled into a mask of anger and she sprinted in an attempt to deter her would-be attacker. If King had hostile attentions, it would have spelt certain death for her. Thankfully, he had no such inclinations.

He stepped aside and tossed the HK417 to the floor. It hit the marble with a loud *clang* and slid across the foyer, coming to rest on the other side of the room. An instant way to diffuse the tension. The old woman stopped immediately and furrowed her brow, confused by the sudden turn of events.

Then Raul stepped through the door and saw them.

At first, nothing happened. The three stood frozen, taking a second to process the sight before them. King made sure to stay out of the way. He did not wish to interrupt such a reunion. Especially after what it had taken to reach this point.

The trio flung themselves together in a tight hug, spilling out a year's worth of emotions. They bowed their heads together and sobbed without restraint, holding each other close, letting the frustration seep away.

King thought better of his position and decided to retreat into one of the adjacent rooms. This was not his moment. He would let them speak. He would let Raul break the news of Luis' demise. He did not wish to loiter awkwardly in the corner and watch events unfold. He had brought the three of them together, and now he would let them become reacquainted in private.

He had a phone call to make.

He stepped into a living room complete with a U-shaped leather sofa and an enormous flat-screen television built into the far wall. More high ceilings. More exquisite decorations. The entire house had a feeling of grandeur to it that directly juxtaposed the grimy warehouse José worked from. King guessed that the man kept his work and home life distinctly separate.

He found what he was looking for in no time. A corded home phone rested on one of the tables just inside the entrance. He picked up the receiver and dialled the number still scrawled on the scrunched-up scrap of paper in his pocket.

José answered on the first ring.

'I assume you worked out I was telling the truth,' he said.

'I did,' King said.

'So there are no hard feelings?'

'I guess not.'

'I'm sorry that I used you for my own interests.'

'Don't worry,' King said, and smiled. 'I would have done the exact same thing.'

'Oh, I know that. I certainly don't doubt what you told me of your past. Not many people could survive what you just attempted. On that note … where the hell is my truck?'

'The Cobra?'

'Yes.'

'I thought I'd park it for you. It's near the ground floor somewhere.'

A pause. King heard José walking on the other end of the line. Then another pause. 'Is that what that enormous hole is in the side of the ship?'

'You're on it.'

'Jesus. That's going to be a hassle to solve.'

'Not my problem. You sent me to die.'

'You sent yourself to die. I covered you in armour to try and avoid that. Let's call it even.'

'I can respect that. I must say — you don't sound too bothered about what I did to Roman.'

'We were business associates,' José said matter-of-factly. 'Not friends. He was a cruel man, just like we all are. You have to be in this line of work. Initially I was mad — but now I get the lion's share of the profits, don't I?'

King shook his head. 'Crazy world. Can I ask a question?'

'Of course.'

'Why?'

'Why what?'

'Why are Raul's family here? You directly disobeyed Rico. He would have found out eventually. He would have butchered you.'

'We were in the final stages of preparing the shipyard assault. At that point it didn't matter what I did. We were hoping to bury him well before he caught onto it. Besides, it wasn't his smartest move asking me to take care of things.'

'Why's that?'

'Ana and I…'

Everything clicked. 'Ah.'

'The things you do for love, hey?'

King smiled. 'I wouldn't know. But I'm glad you've found someone that makes you happy.'

'You got a woman?'

'Not yet.'

'You should find one. Might settle you down.'

'I see that hasn't worked so well for you.'

'Touché,' José said. 'So where does the great Jason King go from here?'

'Somewhere quiet, I think.'

'You enjoy that. I have many hard years ahead.'

'Your decision.'

'Never said it wasn't. I relish hard work.'

King raised an eyebrow. 'You patronising me? Saying I don't work hard?'

'Not at all, my friend.'

'You should hear some stories…'

'I can only imagine.'

'I'm done with that life.'

'You don't seem to be.'

José was right. King said nothing in return, but he found himself thinking hard. He'd lost count of the number of times he'd told himself he was done. Done with fighting, done with killing, done with violence. He'd been through hell down in a small country town in Australia, and now he'd been put through a second round in Venezuela. He began to wonder if peace would ever come.

He thought he might get himself killed trying to find it.

'Want some advice?' José said after a lengthy period of silence.

'I'm all ears,' King said.

'Go find some place in the middle of nowhere. Lay low for a while. Don't talk to anyone. Don't provoke anyone. If someone tries to start trouble, turn and walk away. That's how you settle down.'

'I'm trying, José,' King said. 'Trust me. I'm trying.'

'Can you do it?'

'Do what?'

'If you get provoked, can you ignore it?'

King tightened his grip on the phone. 'I honestly don't know. Seems like I can't.'

José sighed. 'Hate to say it, my friend, but you might just be made for this life.'

'I might just be.'

'Good luck, King. And don't worry about Raul. I'll take good care of the three of them. You have my word.'

The line went dead. King spent a long time cradling the phone in his hand, staring at nothing in particular.

Thinking.

Maybe it was time to shake things up. Just like that, he made a decision.

No more travel. No more hopping from country to country, willingly heading into dangerous locations. Maybe he had been looking for trouble all this time — subconsciously. Putting himself in situations where he knew he could retaliate. He thought back to the crowded bazaar in the heart of Maiquetía, where the madness had begun. If he'd simply stepped aside to let the short thug pass by, none of this would have happened.

He would have continued on with his nomadic existence until the next sign of trouble reared its head.

But then where would Raul be? Still in El Infierno.

Would José's assault on the Movers have succeeded without King's help?

Would it have backfired spectacularly, leading to the slaughter of Raul's family after Rico discovered what José had done?

More than likely.

King sighed and headed out of the living room. Truth was … he probably wouldn't have done anything differently. Even in hindsight.

He stepped into the foyer and saw the two women staring at him with a mixture of awe and disbelief. Their eyes were bloodshot and their cheeks were puffy. They'd been crying.

'I told them what you did for me,' Raul explained. 'What you did for Luis.'

King shrugged. 'Not a problem.'

'They don't speak English. But they want you to know that they will always be in your debt.'

King smiled. Raul's mother crossed the room and held out a plump hand. King took it. Her skin was warm. She squeezed hard, and King noted the gratitude in her eyes. He nodded acknowledgement and smiled back.

He turned to Raul. 'Take care of them.'

'Of course. They're not leaving my sight.'

'Do you need the car?'

Raul paused. He cocked his head. 'You're going already?'

'I've done my job.'

'I know, but…'

'I'm sorry. But I need some space. I have a few things in my life that I need to sort out.'

'Of course. Completely understood.'

Raul crossed the room and held both arms wide. King embraced him and slapped him on the back, hard. 'We did it, brother. We did it.'

When they parted, Raul had tears in his eyes. 'I can't put into words how thankful I am.'

'I know,' King said. 'Don't worry. I get it.'

'How can I contact you?'

'You can't. I don't have a phone.'

'What about your family? Your friends?'

'Don't have any.'

'Is that what this is? You're finding a new life?'

'I've been travelling for a while. Think it might be time to buy a place. Stay in one location.'

'Here?'

'Not a fucking chance.'

Raul laughed. 'I was only joking. I don't blame you.'

'No offence intended, but I've had enough of Venezuela for a while.'

'None taken. I wouldn't blame you if you never came back here. Where are you thinking?'

'Not sure yet. I hear Europe is nice this time of year.'

He turned and made for the door, nodding his goodbyes to the three of them. They watched him go like he was an apparition, someone who had simply appeared to fix all their problems and then shrink away into the shadows. Maybe that's what he was. Maybe that's all he was ever meant to be. He certainly hadn't had time to look after himself.

King stepped out into a dusty Venezuelan evening. His ribs suddenly seared with pain. With all potential threats eliminated, his body had given up on suppressing the feeling. It came fast and strong, making him hunch slightly to ride out the agony. He fought the urge to cough. He knew it would only lead to another sharp burst of searing fire. He tried to ignore it and looked ahead.

The sun had begun its descent, melting into the horizon, casting an orange glow across the Caribbean Sea. The waves sparkled under the rays. He admired the view for a moment. Then he stepped down onto the gravel driveway and made for the pick-up truck running idly in the courtyard.

He got in and slammed the gearstick into drive and rolled away.

CHAPTER 50

Through the open front door, Raul watched the pick-up truck disappear over the edge of the road and vanish from sight. He was left amidst his family. He didn't move for a long time. It was only after King had left that he realised just how incredulous their journey had been.

He turned to his mother and said in Spanish, 'Are you okay?'

She nodded. 'We're together now. We'll get through it. Luis will watch over us.'

Ana said, 'Who was that man?'

Raul shrugged. He didn't know what to say. 'Just a guy.'

'What did he do?'

Raul reminisced on the trail of destruction one American tourist had carved through the darkest depths of Venezuela. He shook his head in disbelief. 'You wouldn't believe me if I told you.'

He walked to the front door and closed it, feeling sorry for whoever decided to cross King's path next.

Read Matt's other books on Amazon.

amazon.com/author/mattrogers23